More
Dreadpunk Tales
of the
Dark and Supernatural

Edited by Bryce Raffle

DEADSTEAM
PUBLISHED IN 2021 BY Grimmer & Grimmer Books
Edited by Bryce Raffle
Copyright © Grimmer & Grimmer Books 2021

Cover art and interior design by Bryce Raffle.

For information, visit:
http://www.deadsteam.wordpress.com

For information about the publisher, visit:
http://www.grimmerandgrimmer.wordpress.com

Book and Cover design by Bryce Raffle
ISBN: 978-1-7773872-5-9

GRIMMER & GRIMMER BOOKS

CONTENTS

FOREWORD VII

NEWGATE 13

THE INVOCATION 46

CECILIA 72

MOTHER OF ROTTEN REEDS & DUCKWEED 91

AT THE END OF A PISTOL 115

A LIVING CELL 138

THE COLOR OF PARIS IN THE SPRING 166

THE GOOD WORK 189

THE SUN WORSHIPER'S GHOST 203

BLOOD TIES 225

THE ARTIST'S HANDS 283

TRAPPED IN THOUGHT 298

RETURN UNTO THE LAND 311

ACKNOWLEDGEMENTS 343

ABOUT THE AUTHORS 344

FOREWORD

BRYCE RAFFLE

L IKE A VAMPIRE RISEN FROM THE grave, we're
back. The decision to do a second anthology
was prompted by the positive response
we've received for the first anthology, and by the
resurgence of the gothic in mainstream media. Even
in works with contemporary settings, there has been
an unmistakable influence of classic gothic works.
The popularity of tv shows like *The Haunting of Hill
House, Castlevania*, and even comedies like *What We
Do In The Shadows,* and mainstream literature, such
as Jay Kristoff's *Empire of the Vampire*, demonstrates
a renewal of interest in the classical influences of
gothic horror.

Which brings us to the inspiration for
DeadSteam. When I came up with the concept for
the first anthology, I had it in mind that I wanted to

showcase the dark, supernatural side of steampunk. Because steampunk takes its cues from a time when engines ran on steam power, the Victorian era has strong ties to steampunk. With that in mind, I began looking to Victorian writing as a source of inspiration for my steampunk stories. In particular, I began looking at the Victorian penny dreadful.

The cheap, sensational stories of the era, known as penny dreadfuls, were sold for a penny per issue. The stories were typically released in weekly parts and often portrayed supernatural entities, such as ghosts, ghouls, and, of course, vampires.

A Feast of Blood, or Varney the Vampire, written by either James Malcolm Rymer or Thomas Preskett Prest (penny dreadfuls were often written anonymously, and *Varney the Vampire* was variously attributed to both Prest and Rymer), was a longstanding favourite, running at an enormous total length of nearly 667,000 words.

Varney introduced many of the common

vampire tropes still common today, most notably the sharp fangs now associated with the undead creatures.

"The figure turns half round, and the light falls upon its face. It is perfectly white—perfectly bloodless. The eyes look like polished tin; the lips are drawn back, and the principal feature next to those dreadful eyes is the teeth—the fearful looking teeth—projecting like those of some wild animal, hideously, glaringly white, and fang-like. It approaches the bed with a strange, gliding movement. It clashes together the long nails that literally appear to hang from the finger ends. No sound comes from its lips."

- James Malcolm Rymer, Thomas Preskett Prest, Varney the Vampire

Penny Dreadfuls, otherwise known as penny bloods, also portrayed the deeds of criminals, such as the Resurrection Man portrayed in *The Mysteries of London*, and Dick Turpin, the notorious highwayman. Spring-Heeled Jack, a popular urban legend, featured in a number of penny dreadful tales.

Further, they often drew from gothic literature for their inspiration, and were often reprints or blatant plagiarisms of popular gothic novels, such as *The Castle of Otranto* or *The Monk*.

As they were either inspired by or ripped off from gothic fiction, dark and stormy nights and fog-thick moors were commonplace. One publisher, as an example of the blatant plagiarism, put out a Charles Dickens penny dreadful imaginatively retitled as Oliver Twiss.

> *"Fog everywhere. Fog up the river, where it flows among green aits and meadows; fog down the river, where it rolls defiled among the tiers of shipping and the waterside pollutions of a great (and dirty) city..."*

- Charles Dickens, Bleak House

In researching the inspirations for the first anthology, I stumbled across an article about dreadpunk, posted on the Daily Dot website. Dreadpunk is an emerging genre founded by Derek "The Dreadpope" Tatum, who on his website dreadpunk.com, describes the genre as the "'costume drama' of the macabre."

> *"I coined the term 'dreadpunk' in early 2015. At the time, there appeared to be a resurgence of interest in the Gothic; most notably, Penny Dreadful was on Showtime*

and Guillermo del Toro's Crimson Peak
was scheduled for release later that year."

- Derek Tatum, dreadpunk.com

I reached out to Tatum for further info on the dreadpunk movement, and he was kind enough to get back to me, describing it as "gothic horror with modern storytelling techniques." Hammer Horror, he said, makes a good comparison, "since that was an attempt to bring "period" horror up to the era it was made."

Besides Hammer, he also referenced Corman's *Poe* flicks, Burton's *Sleepy Hollow*, *Ravenloft*, Coppola's *Dracula*, *Castlevania*, and of course (Showtime's) *Penny Dreadful*.

Diving deeper into the dreadpunk movement, the article from Daily Dot described a "late Sunday night panel at Dragon Con," which gave rise to "a new movement [dreadpunk] that aims to push horror and dark fantasy in new (old) directions."

Its description of "a subversive take on fog-drenched Victoriana, tales of the supernatural mixed with late 19th-century aesthetics, and the recent wave of Gothic horror like *The Woman In Black* and *Crimson Peak*," sounded exactly like what I had in mind for the *DeadSteam* anthology.

The article went on to quote Leanna Renee Hieber (*Strangely Beautiful, The Eterna Files*), who later wrote the foreword for the first *DeadSteam* anthology, and Cherie Priest (*Maplecroft, Chapelwood*). Hieber was quoted as saying that she "love(s) the idea of reclaiming gothic horror," and that "dreadpunk acknowledges the 19th-century roots that gothic horror is built on," while, Priest noted that "dreadpunk is also about subverting dominant narratives and social norms."

Thus emerged *DeadSteam*. As Hieber noted in her foreword for the first anthology, "the engine, the furnace, the terrible beating heart of the Gothic is dread, correlated with the prolific 19th Century tradition of 'Penny Dreadfuls'. Dreadpunk's compass needle is the centuries-old Gothic literary tradition, but it is a cross-genre enterprise reimagined by modern voices."

Each of the stories that follow owes some credit to the writers of penny dreadfuls, who introduced us to fang-bearing vampires like Sir Francis Varney, resurrection men who dredge the dead up from their rest to sell to anatomists, and ghosts haunting the halls of gothic manors on dark, foggy nights.

Bryce Raffle

Newgate

Bryce Raffle

"If it were true that the spirits of the departed are allowed to revisit the earth for certain purposes and on particular occasions—if the belief of superstition were well founded, and night could be peopled with the ghosts and spectres of those who sleep in troubled graves—what a place of ineffable horrors—what a scene of terrible sights, would Newgate be at midnight!"

– George W. M. Reynolds, *The Mysteries of London*

Excerpt from the Journal of Matthew J Harrow, Prison Guard at Newgate

May 31st, 1891

THE CARVINGS ON THE BRICK WALL looked like the sort of thing a child might have drawn. I had five of them at home, so I ought to know. Three boys and two girls, and this was exactly the sort of illustration they liked to make, often sketching in the margins of their lesson pages of their school workbooks. The carvings before me, by contrast to the drawings sketched on paper by my children, had been etched into the brick just above my own eye level, suggesting that the artist was at least a little larger in stature than me. An adult, surely, and a tall one at that, me being only a little under six feet and still having to direct my eyes upward to look at the artwork. If it can be called that.

The subject of the work was a woman in a dress. That was really all the detail I could make out of it. The medium used to render the illustration into the wall, I hesitate to say, was undoubtedly a person's fingernails, for there remained remnants of the artist's chipped nails still lodged in the brick, and great streaks of blood trickled down the walls. Slowly, little by little, probably during the course of several months or even years during their time here, they must have scratched out that same pattern in the bricks until the lines grew deep enough to be discernible. A woman in a dress. I leaned forward, nose crinkling in distaste. The woman was smiling. Yes, the artist had rendered a smile on the woman's face. This was a happy memory.

I turned away from the carving, a hard knot in my stomach as I contemplated what must have compelled the artist to bloody their own hands in order to accomplish this piece of work, as if it were an act of utter desperation. A dire longing for some comfort—anything at all—in an otherwise desolate place. Any distraction from the loneliness, even if it came at the expense of one's own fingernails. Without so much as a piece of chalk, this—this— was the only course of action they could think to take. To chisel, by bare hand, what looked like a child's drawing, into the brick wall.

"Sometimes the mind reverts to a state of childhood," the warden remarked, "under such trying circumstances as these."

I took a step back, almost stumbled. I'd been so absorbed in what I was looking at—so horrified— that I hadn't noticed my own lips moving, or heard any sound coming out of my own mouth. But I must have been speaking aloud, or else the warden had read my own mind, and I am not so superstitious as to assume the latter.

"Trying circumstances," I repeated. The warden sure had a gift for understatement.

"Confinement," he explained, "has a tendency to chip away at one's mind. Much like—"

"Fingernails into a brick wall," I finished for him.

"Precisely." He nodded, turning away from the cell and imploring me to follow, his short, stubby legs quickly carrying him down the hall at an unlikely pace, leaving me with my longer legs to plod along behind him, like a Greyhound somehow outpaced by a Dachshund. The warden was small in stature and nearly as wide as he was tall, and his skinny little legs appeared to be overburdened by the great weight resting upon them, though he walked with purpose and speed, unhindered insofar as I could tell, by his stature or weight. Or his age for that matter, for he must have been nearing seventy, judging by the sharp lines that creased his forehead and the way his skin sagged as if weighed down like an air balloon with too much cargo. He dabbed at his brow with a handkerchief as he walked, the only sign of any fatigue whatsoever.

The iron bars of the cell at my back, I proceeded down the hall after him, trailing behind him in spite of my longer stride as my eyes swept past the long, dimly lit hall, crowded with cells no bigger or more cheerful than the one we'd just exited. Were I to pause to inspect the other cells, I had little doubt that each would provide an equally disturbing scene. Perhaps not the same manifestation of madness, but certainly some manifestation of it. The human mind, as I was quickly beginning to discover, could only handle so much.

"I imagine you're beginning to wonder why I showed you that," said the warden, pausing only to turn and see that I was still following at his heels like the obedient dog that I was. "I will be the first to confess that I have made a few egregious errors of calculation in recent months, wherein human resources are concerned. That is to say that I made a mistake in my choice of recent hires, placing men who—through no fault of their own—found themselves quite out of their depth when it came to handling the difficulties of managing their rounds. The prisoners disturbed them, it seems, and perhaps, I will admit, their salaries did not match the demands placed upon them. For it is not merely the prisoners who face a toll in this institution. It wears on the staff as well, and for some, the compensation does not measure up adequately."

Here, he paused to draw in a great deal of breath and let it out in a great world weary sigh. There it was, at last, the first real piece of evidence that he was tired. Indeed, if his sigh was genuine and not merely put on to emphasize his point, the life of a warden had left him exhausted. He was not the type to allow exhaustion to slow him down, however. Not for long, anyway. He was the type to rally against it. To persevere in the face of hardship. That being said, his roundabout manner of speaking had left me feeling quite lost. If he was coming to a point, I couldn't quite see what it was.

"I will be candid with you, Mr. Harrow. Three of my guards have given up their employment this past week alone, and it has been going on that way for several months now. Not everyone has the stomach for it, you see. Not everyone can endure the burdens forced upon them by such an employment as this."

Ah. And there it was. Mr. Clarke—for that was the warden's name—wished to know if I was made of sterner stuff. That he was not making a mistake in hiring me. I wasn't sure if I had passed the test, thus far, but I needed this job. In that regard, I was as desperate as the artist who'd carved, with his fingers, an illustration into a brick wall. I had mouths to feed and no other prospects. The warden's warning, for that's what it must have been, had done little to dampen my enthusiasm at the opportunity for employment, even if it wasn't the most desirable occupation. And perhaps that meant that I was indeed made of sterner stuff. I opened my mouth to assure the warden of as much, but his speech was not finished. Not yet.

A plump finger jabbed toward me as if to emphasize his point. "You will see humanity at its worst here at Newgate, Mr. Harrow. You will see men hanged with such regularity that it shall become commonplace. You will see desperation such as you have never known, and you must endure it. They will beg mercies and little kindnesses of you, and perhaps even try to bribe their way out of their cells, and you will be forced, as your duty requires it, to reject such demands. They will hate you for it, for that is only natural, as you will come to represent, in their minds at any rate, the very institution that has brought them to their lowly state of confinement. You will come to pity them in turn, and to fear and revile them in equal measure. For these men—and women—are the very worst of society. The criminal underclass. Murderers, thieves, and vagrants."

I tightened my lips. I wasn't entirely certain I agreed with the warden's assessment of the situation, though surely he had seen a great deal more than I had of prison life. But I felt certain that many of the wretched prisoners held within these walls were victims of circumstance. They were not evil, merely misfortunate. I kept quiet on this matter, as I knew that voicing my opinion on the subject would do me little good so far as my chances went in securing the job.

"And you'll be paid pitifully for it. I won't beat around the bush about that. I've had too many quit on me who've fancied that this job might be some sort of vacation for them, or that it would line their pockets with coins. It won't."

"I understand that, Sir," I said. I had no illusions about the pay for my prospective employment at the prison, but it would be enough to keep my children fed and keep a roof over their heads.

The warden sighed again. He dug into his coat pocket for his handkerchief and wiped the sweat from his brow. He turned away from me again, muttering something about having said too much. I think he expected me to walk away then, to fold up my reference letter and leave the prison in search of other occupation. Instead, I followed him deeper into the darkness of the long corridor lined with prison cells.

"There's this as well," said Mr. Clarke. "I suspect that one of the reasons I can't keep the guards from quitting is due to Newgate's reputation."

He left that sentence at that, as though I were simply meant to understand what reputation he was referring to. Its reputation for being a cold, hard place? For being inescapable? Or what?

"Sir?" I said, by way of inquiry.

The warden turned to examine me, to scrutinize my face as though he might find some secrets hidden within my grey-blue eyes or within the white whiskers that dotted my stubble. "You're not superstitious, are you, Mr. Harrow?"

I let out a cough, eyes sweeping past a foul-smelling prisoner who had stripped himself of all his clothing and who was howling wildly at us as we passed too quickly to pay him any mind.

"Superstitious? No," I answered. And it was the truth. I had been to war, after all, in Burma, and what places are more haunted than battlefields? It was not ghosts that haunted me, but memories.

"Good," he answered. "Too many good men lost to foolish notions of spectres and ghouls. We've got enough problems on our hands with the living."

As we walked, a prisoner spat at us through the bars of his cell.

"I can see what you mean," I answered.

Mr. Clarke inclined an eyebrow, apparently impressed by my unflinching attitude as I sidestepped the ball of saliva aimed at our heads and carried on down the corridor.

"I can see we're going to get along, Mr. Harrow. You seem a reasonable man, and that's what we need at this prison. Reasonable men." He muttered this last point, almost as a complaint. I could see he was still thinking about the guards who'd recently deserted him, apparently over a fear of ghosts. I almost laughed, I'm ashamed to say, at the thought of these grown men supposedly turning tail and running over a fear of ghosts, like school children frightened by some specter in a penny dreadful.

"So, I've got the job?" I asked.

Without turning, Mr. Clarke answered the question with one of his own. "You're still here, aren't you?"

London, June 13th, 1891

To Captain Edward Langford of Her Royal Majesty's 41st Regiment,

I sincerely hope this brief epistle from an old friend and fellow soldier will not be thought impertinent. I have known you so long, that I feel assured, you will consider my sincerest thanks for what it is and pay no mind to any complaint that follows, for it does not reflect on you, and I am not ungrateful.

And yet I must be wholly honest with you about the employment I have managed to secure. It is not entirely what either of us had hoped. You were right, I must first tell you, that the horrors of war, which we both experienced back in Burma, have made me well suited to the job. Better than any of the men who came before me, or so the warden continues to compliment me, and you can take that as a complement to yourself as well, Sir, for it was under your charge that I survived the war, as did, I'm pleased to say, the great majority of our regiment, and it was by your instruction and guidance that I came to be as well-prepared for battle as one can reasonably expect. Can a man ever truly be prepared for such horrors? I think not. And still, I did return to London with my mind—and body—relatively intact. My shoulder still gives me trouble, at times (particularly after a long day at the prison) where the bullet pierced it, but that is the worst of it.

But I've gotten ahead of myself, haven't I? I am distracted, I'm afraid, by a number of things, but I'll get to that. I should have started with the news that I did indeed manage to secure the position for which you recommended me, at Newgate Prison. I am, therefore, presently employed as a prison guard, and am therefore in your debt. I cannot thank you enough for your heartfelt letter of recommendation.

This employment means a great deal to me. You will remember fondly three of my young children: Matthew, James, and Elizabeth, who are now twelve, eight, and seven, respectively. Matthew is practically old enough to look after the rest on his own now, and takes after the father for whom he was named. He is a responsible lad, but I hate to contravene upon his success as a student by requiring him to look after his siblings. He must remain in school, therefore, and it is only thanks to my salary at the prison that I am able to afford the luxury of keeping a household staff to look after my children while I am away at work. My beloved Jane is gone from this world. I'm certain you will remember her fondly as well. I am pleased to tell you that she left me with two additional children besides those with whom you are already acquainted: young Jane, who is three and named for her mother, and little Edward, who came into this earth the very day his mother left it. Yes, dear Sir, you may be pleased to hear that I have bestowed upon my son the highest honor I could consider, by naming him after you.

Again, my thanks goes out to you, for without your intervention, I might have ended up in the very prison that I now find myself employed in quite another fashion entirely. That is to say, in the ward reserved for debtors. I am now, narrowly, saved from destitution, by what I hesitate to call a happy employment. I am at all times adverse to troubling my friends—and particularly my superiors—on my own behalf, especially as I now find myself in your debt. But I hope that our longstanding friendship will excuse me this indulgence, as I feel some need to unburden myself. There is a weight upon my shoulders the likes of which I have never known, not even during the war. And you have always been an exceptional friend and a great listener. I beg you, therefore, to overlook this transgression.

As I mentioned earlier, my employment is not entirely what I had hoped—what either of us had hoped. It is a waking nightmare.

As I walk the halls of the great stone edifice that is Newgate, my ears are constantly assaulted by sounds of despair. It is not dissimilar to the sounds we heard at Burma. Awful screeching voices, anguished cries of desperation, it is as though the very bowels of hell have opened up and filled the air with the inhuman wailing of the damned. And they are damned. For once confined to imprisonment within the stone walls of Newgate, little hope remains of their eventual release.

The prisoners are wretched, sad things. If they were cheerful before their arrival to Newgate, they do not remain that way for long. It takes only a matter of hours before they fall prey to that old monster: despair. Their appetites soon leave them, so the prisoners scarcely eat what little food I slide through the holes in their bars. The rest is left for the rats. Some of them try to engage me in conversation, desperate for some human connection, but under the warden's instructions, I am not to indulge them even the slightest of kindnesses beyond delivering their meals. Newgate is a cold place, and I am meant only to add to that coldness, not dispel it with a smile or a word of encouragement.

Those who have been long confined to their life of prison are truly wretched. Their bodies are emaciated, their voices thin and raw as if they've worn out their own vocal cords from screaming at the walls. Only those who've been sentenced to hang have any cheer about them at all. For at least they can see an inevitable end to their suffering.

I take no solace from the shared experiences of my fellow guards. My colleagues vary between only two types of men. They are either callous, cruel men with no regard whatsoever for the prisoners' wellbeing; or they are weak, superstitious men who walk the halls of Newgate in trepidation and fear. They will not last long in their employment. That much is certain, and then we will be left only with the first category of guard.

I mentioned that some of the guards are superstitious. I return to the subject of superstition now because the prison is supposed to be haunted. There is one cell in particular that my fellow guards will not visit, and that includes the cruel, callous guards.

As I've said, Newgate is a cold place. The hall leading towards this cell is frigid. The air is positively frozen. Prior to my recent employment at the prison, I would have categorized myself as someone immune to superstition, but I am ashamed to say that when I dared to venture down that long, cold corridor myself, I initially dismissed the chill in the air as a trick of the wind. The odd architecture that sometimes produces wind tunnels and strange drafts. But the nearer I got to that cell, the more I felt that the cold wasn't just in the air. It was as though the cell were actually leeching the warmth from my heart.

From my soul. It crept through my clothing, crawled the length of my skin, pricked at it like the sharp jab of a knife, and stole all the warmth from my body. The warden told me, when first I met him, that Newgate held the very worst of society within its walls. What sort of person, what vile, evil murderer was held captive in that cell? I shudder to think of it. But if I do not fall into the category of cold and callous, then surely I must be weak and superstitious. I'd never felt that way before in all my life, but I knew fear that day.

I slid the food through the gate in the cell door. Without looking inside at the prisoner held captive there. Somehow, I couldn't manage even that. Even a look through the bars was too terrifying a thought to behold. I turned away and fled the corridor, never to look back.

And I'm ashamed to say, I do not wish ever to return there. There is nothing I would not give if it meant I did not have to go back there. My livelihood. My soul. My dignity. I'd give it all up if I didn't have to return. And yet, I must.

I beg for your advice, and hope you won't judge me too harshly for my weakness. Perhaps it's all just memories come back to haunt me again, from the war. Memories I thought I'd suppressed, risen up to meet me again, somehow taken on the shape of a prison cell.

Your old and ever sincere friend,

Matthew Harrow

Excerpt from the Journal of Matthew J Harrow, Prison Guard at Newgate

July 18th, 1891

I hesitate to put this all down on paper, for surely if my journal were to be discovered and read, my sanity would be put into question, but I must put pen to paper or the last vestiges of my sanity will truly unravel. I must give voice to these dark thoughts or they will work their way out of me in some other fashion. An outburst of violence. A nightmare. An ill-considered letter rambling at length on the subject of superstition. No, I must have some release for the thoughts that plague me, but if I am to put pen to paper, it shall be confined to the pages of my own private journal, for no prying eyes to see.

It had been a good day. A good week even. I have been starting to find some degree of camaraderie or perhaps even friendship with some of my fellow guards at the prison. They are not all so bad, even if they are a superstitious bunch. One such guard, a young lad by the name of Jonathan—or John, as he prefers—told me as we crossed paths during our rounds, a disturbing rumor about the prisoner in the Haunted Cell. I call it the Haunted Cell with no hint of irony or skepticism because I have felt its dark presence now myself, and because that is the name the guards use for it. The Haunted Cell.

Its former occupant—as the cell remains empty, aside from the spectral prisoner—according to John, was the Richmond Murderess, who back in 79 slaughtered her employer and hacked her victim to bits with a carving knife before boiling the poor woman's body parts. She was later hanged for her crimes, though a woman has been seen by some of the guards through the bars of her cell. Her face is famous enough to be recognizable, given that Madam Tussaud's has her likeness on display at the wax museum, and those who have seen her swear that she's the Richmond Murderess. I have myself heard her fiendish cries from down the hall, although I dare not look inside her cell. That being said, I am under strict instructions from Warden Clarke to continue bringing food to the prisoner's cell, which lends some doubt to the rumors being spread amongst the guards. Surely the cell is not unoccupied, and whatever woman they've spotted in the cell must be the new occupant? And yet I cannot shake that feeling of dread which overcomes me whenever I visit the cell.

To further muddy the story I've been told by John, another of the guards swears that the ghost haunting that unearthly prison cell is a man, not a woman. A murderer, not a murderess. The Thames Torso Murderer, says one of the guards. Jack the Ripper, swears another. For each account of the ghost at least shares that in common. Whatever soul haunts that dreaded cell is evil.

Of course, this sounds like the stuff of penny dreadfuls and not an account of the experiences of a prison guard. And I have gotten off topic, for I said that it had been a good day, and I have been rambling again about the prisoner. But it was a good day, for my children were still awake when I returned home from work, still in my guard's uniform. I hung my hat upon a hook by the door, dismissed the children's governess for the night, and spent an hour in the rare company of my young ones.

Little Jane is a wonder, for she has such energy for one so little, and speaks surprisingly well for such a tiny tot. She has little interest in her toys but shows great attention to whatever her older siblings are interested in. She has her mother's eyes, and I only wish that the elder Jane were still around to see her daughter. Elizabeth is learning a great deal in school, and I am well pleased to know that her education is worth something. She can read and write and do arithmetics, perhaps as well as her older brother, James. Such a smart little thing. James is your typical lad, his legs covered in scratches and scrapes from climbing trees and getting himself into trouble. He has so much energy he knows not what to do with it, but he behaves himself well enough in my presence and listens attentively. Mathew takes after his father and is therefore stoic and quiet. He takes charge of his siblings as though they are his own offspring, and there was little for me to do when it was time for the children to go to bed, for Mathew had it all well in hand on his own.

With the children well in hand, I decided to run myself a bath, for even in such a cold, stone building as Newgate, in the thick wool of my uniform, I manage to work up quite a sweat making my rounds, and frequent bathing is the only remedy for the resulting stench of a hard day's work.

I filled the tub as much as I could manage without the modern conveniences of the modern plumbing some homes these days are blessed with. I can afford no such comforts on my meager salary and make do by boiling the water in the kitchen and filling the tub one bucket at a time. Steam rising from the waters, I stripped myself of my uniform, and with little energy left in my reserves, left it lying in a pile on the floor, while I climbed into the water.

Steam filled the room and fogged the mirror while I scrubbed until the water turned a dark, murky grey. By oil lamp—for again, my house lacked such modern conveniences as gas lamps—the water was so dark it almost looked like tar. Black and murky and stinking of sweat and soap commingled.

Outside, it had begun to rain in earnest. In London, as constant and grey as this city is, it almost never seems to pour. It rains. It drizzles. It mists so lightly sometimes one wonders if it's raining at all and wonders at the dampness of one's clothes. It fogs. It is in a constant state of some degree of dampness. And yet it never pours. But tonight it did. The rain hammered at the window with such fervor I almost feared it might hail and crack the glass. I couldn't afford the expense of replacing the windows if it did. But soon enough the downpour slowed and much to my relief the great gobs of rain pelting down against the glass turned to little droplets that formed thin rivers that trickled down the glass.

It was mesmerizing watching the water run down from the comfort of my warm bath. Hypnotic enough that I must have drifted off. My head slumped against the back of the tub, and when I woke, she was there.

Hanging from a noose, the rope firmly tied to the chandelier, she hung there in front of me. Face bloated and purple, her eyes white and blank. The corners of her eyelids crawled with maggots and flies buzzed around the edges, looking at first glance almost like kohl, as though she'd put them there on purpose. Blood dripped onto the white tiles that lined my bathroom, spilling out from her neck where the rope had dug in so deep as to carve its way through the first few layers of flesh. It was thick and gelatinous, staining the rope a dark red.

I scrambled back in the tub, spilling pools of murky water onto the floor. The water had gone cold (how long had I been asleep?), but I hardly noticed.

And when I recovered myself, just as suddenly as she'd appeared, the woman was gone.

She was gone.

But the memory of her was not. She plagued me long afterwards, leaving my heart hammering against my chest the way the rain had pounded against my windows: so hard I feared it might shatter something if it pounded any harder. I scrambled out of the tub, slipping hard on the puddles I'd spilled upon the tile. I went down hard, nose first against the floor. Blood welled from my nostrils, and again, bright drops of crimson spattered the tile. This time the blood was real.

Winded, I pulled myself to my feet more clumsily than I usually am, and tried to stop the flow of blood with my bath towel, staining it red. I cursed myself for being so frantic, and the words came out in a hoarse whisper. I'd fallen harder than I'd thought, probably broken my nose and maybe a rib or two. I placed one hand, gingerly, upon my chest, but no, there was nothing broken. Just bruised. But by God, did it ever hurt to breathe!

After what seemed like an hour, the bleeding finally stopped. Limping, I made my way over to the tub and pulled the plug. Swirling, black waters gurgled as it drained out of the tub. I wiped the bloody floor with a rag and wrapped the red-stained towel around my waist, then made my way down the hallway to my bed chambers.

There, I tossed and turned beneath my sheets until finally, in a fit of frustration, with the light of morning already finding its way through the gaps in my curtains, I got out of bed. I dressed myself and made my way to my writing desk to find my journal.

And now I've come full circle. Damn it all, should this journal ever be discovered and read, I would surely be deemed insane and put in a cell not unlike the one that haunts me. Not at Newgate, of course, but at Bethlem Hospital, with the walls of my prison padded for my safety. With doctors there to treat me with that new electrical shock therapy that is so much talked about these days. God help me. But I saw what I saw, and it must be put on paper, for without some sort of release from the prison of my own mind, I would truly lose my grip on reality. I would truly crack.

And I cannot speak of this to anyone, except perhaps to my fellow guards, but I fear that if I do, it will work its way back to the warden, Mr. Clarke, whose former opinion of me as a rational, reasonable man will be changed, leaving him no choice but to dismiss me. And what should become of me then? Destitution, that's what. For I have mouths to feed and bills to pay.

So back to Newgate I must return, to that place of horrors that follows me now wherever I go, haunts me even when I'm not there. Even in my own home. Back then, to the prison. Back to that dreaded corridor to put food in an empty cell for the rats to eat. And I must keep my mouth shut. For fear of dismissal, and fear of being sent to Bedlam. I must remain silent. But I saw her.

I swear to god, I saw her.

An Excerpt from "The Chronicles of Newgate,"

By Arthur Griffiths, One of Her Majesty's Inspectors of Prisons

How desperate was the case of the bulk of the inmates of Newgate will be amply set forth as my narrative proceeds. A few brief facts will suffice here to give a general idea of this foul prison house. The whole place except the press yard was so dark that candles, "links or burners," were used all day long; the air was so inconceivably disgusting, that the ventilator on the top of the prison could exercise no remedial effect. That malignant disease, the gaol fever, was chronic, and deaths from it of frequent occurrence. Doctors could be got with difficulty to attend the sick in Newgate, and it was long before any regular medical officer was appointed to the prison.

Evil was in the ascendant throughout.

London, October 1st, 1891

My Dear Friend, Matthew Harrow,

Please excuse the untimely nature of my reply. I have not been in good health these days, I'm afraid, and it has taxed me more than you might think to come up with what I hope will be a suitable reply to your letter.

First, may I extend my condolences regarding the terrible news about Jane. What a terrible shame! You are right to say that I would remember her fondly; I do. My memory fails me now at times, a symptom of my age, but I cannot fail to recall the many times you and your wife have invited me to your home over the years. It has been some time now since I was in good enough health to attend one of your dinners, but I remember such happy occasions with such fondness that it fills my heart with warmth to think of it. But Jane, beautiful, kind Jane. She will not be forgotten. That much is certain. What more can I say on the subject? It would not do justice to her memory.

And while condolences are in order, so are congratulations! Although I have yet to meet your youngest daughter, Jane, I remember hearing that you were expecting her, and I believe I sent a letter to congratulate you when I heard that she'd been born in good health. I hope I did, and if not, do forgive an old man for his failure of memory. I did not know that you had been expecting a fifth child to join your family, and I am humbled that you should think to name him after me. Edward is a fine name, if I may be so bold as to say so, and one that I shared with my father, as well as his father before him.

And now I must turn to the very sobering subject of your present employment. I am deeply sorry to hear of your troubles at the prison. If you are able to find for yourself some employment elsewhere, I would not be offended in the least. In fact, I would take great joy in hearing that you had found some happier circumstance for yourself, and would be amenable to acting as a reference once again, if that would be in any way helpful.

If not, then I can only think to suggest that you do what you can to dispel with the superstitious rumors spread amongst your fellow men. Let the facts speak for themselves. For surely the warden must keep some record of the prisoners who dwell within his walls. An account for the sentences of the captives and a list of precisely where they are to be confined. What I mean to say is this: there must be some record of precisely who is being held in the cell your fellow guards refuse to visit. Would it not be of some reassurance to know for sure?

And if the warden will not tell you, his records surely will. You still remember that old trick I showed you back in Burma, don't you? With the butter knife?

Your ever faithful friend,

Captain Edward Langford

Excerpt from the Journal of Matthew J Harrow, Prison Guard at Newgate

October 19th, 1891

I stared at Captain Langford's letter with no small measure of surprise. The trick with the butter knife? Of course I remembered it. It was a means of lock picking. But did he really mean to suggest that I should break into the warden's office? I was accustomed to the captain getting me out of trouble, not into it. I read and reread that final paragraph before coming to a conclusion. I folded the letter shut, pocketed it within the inside coat pocket nearest to my chest, and crossed the short distance from my parlor to my kitchen. There, I found a butter knife. I picked it up, held it by its handle.

The knife lingered in my hand a moment. I had caught a glance at my reflection and was surprised to see how disheveled I looked. How old. How tired. I hardly recognized myself. My nose was crooked from my recent fall in the bathroom, and there were heavy bags beneath my eyes that reminded me of what I'd written about the warden after our first meeting back in May. Like an air balloon overladen with cargo, the skin beneath my eyes was beginning to droop down as if even my skin was too tired to stay upright.

With a grimace, I spun the butterknife between my fingertips, turning my reflection away as I tucked the knife away into my pocket, beside the letter.

When I arrived at the prison, I made my first rounds and then my second before returning to the warden's office. I needed to make sure Mr. Clarke was not in before I picked the lock, or else I would have no way of explaining myself for the intrusion. I had decided, during my patrol, on a course of action. I would have to knock on the door, and if the warden answered his door, I would simply claim to have needed his help with some matter. Perhaps with a prisoner who was giving me some trouble. I had no shortage of such complaints as it was, so I would have no trouble coming up with a suitable lie along those lines.

But the warden didn't answer, so he was not in. A quick glance down the halls in both directions told me I was alone, apart from the prisoners, but I was out of their view from my angle at the door. I drew the butterknife from my pocket, heart hammering as I slid it between the door frame and the door. I felt like a criminal, like one of the poor bastards I was charged with guarding. I was supposed to be upholding the law, not breaking it.

But I needed answers.

I worked the knife between the locking mechanisms of the latch and with a few quick taps, the latch made a little pop, and the door creaked open. My heart started pounding again at the sound of the door swinging open on rusted hinges. It was too loud, I thought. Too loud by far. If anyone heard it and came running, I was done for.

But no, I was getting worked up over nothing. It wasn't that loud really. Not compared to screaming, shouting prisoners or the clang of a tin plate being slid through a cell door.

I shoved the door open and took a moment to let my eyes adjust to the dim light. I didn't dare strike a match and draw attention to myself. There were a number of books on the warden's desk, strewn about in a disorderly manner. In Mr. Clarke's defense, he wouldn't have been expecting company and would have had no reason to tidy up. But I turned my attention to the one book he'd left open and dog-eared, for that must surely be the one most up to date.

It took me less than a moment to confirm that this was indeed the warden's record of prisoners, and his penmanship was neat and easily legible, with the exception of a few blotches of spilled ink that marred the page. It didn't take long to find the Haunted Cell in his records, either. Less time than I'd expected by far, a matter of seconds, rather than minutes.

For there it was. Cell Number 23, the cell number that corresponded to the dreaded cell all the guards at Newgate had come to fear. The very cell that had caused so many of Mr. Clarke's men to leave their postings in search of another job somewhere else. The cell that had been the source of my nightmares for several months now, and the cause of so many sleepless nights.

I tore the page from the book and tucked it into the same pocket that contained Captain Langford's letter, and with that in hand, escaped the warden's office with no one any the wiser that its threshold had been breached.

It was not until much later that I returned to my own home that I was able to unfold the letter and examine it fully, without fear of being discovered. Only then did I comprehend the words on the torn-out page from Mr. Clarke's record book.

A Record of The Prisoners at Newgate Gaol, Compiled by Warden Henry Clarke

October 14th, 1892

Cell Number: 21
Prisoner Number 82: Charles Burroughs
Age: 13
Sex: Male
Trade, &c: Labourer
Date of Conviction: September 8th, 1892
Sentence: [Illegible]
Sentenced by: Lord Chief Justice Ratcliffe
Offense charged with: Stealing a waistcoat, the property of Peter Bower
Date of Sentencing: September 8th, 1892; to be confined at Newgate until September 8th, 1893, permitting good behavior

Cell Number: 22

Prisoner Number 161: John Hoskins
Age: 30
Sex: Male
Trade, &c: Bricklayer
Date of Conviction: December 1st, 1889
Sentence: Death
Sentenced by: Lord Chief Justice Henbridge
Offense charged with: The willful murder of Charles Watkins
Date of Sentencing: January 8th, 1893

Cell Number 23

Prisoner Number 161: [Name Illegible]
Age: 43
Sex: Male
Trade, &c: Prison Guard
Date of Conviction: October 14th, 1892
Sentence: Awaiting Trial

Excerpt from the Journal of Matthew J Harrow, Prison Guard at Newgate

October 12th, 1891

The dates are wrong. An error of transcription, no doubt, that comes from fatigue and absent-mindedness. I've never known the warden to be absent-minded, but have any of us not made such an error when writing a letter? The mind slips sometimes, such that we write the wrong year, or month, or forget our own birthdays. We skip months at a time, and fall behind.

The warden's records reflect only this sort of error. For the most recent instance of a prisoner being admitted to the Haunted Cell is dated for next year.

October 14th, 1892. An ink blotch prevents me from reading the prisoner's name, but the gender is male, thereby contradicting the narrative of the prisoner being the Richmond Murderess. Who was it that I saw hanging from a noose in my bathroom, if not her? The mind falls back again, turns back time like a wrongly dated letter, turns memory upside down. The woman on her noose swings from the rope until her face comes around to meet my eye.

Her face, bloated and purple and swollen almost enough to be unrecognizable. Almost.

I've never been to Madame Tussaud's, where the Richmond Murderess's face is put on display for all the world to see. But I'm sure it's not her. The hanging woman, I know her. Know her intimately. It's Jane.

My Jane.

But she didn't die hanging from a noose. She died giving birth.

Didn't she?

The memory shifts and turns like the rope from which she hangs, spins and pivots and digs into the skin. The memory is buried beneath mounds of dirt. Six feet deep and worm-ridden, maggot-eaten. It swarms with flies.

She didn't die giving childbirth. The child died.

Edward. Died in her arms a few moments after he came into the world. Stopped breathing. It nearly broke me. It killed Jane. I can still hear her sobbing. Her unearthly, inhuman moans as her child stopped breathing. I can hear her still each time I round the corner towards that dreaded corridor, towards the Haunted Cell. Good God, how could I have forgotten that it was her? It was my Jane that swung from the noose. A noose of her own making, our

Lord in heaven, how did I manage to forget that awful moment?

But our child wasn't dead. His breathing hadn't stopped. It was simply too shallow for her to detect. Too faint and frail, but the boy recovered. I remember now. Remember screaming at Jane to just wake up and look at her boy. He was alive, god damnit, and why did you have to go and do a thing like that? Why, god damnit, why?

I turned my gaze to the warden's records again.

Cell Number: 23

Prisoner Number 161

Cell 23, the number belonging to the Haunted Cell, drew my eye as easily as if it had been written in red ink rather than black. As though the letters had been done in boldface type. An overzealousness with the ink well had rendered the prisoner's name entirely unreadable, but the prisoner and I were of an age. And of course it did not go unnoticed that we shared one another's occupation. A 43-year old prison guard awaiting sentencing. What were the odds?

And what was I to make of the warden's clerical error? His jumping ahead in time?

From the notes of Dr. J Mayhew, alienist, after his visit to Newgate Gaol

October 24th, 1892

The human brain is the most fragile of organs; when a soldier goes to war, for instance, and is fired upon by enemy insurgents, it is not the body that is most at risk, but the mind. The arm, if injured, can be amputated (at great risk to the body and with a great deal of pain, but we know that man can survive the loss of his mind), but if the brain suffers such a trauma, there are few if any remedies. It cannot be amputated, cannot be replaced by means of surgery, even if a willing donor were available. And yet, trauma to the brain is not limited to physical damage. We alienists have come to understand that trauma inflicted upon a person's psyche can cause devastating effects to the mind as well. Some of these effects have been well documented and supported by a great deal of evidence. Sometimes they manifest in unexpected ways.

The mind is unpredictable. Fragile, unpredictable, and unreliable. It unravels after too much isolation, too much confinement, too much trauma.

My latest patient is a former guard at Newgate, now one of its unfortunate inhabitants. A jailor turned prisoner. He makes for an interesting case and has claimed a great deal of my attention—and fascination—for the last few months.

His mind is fractured in a number of ways that I have seen before—and in ways that I have not. He has come to believe that the cell in which he has been imprisoned is haunted. By whom, I inquired? He explained that his late wife took her own life after her newborn son expired mere moments after he was born; it was only later that my patient discovered that his son still lived. She had taken her own life—committed that great cardinal sin—for naught. This sort of trauma, as I alluded to earlier, has a devastating effect on the mind, for any rational man knows that ghosts are a phenomenon that takes place solely in the mind. A haunting is merely this: past trauma revisited upon the brain when triggered by duress.

This is not the only trauma my patient has experienced, nor is the haunting the only symptom of his stress.

I alluded earlier to the trauma a soldier faces when he marches off to war, is fired upon by enemy soldiers, or when he fires upon others. The things he sees and feels during battle do not stay on the battlefield. They come home with him when he returns from war. They remain in the mind. My patient was at Burma. I can only imagine the sort of trauma he experienced while at war, but it is clear that he brought them home with him. And it is clear that the damage inflicted upon his mind were triggered when his wife took her life, and again when he took up employment at Newgate Gaol. The suffering of the prisoners and the rumors of the prison's superstitious origins proved to be too much for him.

His mind has become fractured, such that he seems to experience his life out of sequence. Time is out of order. In his mind, the year is still 1891. In his mind (and in his mind alone), he is still a guard at the prison, carrying out his patrol through the prison's many halls, and approaching cell 23 from the outside, still a free man. He approaches his cell with trepidation and fear, perhaps because there remains some subconscious part of him that understands he is in reality a prisoner, that the only one haunting the cell is he himself.

He is often quiet during our interviews, sometimes saying a few words, and other times saying nothing at all. His journals have been a great deal of help to me in understanding his case, although it is gruesome to look at. Without a pen or paper, he has taken to writing on the walls. With what instrument? His bare hands, scratching at the brick until his fingernails are stripped raw and the blood is thick enough to coat the brick walls with red ink. I've seen this sign of madness elsewhere, in other cells, and I suppose, so has he. Perhaps that's where he got the idea.

I've asked him about it, and as usual, he says very little during our meetings, but recently he told me that he needed to write it down.

"It is the only means I have of release. If I don't let it out somehow," he explained, "my mind will surely fracture."

"I see," I told him. What I didn't tell him at the time was that it was already too late. Too late by far.

THE INVOCATION

ROSS SMELTZER

AT 11:01 PM ON A THURSDAY evening, after a dinner of stewed eels drowned in sherry gravy, five men and women filed into a dimly lit parlor and crowded around a table. They had convened to find a lost girl. This task was a complicated one, for the girl had died six months earlier.

They had until midnight.

Their guide, Robert Leigh, commanded the group members be seated, shut their eyes, and clasp their hands together. His tone was grave but definite. He had told them over dessert that they had to contact the girl by midnight or else she would be lost to them, forever wandering in the dark maze of the dead. He had slurred his way through those words, such was the potency of the champagne served.

"Let us pray," he whispered. "Rending the veil demands perfect faith."

The group members nodded and did as they were told; they could hardly do otherwise. Leigh came recommended. He'd conducted scores of seances in Birmingham and in the north of England and had insinuated himself into the highest strata of London society. His guests this evening included the hostess of the night's festivities, the Countess of Warwick, Evelyn Kitchener, and her rather sullen husband. Aside from the Kitcheners, Catherine Browne and Robert Villiers were in attendance. Browne and Villiers were, unbeknownst to Leigh, journalists writing for the *London Journal,* reporting on the "medium mania" sweeping through the capital. They had been colleagues for years, and rivals.

Each had private reasons for their attendance.

All was silence, save for the clipped ticking of a clock in an adjacent corridor. All was dark, save for the amber light cast by a single ornate candelabra. The spectral glow cast by the gas lamps burning on Regent Street was dampened by the velvet curtains that smothered the room.

They prayed. And they called out to the lost little girl.

By 11:17 PM they had not found her.

"We must be patient," Leigh murmured.

The group members continued to pray. Their

mouths moved but made no sounds. Their hands grew clammy and cold. Robert Leigh eventually spoke, addressing the spirit of the little girl. Leigh spoke to her in gentle tones, like a doting father, imploring her to make her presence known. He wasn't quite certain she knew she was dead. Delicacy would be required.

The clock ticked. Midnight neared.

"Give us a sign, so that your dear mother, my gracious benefactress, the Countess Kitchener, can be put at ease," he said, addressing the stillness of the parlor.

As his last syllables dissipated, the table lifted off the floor. It hung in the air as if suspended from an invisible cord. It trembled.

The Countess's breaths caught in her throat.

"A most auspicious beginning," Leigh said. "The spirit has given us a sign of her presence. Leigh was a powerfully built man with a blocky, boyish face and an archly forked beard. His eyes glimmered in the lamplight like opals. "We have a guest from the realm beyond, friends. We are not alone."

The Countess gasped. She was wearing an ebon sheath of parramatta silk, trimmed with extravagant quantities of crimped crape. Her face was hidden behind a black veil. Such had been her attire ever since her daughter's death.

The clock chimed. It was midnight.

The table rocked and spun and swayed drunkenly, as if it were on the deck of a storm-tossed freighter.

The front door of the house yawned open. The

Countess screamed. Her husband leapt from his seat and turned towards the open door.

Another guest had joined them in the parlor. The guest oozed into the parlor, casting a wraith-like, fluid shadow across the far wall.

The guest was an old man.

"Levitating tables has been out of fashion for years, Herr Leigh. You might have given your customers something more to see," the guest said, his tone mocking, sardonic. He was a stooped old man with the posture, gait, and manner of a vulture. Delicate spectacles hung suspended at the precipice of his beak-like nose. The eyes behind those spectacles were deep blue. His pale lips would have looked sensual were they not bent back in a crooked sneer. The man spoke with a German accent.

The table fell, and its spindly legs clattered on the floor.

"How dare you!?" Leigh roared, standing, his fists balled up and white with rage. "You have broken the tenuous threads of connection that I had only just begun to forge. Dearest Anne, the daughter of my good hostess, the Countess Kitchener, might have been on the verge of materializing this very night. Thanks to you, her suffering, tormented parents have been prevented from laying their eyes on her for one last time."

The Countess wailed. Her husband's eyes narrowed, and he glared at Leigh from across the table.

"Her name was Eva," the old man with the German accent said. "And she wants you to go."

Leigh's face blanched.

The Countess got up from the table, gasped, and began to sob. She rushed from the room and her wails carried through the halls of the house like a sullen wind.

"Leave here," her husband growled, addressing Leigh. "Her name *was* Eva. Now, if you excuse me, I need to find my wife." He charged into the nearest corridor and his shouts echoed in the halls.

Leigh was shown from the house by an embarrassed-looking valet.

The old man stalked further into the parlor, where two guests remained. He was smiling mischievously as he removed his tattered grey overcoat and his rumpled top hat, revealing a pale bald head.

"Professor Mors, I am so very glad you accepted my invitation," Villiers said. "I thought it best if an expert were included in tonight's proceedings."

"Indeed," Mors replied, seating himself in a high-backed velvet chair. The folds of his black suit spread around him like wings. "I hope I could help you with your story, Mr. Villiers." The old man helped himself to a pour of Madeira, downing it in a single draught. "It is tragic that charlatans like Mr. Leigh profit off such despair."

Villiers agreed. He then motioned to Catherine: "Ms. Browne, I would like to introduce you to Professor Hieronymus Mors, lately an esteemed physician with the University of Munich, now conducting research at the London Library. Have I got all that right, Professor?"

The old man nodded slightly.

"I have heard much about your work," Catherine said. "But Herr Professor, I must know: how did you know the little girl's name?"

"Her death was reported in *The Times*," Mors replied blandly. "She was claimed by the cruel scythe of typhus. Had Mr. Leigh bothered to learn much about his benefactress, he would have known it." Mors poured himself another drink.

"But you said she wanted him to leave," Catherine said.

"She did," Mors said. "She's not a very friendly little girl. In truth, I have found, in my research, that the change of state occasioned by death can have *unpredictable* effects on personality. The dead are often rather less pleasant than they were in life." He chuckled, but it was a stringy, strangled sound that came out. "Far less pleasant," he added.

"How do you know?" Villiers asked.

Mors smiled. "That is my secret, my boy," he said. "I know much about the dead. They are my life's project."

"In your writings, Professor Mors, you claim that you can communicate with the dead. I think I speak for myself and Mr. Villiers: we want to know your secret," Catherine said.

"It is not so difficult to speak with the dead. Alas, Fraulein, I'm no good as a teacher," Mors replied. "My last apprentice, Amelia, came to a rather bad end. A terrible accident, I'm afraid."

"We have learned of too many common cheats

among the spiritualists," Catherine said. "But we want to know if their promise can be fulfilled, if the living can ever contact the dead." Villiers again nodded. He was growing annoyed by Catherine's dominance, by her eagerness to overshadow him.

"It can be," Mors said. "I have only seen only a little, as if I am peering into a darkened room through a keyhole. Much is hidden from me."

"Perhaps you could see further if you had students to aid you," Villiers offered.

Mors' shriveled face was split apart by a strained, tortured rictus, revealing a mouth filled with blackened teeth. His eyes glittered in the amber light. "Well, then, my young students, let us talk of the realms beyond, of the lands of the dead."

Blank eyes peered from a shriveled grey face. Brittle hair clogged with blood that was the texture of tar. Death's caress was not kind.

The dead woman lay sprawled on an old wooden table. Her limbs were bent wrongly, and her hands had become palsied, arthritic claws. There was a dusty emerald ring on one of her fingers, and a deep puncture wound in the right side of her neck. It had been made by a slender blade with a needle-fine point. It would not have killed her instantaneously.

Catherine and Villiers stood beside the table. Neither flinched. Their expressions were impassive, mask-like. The months with Mors had accustomed them to the disquieting appearance of the recently disinterred. And the smell.

This was a night they had prepared for.

"Are you ready?" Villiers asked her.

"Yes," she said. "I remember when my first kitten was buried in my family's back garden. My sisters shied away from it. They were frightened. I was fascinated."

Villiers nodded glumly. Her intensity frightened him sometimes. She'd changed so much.

Ever since the night in the Kitcheners' parlor, the pair had studied under Mors, mastering the complicated rituals and alchemical preparations Mors said would enable them to speak with the dead. Villers had learned how to collect black henbane, belladonna or mandrake, how to transfigure them into poisons and potions. He had studied the works of ancient Kabbalistic bone-conjurers. He had memorized incantations that would have, three centuries earlier, been condemned by the Catholic Church as *maleficium*, and would have led to his execution. He slept with the *Munich Manual of Demonic Magic* at his bedside.

His relationship with Catherin had changed. Where once they had been colleagues, now they were competitors, like schoolchildren jockeying for the attentions of a fickle headmaster. Catherine, the fifth and final child of an Anglo-Irish peer and colonial administrator in Assam, was accustomed to such competition; she had fought for the love of her father. Villiers found his brand of chummy, unctuous charm unequal to her relentless striving.

She out-studied him, out-read him, and daily out-smarted him. She was Mors' favorite.

But Villiers had a reason to be there. He knew that Catherine hungered for knowledge. He knew she *wanted* to know what was beyond the veil, but her motives were those of the dilettante. She was thrilled by things forbidden, and she reveled in the possibility of knowing secrets that others did not. But she was a dabbler. Villiers knew he was different. He *needed* to know. His hunger was greater than her curiosity.

But the gleam in her eyes gave him pause.

Villiers was wrenched from these thoughts by the sound of footsteps on dry boards.

Mors descended the stairs and entered the room, his basement study, carrying a candle and a gray book, secured with a clasp lock. It was coated in a trailing membrane of dust and cobwebs. His candle cast an ethereal glow, leaving the basement's dark nooks shadowed.

"Good evening, my students," he said.

Mors set the book down on the table and stared at his students. A vial of pink liquid hung from his wasted neck. Villiers knew the vial contained a mixture of milk and blood.

The study was dark, lit only by a ring of tallow candles whose wax dripped onto the earth floor, collecting in viscous pools. Rats slunk around the margins of the room, squealing.

"Who was she?" Villiers asked, motioning to the

corpse on the slab. "Where did she come from?" Catherine glared at Villiers.

"That is another of my little secrets, my boy," Mors hissed.

Mors opened the book using a key he withdrew from his overcoat. Villiers studied the book for the first time. Its front cover was engraved with strange arabesques that seemed to writhe and squirm. Villiers had to look away from the book. It made his head spin and his insides churn.

"Are you ready to begin this working?" Mors asked. Holding the candle aloft, Mors exaggerated the highlights of his face, leaving the hollows of his eye sockets and the deep crevasses of his cheeks and jaw wreathed in shadow. He looked like a talking skull.

"Yes, I am ready," Catherine answered, speaking quickly, wishing to demonstrate her zeal.

"Give me what I need to prepare the circles, Mr. Villiers, if you please," Mors said.

Villiers probed the pocket of his suit jacket for a piece of white chalk. He could not find it. He checked his vest pocket next, finding it similarly empty. He cursed himself.

"I have an extra," Catherine said. She withdrew a nub of chalk from the folds of her green skirt. She handed the chalk to Villiers, who then handed it to Mors. The old man shook his head, and a few lank strands of white hair fell before his eyes.

"Details matter, Mr. Villiers. The art of the necromancer is no different from that of a painter. A painter without a brush is not a painter at all. A necromancer without a magic circle leaves himself--or herself--open to the predations of the otherworld."

Mors carefully drew a thick circle around himself. The bone-white of the chalk glowed against the black of old loam. Then, Mors drank deep from a flask hidden in the pocket of his waistcoat and consumed a stale hunk of black bread. The vinegary smell of the liquid he consumed did not mix well with the earthy, fungal dankness of the dead woman. There was a wrongness in the air. It filled Villiers' mouth with the tang of metal, with the taste of spoiled milk.

"Now, my students, what have I done?" Mors quizzed. "Why did I consume these things?"

"You consumed unfermented grape juice and black bread. These are symbols of death, and they propitiate the dead," Villiers said, seeking to atone for the most recent of his many humiliations. He was not the student Catherine was. She was poised and self-assured. He was a bumbler.

"Good," Mors said, still chewing. "And why have we gathered here tonight?"

"We are opening the West Gate, a working which must be done when Orion is at its zenith in the night sky, as he is now," Catherine said.

Mors smiled broadly. "Impressive, my dear. What must I do next?"

Villiers scrambled to think of the next step in the working. He had been studying the manuals of High Necromancy for months, learning Latin and French and German to extract their secrets, but his knowledge now deserted him. He looked down at the table, at the dead woman, and his eyes locked with hers. They were black, fish-like; her grey tongue lolled out of her mouth like a slug. Villiers felt overcome by shame and guilt that seethed in his guts like turned meat. At least Catherine's silence told him he was not alone, that she didn't know the next step in Mors' working either.

Catherine spoke first, but her words came out in a tentative burst: "there are no invocations necessary for the summoning, no sacrifices, no rituals. All that is necessary is the purity of the scholar's desire, which is its own silent language, calling out to the dead. We must call out to the dead with our thoughts. They will come to us."

Mors shook his head. "My students, you have come far, but not far enough. There is much you still need to learn." He laughed, but the sound that came out was thick and mucoid, and it soon became a wracking cough. The old man doubled over and heaved. Villiers was struck by how sick the old man looked. He remembered his wife. Her cough. Her handkerchiefs stained with black blood. Her pale skin, cool to the touch.

He remembered her coffin being lowered into the earth.

He remembered collapsing into the wet grass beside her and watching clods of dirt being tossed onto that coffin. Rain falling.

He pushed those thoughts away. *Not now.*

Mors studied his two students, then extracted his spectacles from his pocket. He placed them on the edge of his hooked nose, and then began to flip through his book, his spindly fingers filing through the pages like a skittering spider.

After arriving at a page filled with frantic scrawling, he withdrew a long stiletto from his pocketblade gleamed in the lamplight. Ruby droplets trailed its keen edge and stained the old man's skin. He let out a sigh and let the blood flow.

"Leave me," he exhaled. "You are not yet ready to see what happens next. Tonight, I will attempt something new."

"I am ready, Professor," Catherine said. "I have learned so much. I have come so far."

Mors scowled: "Contradict me again, Fraulein, and you will be a dead woman. You have learned nothing. You know nothing. Go now. Wait for me in the library above."

Villiers and Catherine walked from the table and ascended the stairs to the rooms above. Mors' library was located on the second story of the ostentatious mansion he had purchased from the widow of the late Sir Gideon Phillips. Phillips, a book collector of staggering means and equally staggering eccentricities, who had been found floating in the Thames soon after Mors' arrival in London. Mors had been fortunate to inherit the dead man's collection of rare books and antiquities.

As they reached the top of the stairs, Mors began to read out from his book. His words were fractured, spiky and strange. The old man was speaking in a language Villiers had never heard before. He had a feeling it was a language the living had not heard in a very long time. It was a tuneless tongue, drawn from the deep desert, an inheritance from antiquity. It was a language that should have been forgotten.

Just as the pair left the basement, sealing it behind them, Villiers glanced down and saw a twitching shadow on a far wall. He could have sworn it was the shadow of a woman sitting upright.

A hand extended.

A head turned.

He turned away, unsure if he wanted to see more.

The library was a claustrophobic space, with its crimson curtains and darkly paneled walls. The floor was thick with a bedlam of Persian rugs. A low flame burned in the fireplace, providing the room with its only light. Books lay piled on the floor, like stalagmites probing skyward. Papers and parchments were scattered across Mors' desk.

Villiers had tried to study some of those papers. He hadn't made it very far. Half of what was written in them seemed like nonsense. The other half seemed like madness. Distinguishing between the two seemed impossible.

Catherine flopped into a chair and stared at the fireplace. Her long, coltish legs sprawled over the sides of the chair and she toyed with a wayward strand of her chestnut hair.

Villiers stalked the room, his hands folded behind his back, and listened to the ticking of a distant clock. A soft rain pattered on the windows.

"Did you see his knife?" Catherine said.

"Yes," Villiers replied.

"And did you see that dead woman's wound?"

"Yes."

They left the implication unstated, neither quite willing to give public voice to their private conjectures.

Villiers continued to circle the room, studying the titles of a thousand obscure volumes. Occasionally he withdrew one of the books from their shelves. He saw pale folios penned by half-crazed Cathars and leather-bound grimoires decorated by Ottoman miniaturists, scrawled with fanciful illustrations of tusked demons and scimitar-bearing angels. He wondered which ones contained the secrets he sought.

And that's when he saw it.

A small photograph carelessly tossed atop a mildewed volume that reeked of stale soil.

It was a humorless woman with a doughy face. Her hands were folded in her lap. There was a ring on one of her fingers. The woman's misery was plain. Her inner anguish and torment were written in her eyes. He recognized her.

"Amelia," Mors murmured. "As I said, she came to a rather bad end." He coughed.

Villiers started and Catherine leapt from the chair. The old man had entered the library without a sound.

"I didn't hear you come up," Catherine said.

"You ought to be more attentive to your surroundings, Fraulein. For all your cleverness, you can be a very silly, abstracted girl. Amelia was just the same."

The rain was picking up outside, lashing the walls.

"What happened to her?" Villiers asked, knowing the answer. "Or is that another one of your secrets?" He returned the photograph to its place on the shelf, but not before looking at its reverse. There was a rust-brown stain on it.

Mors chuckled and slithered further into the room, creeping in like an evening fog. He was carrying his book and his hand dripped blood.

"I think you know," the old man replied.

"Why did you kill her?" Villiers asked.

Mors sat in a chair facing the fireplace and held his spidery hands before his face, as if to examine his wound. "Procuring corpses has always been difficult for me. They are expensive to source. Amelia's limitations as a student made her an excellent candidate as a research subject." Mors let the words hang in the air, before he spoke again: "She was magnificent tonight. She lived again--briefly."

"You killed her for a parlor trick," Villiers said.

"If that is what you think, you have not come as far as I thought, Mr. Villiers," Mors replied. "We work upon the bodies of the dead, dredging the souls of subterraneous spirits out of their resting places, alluring them into their carcasses. It is a beautiful art. It is like sculpture. We imbue dead things with life. Who else can say the same? If you had seen what

I saw in the basement tonight, then you would know what we do is far more than a mere 'parlor trick.'"

"What was she like, just now?" Catherine asked, her eyes wide and wondering. Villiers knew her misgivings had been dispelled.

"How badly would you like to know?" Mors asked, withdrawing his knife from his pocket.

"Very," Catherine said. She was sitting up straight now and her bored eyes had become keen, vital. Villiers walked towards the fireplace.

Mors gingerly placed his knife on the table, then slid it between them. It sounded heavy on the old wood. Then, he spoke: "Tonight, you have a test: one of you will kill the other."

The knife gleamed on the table, cold and silver and deadly.

"I confess, my students, that I have grown weary of teaching the pair of you. And I will admit that I require further subjects for experimentation. Amelia, poor thing, proved entirely inadequate. The dead are unpredictable, it seems."

Neither Villiers nor Catherine moved. Their eyes were fixed on the knife between them.

Mors spoke again: "Whoever does this thing will learn my final lesson. The dead can be made to rise with but a word. I know that word."

It happened so quickly.

Catherine's gaze shifted from the knife to Mors

and back to the knife again. She pounced on it and lunged for Villiers. The knife hissed in the air. He fell backwards, and the blade missed his throat by inches.

She swiped at him, tossing aside chairs and books, careening forward. She was moving quickly, without control, without her customary precision. She unbalanced herself, tumbled over a velvet-fringed ottoman, and snarled. The knife slipped out of her fingers and slid onto the wooden floor. She hurled herself on it and grasped it with both hands.

Villiers backed into the corner of the library. "You don't have to do this," he said. "I don't want to kill you." That much was true. But he knew he could if it came down to it. It was the only way.

She circled him, wary, plotting her next move. He had retreated behind some stacked books.

"How much is this knowledge worth to you?" Villiers pleaded.

"I've come so far, seen so much. I want the key to unlock the final door," she said.

Still seated by the fire, Mors was smiling.

Catherine lunged forward again, and Villiers recoiled, before spinning around a stack of particularly mouldering volumes. He took one of them in his right hand as he dodged her frantic blows. She lunged again, aiming wide, and he caught the knife with the book. The blade stuck deep in the book's tough leather hide. Disarmed, Catherine shrieked and leapt on him. She coiled her fingers around his throat. He tossed the book away and did likewise.

The pair were locked in a deadly embrace, choking the life from one another.

Villiers felt her fingers dig into his corded muscles, felt his consciousness failing him, felt his body's strength draining away. His eyesight faded and the room and the woman looming above him became a blur.

There's no other way, he thought.

He thought of his wife propped up in bed, surrounded by white pillows; he thought of her ashen skin, and the droplets of blood glazing her lips; he thought of her pale eyes sunken in the cragged ruin of her lovely face, the lingering fatigue in those pale eyes, the overwhelming exhaustion in those pale eyes. He thought of her coughing fits, and of the relief in those pale eyes when the last of those fits subsided, when at last she was dead.

You must see her again.

You can recover what you have lost.

You can see her again.

There's only one way.

He dug his thumbs into Catherine's throat. He felt her muscles yield to him, and as her grip slackened, he gulped down air. Blood trickled from the edges of her mouth, stained her gritted teeth. Her lips turned blue. Her eyes faded and swam. And her fingers fell away. Her body surrendered and sank to the floor. She lay still. She stared at the ceiling, seeing nothing.

Villiers stood, rubbed his throat, and staggered

towards the fire. He wrenched the knife from the old book.

"Bravo, Mr. Villiers! Fraulein Browne, for all her gifts, lacked your commitment. I sensed this from the night we met. Come and rest by the fire, and I will tell you all that I know, of the secret worlds of the sleeping dead, and of the Invocation of Usapháis."

Villiers clutched the knife in his balled fist as he crossed the disordered library and approached the old man. The sickly pink light of dawn was filtering through the curtains.

Villiers' footsteps echoed against the wet stones of the cobbled streets. He rasped as he walked, and his throat screamed in agony. His neck was daubed in darkening bruises. He'd tied a scarf around his neck to ward off the curious.

He crept through the darkness. A thick, mustard-yellow mist slunk through the chaotic warren of back streets and alleyways. He was picking his way into the poor quarters of north London, towards Highgate Cemetery. Towards his wife.

The weather was perfect for his purposes. He doubted anyone could make out the outlines of his hooded lantern from ten paces away.

The bloodied knife he'd taken from Mors lay at the bottom of his pocket. It felt heavy, dangerous. He knew it was crusted with dried blood. Mors' blood.

You have killed, he thought. *What has become of you?*

I have killed to restore life. And I have killed to rid the world of evil.

Killing Mors had not been very difficult. He'd done it only hours before, after hours of study and toil, after the old man had taught him the words of power, the incantations that would enable him to bring back his dead wife. The old man had looked surprised when Villiers had gutted him the same way the butchers on Hornsey Road would do a fattened hog. As he lay dying, the old man had laughed and said: "That was a very rash thing to do, Herr Villiers." The old man had laughed. "There is much you do not know," he'd said, before he'd spilled his insides onto the floor.

Villiers tried not to think about it, to push those thoughts away. He had work to do.

He reached the spiked gates of the cemetery and forced them open. He looked for night watchmen and patrolling policemen on their night beats. He didn't want to be questioned or disturbed. His presence would be difficult to explain at such a late hour.

It was nearly midnight. Nearly time for the invocation.

He entered the cemetery and walked among a labyrinth of white stone tombs. He passed ruined angels whose beatific faces had been eroded to blank masks and tombstones sinking into the tangle of long grasses and wildflowers. He tripped over a disinterred femur, perhaps dropped by a neglectful gravedigger. Villiers knew that coffins in London were often stacked in pits in shambling piles, the topmost of which could be just inches below the earth's surface. In London, the bones of the dead had a way of finding their way back to the surface.

He knew where he needed to go. He knew the cemetery's layout by heart.

It did not take him long to find the crypt he sought. It reared out of the low, slinking fog, opulently decorated in the Gothic fashion favored by the well-to-do. It had been purchased by Alice's father, a prosperous banker. A journalist like Villiers could never hope to afford something so lavish, even for one he loved so dear.

Villiers stood before the crypt and let his hands run down its cold stone skin. It was new, only months old, but it would soon fall into disrepair, just like the rest of the cemetery. It was already dyed green by lichen and moss. It would yield like all the other tombs. Highgate had been opened decades earlier, as a garden cemetery for the rich. Steadily, it had been overcome by the forces of rot and ruin, given over to the weeds and the thorns.

The moon was high, glazing the tombs and crypts in a soft blue glow. It was time.

Villiers took a crowbar out from under his overcoat and forced open the lock to his wife's crypt. It came away without difficulty. He paused after he yanked the lock away, listening for signs he had disturbed the night watchmen. It wasn't likely. The man had probably drowned himself in cheap gin. The cemetery was silent.

He peered into the crypt and saw the coffin. Her coffin.

Her prison.

He hefted his crowbar in both hands and smashed the coffin apart. The moldy wood crumbled, revealing his wife's body. He yanked away the remaining wood, exposing her fully; her grey skin, peeling away from her bones in ragged ribbons; her eyeless and gaunt face, the thin skin pasted to the bones beneath; her sagging flesh, void of muscle and form; and her white dress, lashed with dark gore. It was her. He wept.

"You are just sleeping," he said, tears streaming from his mad eyes, staining his cheeks and his stubbly jaw. "I will wake you. I will make you whole again."

He knew the words now. He knew the secret.

He stood over her, in the entrance of the crypt, and collected himself. He had waited for this moment, ever since that night, nearly a year ago, when Alice had been wrenched from him forever. He had dreamt of speaking these words. He recited the words Mors had taught him, the words from the *Book of the Dead*, the words of the mad prince Usapháis, the cursed priest of Apophis who had been found murdered in a cell locked from the outside. The gnarled words rolled from his mouth and filled the silence of the crypt.

Villiers spoke slowly, deliberately. There could be no mistakes. Mors had been adamant about that. He forced himself to be calm, to steady his breathing.

I will see you soon. I will hold you soon. I will make you whole again. The thoughts churned in his mind.

Shadows gathered in the corners of the crypt.

They writhed and swirled like eddies in a dark pool, like waves rolling across the night ocean. He focused on those shadows, called them to him, and directed them towards the body in the coffin. The shadows crawled up the body, twining around the legs like snakes, and slithering up her belly, pouring themselves into the void between her breasts, and seeping themselves into the nostrils.

An eyelid twitched. It opened. The eye beneath was long gone. In its place, a pale green fire burned.

"Welcome back," Villiers said. Triumph filled him. He had done it. He had called Alice back from her rest. He had triumphed over death.

She sat upright in the coffin and stared, then moved in a jerky, reptilian way. This was odd, since Villiers had not directed her to do anything at all.

Her jaws creaked open. Her gums had receded and grown black. Her teeth gleamed. They looked long and keen.

She stood. She lurched for him. Her claw-like hands reached for him.

Something wasn't right.

Villiers wept uncontrollably and withdrew. "I love you. I missed you." he said, over and over again, pleading. He recited all the words he knew, all the incantations, all the chants. All were useless. The lurching body of Alice Villiers would not stop. She kept coming, kept reaching for him.

He staggered from the crypt, and fell on a piece of crumbling stone, and felt his ankle snap.

She was coming closer. Moving faster. Reaching. Always reaching.

Mors dragged himself away, into the long, wet grasses. He recited the words of power again, speaking them faster, louder, screaming them out. But they were wrong, all wrong, strangled by his sobs. He remembered Mors' words from months ago: "The dead are often rather less pleasant than they were in life."

He couldn't believe what was happening, that he'd come so close, that he'd learned so much, that he'd killed for her, that he'd courted madness for her, that her cold, clammy hands could wrap themselves around his throat, that those cold, clammy hands could feel so vital and strong, that his dead wife's corpse could contain such impossible power, that Alice Villiers could throttle him so easily.

In a room lit by a single candle a woman was seated at a low table, draped in rich green cloth. She was flanked by four others, one of whom was weeping. It was the murdered man's sister. Their heads were hung low, in prayer. The woman yawned and brushed some crumbs from her white dress. She glanced idly at her watch. The clocks in the house had been stopped at the time when the police estimated the man had been strangled to death.

It was almost midnight. It was almost time for the show to begin.

She addressed the still and silent and very

cold room: "Robert Villiers, give us a sign of your presence." She tried to muster as much enthusiasm as she could, but it was hard to say the words with conviction. She'd conducted the same ceremony four times this week. "Give us a sign," she repeated.

The candle flickered. And went out.

CECILIA

E. SENECA

LET ME TELL YOU OF MY sister, and what became
of her; the peculiar fate that even now still
haunts my nightmares.

She was always an odd girl, much given to intro-
spection as a result of her sickly nature. A fragile
thing, Cecilia spent a good part of her childhood
confined to a chair on account of broken bones. I
devoted all my spare time to wheeling her about,
keeping her company so she would not become
lonely. Long hours we spent outside on the green,
and she would listen with sparkling eyes as I read
to her from whatever book she would eagerly
press into my hands. The pain she suffered did not
seem to touch her when we were together, and it
heartened me that I could bring her such joy in the
hours we shared. I thought of her daily when I was

away tending to Father's business, and yearned to return to see her smile as soon as I possibly could.

It was following one of my extended absences that I noticed a change had come over her. She had, for once, not suffered any particularly debilitating injuries: but a curious set of bruises marred her pale, thin wrists and the column of her throat, as far as along her cheekbones when I found her sitting alone in her room. She smiled up at me, but there was a curious absence to her limpid brown eyes, an almost hollowness to her gaze that chilled me down to my very core.

"Hello," she said, and when she took my hands, her fingers were limp and clammy like wet leaves. As I squeezed them, she made no effort to return the gesture, and I feared that some new torment had befallen her, some new failing of her mishap-prone body to tear her further away from me.

"Cecilia, what on earth happened to you?" I kissed her cheek, and that too was frigid although she sat mere feet away from the hearth. "You're so cold, and what are all of these bruises?"

"Oh, nothing..." As I smoothed the lank, wispy strands of hair away from her brow, she leaned into my palm. "I went out on a walk a few days ago. Out to the wood beyond the meadow—you know, by our favorite place?"

"The wood...?" Certainly, I recalled the wood and its dappled shadows and rustling leaves that would often be a backdrop to my voice. "Why would you go there?"

"I didn't intend to, at first. Oh, sit down, Sam."

She tugged me into my customary chair by her side, and it seemed that my presence had grounded her slightly, for some of the focus returned to her gaze as she spoke. Still, I maintained my hold on her hands, hoping both to warm them and to draw her back to herself. "I wanted to see the flowers in the meadow before they wilted—the daffodils are so lovely this time of year, you know, I wish you could have seen them with me—and the weather was so nice that I brought lunch with me. And then..."

She trailed off, staring into space with a vacant smile. I waited, but no response came. "Cecilia?"

"Oh, yes." She shook herself, brushing a lock of hair behind her ear, her lace-edged sleeve sliding down her wrist with the motion, revealing more of those curious, round purplish bruises dotting her arm, no larger than a coin. "I sat outside for a while on the grass, and then—" her voice became soft and wondering, "—it seemed as though I heard a voice, calling out from the trees."

A voice? That couldn't be possible. I had been out there with her more times than I could remember, and all had been completely ordinary. I wanted to believe her, but I could not help wonder if perhaps the sun had addled her senses. She had occasionally made comments about hearing or seeing strange things, but whenever I had gone to look, there had never been anything there. And it had been years since the last time she'd said such a thing. For the habit to return suddenly like this was strange... "What kind of voice?"

"Hmm, it was a very pretty voice, like a wind

chime, soft and tinkling, but it was also whispery... I've thought of it as the voice you imagine a rose would have!" She pulled her other hand free of mine to clap them together in delight. "But it didn't say anything in particular, almost as though it were singing a wordless song."

I took one of her hands back, finding it still cold. "So you went after it, and that's how you hurt yourself, then?"

Cecilia laughed, merry and completely carefree. "Yes, exactly. I got caught on a nettle bush! So I came home."

Nettles? But nettles would not leave such regular bruises. It was so painfully incorrect, yet she did not appear to be lying, and she would not conceive of such a pitifully transparent lie if she wished to lie in the first place, surely. At a loss for words, I did not know whether to believe her or doubt her. Perhaps it had all been nothing but a dream beneath the spring sunshine.

But I did not wish to spoil her mood. Squeezing her hand, I said, "Be careful when I am not around, Cecilia."

"I will, I will."

Yet however sunny her smile was, the chill that had sunk into my bones refused to leave.

There is much to be said for the force of curiosity. I had only a matter of days at home, but I was compelled to head out to the wood to witness with my own eyes that which Cecilia spoke. I left the house at the crack of dawn, drawing my coat around me as the remnants of early morning frost crackled beneath my boots, and the chilly air nipped at my cheeks as I hurried through the fields and beneath the cold shadows of the trees. 'Twas a sprawling estate which we had, though all its splendor meant little when it could not cure Cecilia of her ills, merely comfort her.

The meadow stood just the same as ever, with the yellow heads of the daffodils anointed by dew glistening beneath the pale rays of sun breaking through the clouds. Beyond, at its northernmost edge, was the wood, the cluster of trunks dark and forbidding despite the light. What was more, it was far enough that I could not see how Cecilia could have heard anything without being near it. Our favorite spot was the bench by the honeysuckle bush, which was rather close to the path on which I stood, beside an old oak to offer shelter. To hear even the sound of the branches or the call of a bird, she would need to be in the center of the meadow at the very least. But that in and of itself was not so strange, that she would be walking among the wildflowers...

I followed what I guessed were her footsteps, picking my way through the meadow, ears pricked as insects stirred and fluttered away, the sunlight beginning to melt away the thin mist that hung over the banks of the flowers. The dew smeared onto the ends of my coat, and though I listened, I could discern no sound but for the minute rustling of the leaves and the stems crunching softly underfoot.

When I reached the edge of the wood, where the shadows of the canopies fell a scant few inches from my feet, I halted, peering uneasily into their depths. Seldom had I reason to come this far, much less venture beneath the branches. And however much I looked and however little I saw, I had but little inclination to go forth. A nameless discomfort crept over my soul as I gazed past the first-line guardians at the dank shadows gathered at the bases of the trunks, a chilly foreboding seeping through my veins.

It was then that a gust of wind swept past me, and shuddering, I curled deeper into my coat, in the process chancing to glance down, and I saw the trail of flowers leading into the wood. Red and yellow petals swayed in the breezy aftermath, beckoning me down a hitherto–unseen path. I regarded them warily, but curiosity bade me step inside—not merely curiosity, but the desire to confirm what Cecilia had seen, to assuage my fears and banish my doubts. My wish was that there was nothing at all here, that she had simply fallen into a daydream, but I would not know until I ventured beneath the sharp-edged leaves.

The very fact that I felt such apprehension for something so simple was totally absurd, and that thought was enough to jolt my heavy feet into motion. There was nothing here, and I would be certain of it.

As soon as I strode past the initial trees, it seemed as though the rest of the world fell away, and a horrible, deafening silence descended as the myriad leaves blotted out the golden morning light, reducing it to a mere handful of thin shafts slanting across the path. Tiny motes of pollen thrown up by my steps glinted as they danced in and out of shadow, and the only motion that I could discern was the swaying of the flowers, to and fro, to and fro, in some hypnotic rhythm that lured me onward, onward. How were these flowers flourishing so abundantly with so little sun?

I followed the path as it curved toward the heart of the wood, and as the shadows grew deeper, I became aware of *something*—a noise, but it was more than merely a noise. It was a whispering susurrus of leaves when the gallery of branches above me was stock-still, a sound that reminded me for all the world of a deep, full-bodied sigh of wistful, yearning anticipation. There was something *hungry* in it, as if a tantalizing meal waited just out of reach.

I froze in my tracks, heart thudding in my throat in the grip of pure terror. The utterly irrational thought lanced across my mind that the wood was *alive*, and not in the conventional sense, yet at the moment, it felt completely plausible. If not the wood itself, then something lurked beyond the point where I'd halted: something within the swirling shadows but a few feet away, something just past the curtain of darkness that seemed as thin and fragile as gauze; something *breathing*, warping the space around it.

While I still remained in possession of my faculties, I turned and ran headlong down the path whence I came, heedless of the flowers plucking at my ankles like burrs, attempting to pull me back; ran until I burst out of the wood and into the blinding glory of the sunlight, only stumbling to a standstill when I reached the middle of the meadow, gasping for breath. And it was only then that I looked back, staring at the wood as my skin prickled horribly with gooseflesh.

Perhaps I had been wrong; perhaps this entire episode was nothing but my mind playing tricks on me. But my every instinct rebelled at the idea of setting foot in there again. I did not know what resided there, and I did not wish to. I no longer had even the shaky reassurance that such impossible things did not exist. Rather than waste my energies on this, I ought to do what I still could, which was ensure that my dear little sister never returned there again.

I picked a handful of daisies for her as a souvenir, and returned home.

During the week when I remained at home, Cecilia was more herself. The distance that had appeared in her eyes that evening did not return, although her bruises took rather longer to disappear than they ought, even for her, and for such shallow wounds. They remained, stark on her pale skin, catching my eye every time she moved despite her attempts to conceal them with long sleeves. She insisted that she felt no pain when I probed them, and we did not speak of what she had supposedly heard, nor what I had supposedly seen. I was only too eager to forget the entire episode, and to my relief, she did not request that we take an excursion to the meadow despite the very fine weather.

For those scant few days, I could almost believe that all was normal.

But when I closed my eyes at night, behind them swam the image of the shadows that I had merely glimpsed; the silence of the manor mirrored the hideous silence of the woods; and I could not help but picture the grasping leaves that had tried to reel me back swarming over Cecilia's shape, leaving those scratches and bruises that she so casually dismissed. My sleep was but fitful, and I could not explain to her my fears when I could scarcely comprehend them myself. The best I could do was entreat her not to return to the wood.

It was this that I begged her not to do as my hour of departure neared. Never had I more wished that I could remain! Never had I more loathed my duties! The sense of foreboding that had gripped me since I had witnessed her bruises only grew heavier with every passing minute, and it seemed as though now—however outwardly well she appeared—she needed my presence more than ever, even if she herself was not aware of it. Yet I could not rationally explain my fears, and not rationally provide any justification for acting out of the normal. All I knew, with a sickening sense of horror, was that she ought to stay as far away from that copse of trees as she could.

As I held her hands, her fingers felt so very cold beneath my own, her slim body so very fragile in the spring breeze, and she looked like a china doll in the way the heavy frills of the dress hung off her frame.

"Cecilia, promise me you will not go to the wood. Not alone. Please."

Innocently she tilted her head at me. The chain of daisies she'd made with my gift still sat upon her head, curiously refusing to wither. "But why?"

"Just promise me. It isn't safe."

Her brow furrowed in confusion, but nevertheless, she nodded. "I promise, Sam."

"Thank you. I will return in a fortnight... Hopefully by then, these will have disappeared." I ran my fingers over the bruises on the backs of her hands, and they felt curiously rougher than I remembered, contrasting sharply with the rest of her thin, smooth skin. Perhaps it was a sign of their healing, I thought, foolishly unwilling to fully give up the last dregs of my hope.

"Oh, Sam! Don't worry about those, they'll be gone soon." She kissed my cheek with her soft, rosebud lips. "Now, you must hurry, otherwise you'll miss your train and Father will be unhappy with you."

This was true, but leaving her was almost physically painful when I could not shake the sense that some impending doom was approaching, like the creeping shadows I saw behind my eyelids.

Alas, all of my meager efforts amounted to nothing. When I anxiously returned home after a two-week absence, I found not a Cecilia who was hale and hearty, but one who was distracted and sickly. It was early evening by the time I arrived, and she was already abed, hours before she usually was, and her absence in coming to greet me sent a lurch through the pit of my stomach. I hastened to her room, and found her buried beneath the blankets, her face scarcely visible beneath the layers pulled up to her chin.

Her eyes were closed, dark shadows visible beneath them even in the dim light, and a fug of sickness hung over the room, palpable from the very moment of entry, stifling and uncomfortable. I crept slowly across the carpet, not wishing to disturb her obviously shallow rest, however much I wished to see her smile at me. I stopped a few feet away, holding my breath, my twin desires warring with each other as I took in how sallow her cheeks were, how pallid and waxy her skin.

Worst of all, the bruises were still there. If anything, they were darker than before, deep black spots on her face almost like holes. The sight of them rooted me to the spot, unable to avert my gaze. Completely bloodless, they resembled blotches of ink, but deeper in hue than anything man could create, as if the very substance of her skin had been eaten away from within and this gaping emptiness was all that was left, so deep that even the flickering light of the embers could not reach its bottom.

I must have made a noise of some sort, for she stirred presently, mumbling, "Sam...?"

Jolting out of my stupor, I fell to my knees by the side of her bed, my hand hovering an inch away from her feverish forehead, not quite daring to touch her. "Yes, yes, I'm here."

"Oh, you're back," whispered Cecilia, barely audible. "That's—that's good. I—I missed you."

"I missed you too..." The question came to my tongue, impossible to suppress. "What happened...?"

She made a vague noise, eyes still closed. "Don't worry about me, I'll be fine. We can... go out, tomorrow, the weather's been so nice... Out to the meadow, to have a...a picnic. Make more daisy chains." Yet still, the one from before sat on her nightstand, making my heart twist in my chest.

"Of course, as soon as you feel better. There's nothing to worry about, I'm here now."

The corners of her mouth curved upward, and a few of the tense lines in her forehead smoothed out. "Will you stay with me tonight...? I feel better if you're close. I'm sure you'd much rather sleep in your own bed, but..."

"I wouldn't be anywhere else."

The bang of a door slamming shut startled me awake. Having dozed off into an uneasy slumber in a chair, I jolted immediately into disorientation as pain shot through my neck. The room was dark, the embers nearly extinguished in the grate. A cold draft blew past me, and I wondered just who had placed the extra quilt over me, and who had left the door open. Perhaps one of Cecilia's nurses, come to check on her? But as my vision began to adjust to the gloom, I saw there was no one there, only a thin vein of moonlight creeping through the doorway to gild the bed frame. I followed it with my eyes towards the head of the bed, and my heart sank as I realized I was alone.

Cecilia was gone.

I sprang to my feet, peeling back the bedclothes—but the bed was empty, the sheets cold to the touch indicating that she had already been gone some time. Seizing my coat from the chair I'd flung it over and a lantern, I rushed into the hall, where I saw the chill came from one of the side doors hanging ajar into the starry night, and realizing my worst fears. There was only one place she could have gone. But why, and how in such a condition? Where had she found the strength to rise; what infernal cause could have granted her the energy?

I ran faster than I knew I was capable of running, pelting out into the cold. Beneath the silvery light from the heavens, I could discern footprints in the frost, small and dainty enough to be hers, weaving unsteadily across the grounds and down the path that led to the meadow, and the wood. I didn't know which I dreaded more—finding her collapsed on the ground out of exhaustion, or not finding her at all. How far could she have gotten, how long had she been gone? And how had I slept through her departure?

The meadow spread out before me, almost white with hoary frost, white like my breath, making clouds in the air before me. Each stem, each leaf, each petal was perfectly still and frozen under the alien face of the moon, a painting in monochrome—how surreal it all looked, how dreamlike! It was only the frantic thudding of my heart and the rasping of my breath that told me the world around me was real, the savage beat of fear resonating through every fiber of my being. I had hoped to see her here, among the flowers, or perhaps on our bench, but there was no sign of her or any living being other than myself, the only testament to her passage being her footsteps cutting straight through the daffodils, leading directly towards the wood.

How tiny and meager my single candle's flame in my hand as I crossed the meadow, how it flickered and guttered in the wind despite its glass shield; how feeble it was as I reached the edge of the wood in a matter of heartbeats and held it up to the wall of trees. They loomed over me, their leaves rustling at me aggressively, warningly. I could almost hear words in that painfully loud noise, demanding that I turn back, that I leave, that I extinguish the fire I held dangling in my fingers. But I would not, I would not depart until I had my sister in my arms. I stared into the thick shadows, pushing down my instinctive fear, and strode forth.

The darkness of the wood was almost absolute. Only the sparsest rays of moonlight sidled through the canopy to supplement that of my lantern, which threw only the smallest circle of light before me, its orange glow painfully artificial. All around me, the trunks towered, ancient and impenetrable, and dozens of tiny unseen hands grappled at my ankles while the leaves sang in their throaty voices, the wind itself their breath, swelling and shrinking as their respiration. Finally, I heard it, what she had spoken of—the song.

It began slow and faint, but with each step I took, it grew louder, weaving through the trees: a song without words, a haunting melody comprised of nothing but a single voice, rising and falling. It sent a powerful frisson reverberating through me, rattling me down to my very bones. The silvery, dulcet tones of it made me want to close my eyes, to remain in place and sway to its rhythm, to its impossible beauty, but I could not let myself be lulled by it. I had to keep going, even as each note plucked at my blood, for as beautiful as it was, so too did it cause me fear, its freezing touch interwoven with the wonder I felt.

With every step forward, I felt acutely how alone I was, how isolated from the rest of the world. The place whence I came did not seem to exist beyond the trees: there was only the wood, cutting me off from everything I knew. I inhaled a shaky breath, and summoned up my voice to call out my sister's name.

"Cecilia!"

It barely carried, sounding small and faint even to my own ears. I could not see where I was going nor what crunched beneath my feet. As I caught myself on the trunks as I went, the things that tore at my boots pushed me in directions I could not see, and with the roots tangling under my soles, I was powerless to stop them. Besides, I thought desperately, perhaps they would guide me to her. If they were strong enough to compel me, they would almost certainly mislead her. Perhaps she'd fallen, and they had whisked her away, like a procession of fairies.

How long I was in the wood, I did not know. There was no escape. All around me, the trees looked identical no matter which way I turned, branches blocking my path and snapping against my body as I pushed past them, frost stinging my face. No matter how high I held my lantern, I could discern nothing different, nothing but an endless parade of wood and bobbing leaves. I seemed to be walking in circles, with only the tug of the flowers to direct my feet, and the song, slowly growing louder and louder until it seemed to ring in my ears, to thrum in my veins.

And so suddenly, the flowers hurled me forward, and my shin caught on something, sending me tumbling to the ground, desperately protecting the lantern with my body. I heard the glass crack, but the flame mercifully held, and frantically I scrambled to my knees, righting the lantern.

I was in a clearing. Was this the heart of the wood? I held the fire up, but here the canopy was so thickly tangled that the sky was no longer visible, a roof of darkness far overhead like that of a cathedral.

It was then that I realized the song had ceased,

and instead, there came a faint, slight giggle, girlish and soft, that turned my blood to ice.

I strained my eyes again, searching the swirling, woolen darkness before me, and something rustled as I stood and forced myself to take a step forward, and then another, and another, terror clawing at the inside of my chest.

With four steps, I became aware of another living being in the clearing with me; with five, I could make out moving extremities; with six, the gleam of what appeared to be eyes; with seven, I finally bore witness to what it was.

An entity sprawled on a bed of daisies—an entity which only tenuously resembled a human being. Its legs were composed of dozens of intertwined, feathery roots teeming with prehensile hairs; its torso slender and green and thorny, visible through the translucent, iridescent petals growing from its long throat; its arms, resting limp by its sides, comprised of several enormous, sharp leaves pulsing with thick veins and tiny flowers blooming in between them. Its head lolled against a tree, masses of pale hair-like vines cascading down its trunk, twitching minutely.

And its face—oh, its face! Its face was serene, white as the moon, but as it stirred and mumbled something incomprehensible, its face pulsed, revealing thousands of crisscrossing patterns like the face of a sunflower, the black underside of the mosaic briefly visible. There was no nose, only a gash for a mouth that hung open just slightly, and a pair of enormous eyes that lay closed, fringed by incredibly thick crimson eyelashes.

As it stirred again, something tangled up in the collar of buds around its neck gleamed, catching my eye, and my breath caught agonizingly in my throat as I saw it was a chain of daisies.

That unconscious sound shattered the fragile calm. The creature opened its eyes; horrible, revolting eyes they were, horrendous in their massive size and filled with half a dozen swollen irises of irregular size and shape and the most shockingly vivid blue.

It opened its awful mouth, revealing rows of needle-sharp teeth, and gave an erratic lurch perhaps in an aborted attempt to rise—but I did not wait. Panic and fear and horror swelling to a crescendo in my chest, I whirled and ran for my life, tearing through the branches and tripping over roots, sheer terror propelling me onward as the song began again. This time it was infinitely more sorrowful, rising higher in pitch and volume, but the fear did not allow me to stop until I burst from the trees and stumbled into the meadow, rolling to a wheezing halt in a bed of flowers and staring at the wood with smarting eyes, fully expecting that cursed creature to pursue me and having no strength to run further.

As the seconds dragged by into minutes, nothing happened; only my gasping filled the night air beneath the cold unfeeling stars, and the wind swept around me, petals tumbling away across the frosty grass. The leaves of the wood rustled a scant few feet away, oppressive and savage, but there was no other motion. The unreal nature of the scene before me began to fade, and the truth of what I'd seen began to sink into my consciousness, and with it, the stifling weight of grief.

With nothing else to do, I picked myself up and limped home.

This was some years ago. The estate and the grounds belong to me, now. Many a time I have contemplated razing the wood, to put an end to its perpetual dark shadow cast over my days. But I have never been able to bring myself to do so, for when I close my eyes, what I remember most clearly is that monster reaching out for me with its leafy hands, its hideous eyes staring at me.

Whenever I see that image in my mind, I push it down and lock it away. I do not try to think of it, nor what it is. I believe—I believe very truly at the bottom of my heart that it was her, but I cannot bear the thought of what awful transformation she underwent to become that *thing*, and whether or not it was her will. I can only hope that it was, for the alternative is too horrid to contemplate, even if the reasons for such a change are beyond my comprehension. Certain things are best not pondered, and I prefer to think of my sister as dead, stolen by the illnesses that perpetually laid siege to her fragile body.

But on cool, clear nights when I have enough liquid courage in my veins, if I sit on the bench by the meadow, it seems that I can hear a faint singing emanating from the wood. But I do not dare set foot within its shadows.

Mother of Rotten Reeds & Duckweed

Artoria Sahnow

IF I HAVE A SOUL, THEN I do not know if it sings. I'd never given much thought to the idea of a soul—there was never any call for such nonsense. When you know you're already on God's wrong side, the best thing is to put it out of mind until the end comes.

It was a hazy, drizzly London night when Mr Jameson called for me. A cab picked me up from Piccadilly Circus around ten, and just on time—I'd spotted a pair of hard-looking boys in bowlers arming their way through, one walking sort of stiff, which meant he had a poker in his trouser, no doubt. They were speaking to some of the other lads, who were playing bluff, and distracted the two thuggers long enough for me to accost the hansom, make sure it was mine, and abscond from the villains.

Ten was our usual time, although I hadn't seen Jameson for some months. In our heyday, we would meet fortnightly, but he had suddenly dropped off contact, and the handwritten letter I had received that day was the only sign that he was even still alive. I had never been to his house before—it was a glorious one, like nothing I was destined for. His manservant led me into the parlour, where Jameson was sitting with a gin. He was dressed in a fine smoking jacket, every hair in place on his handsome head, his moustache growing out from last I saw him, albeit still just as groomed.

"Welcome, William. Please take a seat. It is wonderful to see you again," he said.

The manservant left us. I sat down, looking about the room. A painting hung on the west wall, two gentlemen standing arm-in-arm. I recognised one of them as Jameson. The other was a soft-faced, clean-shaven man, tall and thin, a look of distant melancholy in his eye.

"Glad to see you, Mr Jameson. You've got an awful nice place here."

"Thank you, William. Sorry for being silent for so long. My wife has taken a devastating turn, and we are unsure of whether she will pull through. As such, I must remain by her side until the end comes."

"I'm sorry to hear that, Mr Jameson. Really."

"It was expected even when we married. Although I cannot love her as she loves me, still I adore her as a woman of wit and beauty. As such, you and I,

William, will not be," and he hushed, "meeting for some time. But that isn't why I called you here. I would ask a considerable favour of you. One of my long friends has not contacted me in some time, and I am worried about his possible condition. My friend, the gentleman Zachary Jackson—you can observe him in that painting—used to send me a letter from Liverpool once a year, and I one back, on consistent dates. We were the closest of companions, from early youth to our days in the theatre; Zachary was an unearthly performer of opera. Our letters were long-form pieces; as such we didn't have reason to send them in excess. His mind is exquisitely detailed..."

Jameson looked off for a second, and I saw a hint of the same melancholy I'd felt from the eyes of his painted friend.

"Last year, I had assumed his letter had been lost; now that the date has passed once again and I have received nothing, I can do naught but fret. If my wife were in good health, I would seek out Jackson myself; as it is, I will not be able to leave for some time. My worry for Jackson's health is great, however; I would ask you to seek him out. I would pay you well for your work; ten pounds, I would offer."

Of course, I agreed right away. I could feel the sorrow leaking from the noble Mr Jameson, for a start—I'd have agreed just down to that. But I also needed to get out of the city for a while, and ten pounds was a chump's fortune. I told Mr Jameson my plight—some taffy prick had fucked around with my lovely Ada, not paid him what he owed, and then threatened to tell the law that Ada was dressing up womanly to let men have it with him and get paid and all that, and Ada was distraught. He was saying he was going to top himself off. So I paid the taffy prick a visit and got that money and made sure he wouldn't be speaking to anyone. I'd just meant to give him a scare...but I went too far and knocked all his teeth out, and left his jaw all fucked up and broken, and in front of his kid, too. I'd heard he had some villainous connections, and his boys were already looking for me, so I needed to get out of the city until it calmed down, or else use Jameson's payment to leave London for good upon my return.

Jameson let me stay the night in one of the many spare rooms, and I'd hoped he might visit once everything was quiet, but he didn't show. The next morning he had me some nice clothes brought in—said he'd have had them tailored but what with me needing to be off, these would do—and they did. Lovely garments. I'd never felt so sweet—stovepipe and all. In a quiet moment, Jameson gave me a kiss on the lips, but nothing more. His wife called shortly after, and he had to attend to her. His manservant led me out to the carriage—great big thing, with two lovely stallions harnessed—and we were away.

I'd never been out of London in my life, and the first day I enthused at all the sights I saw. By the second day, my arse was hurting, and shitting outside wasn't much fun either. Just wanted to get to the bloody destination—Toxteth it was called, in Liverpool. Cab driver said Liverpool was going to be bigger than London before long—all manner of people were coming through, and with the Irish in large number the city had doubled in size in just a couple decades. My interest was piqued, but I knew I had other business to attend to first.

I'd have been fit to stay in Liverpool the first night—it really was a wonder, New York of the North they called it—the docks were still brimming with activity, and the pubs were raucous. But with handsome Mr Jameson's sorrow in mind, I pushed on to Toxteth.

Cold blew the wind that night, the mist lying low upon the Mersey. Dock bells clanged distantly. The last stretch of the journey was rough, the glorious carriage swapped for a rattling cart that knocked my arse right out of shape.

The main street of Toxteth was wide open and dimly gaslit, the fog of the river creeping all from the banks and leading these couple miles inland, breathing softly on the cobblestone and dirt tracks. The first few rows of houses we passed were slummy, hastily constructed, but past them were real big ones, mansions like Mr Jameson's. I supposed Liverpool was just like London, then: the rich side-by-side with the poor, all sharing the same grubby water. There was an overgrown aspect to this city, though—wilder, as if nature and man had not yet made peace.

I arrived, finally, at the Phoenix Inn, which surrounded itself on one side by narrower streets of common housing and the other by grand abodes. It overlooked a sizable park, at this time a shadow-cloaked undulation, within which I fancied the sight of shimmer, possibly a small lake.

"What hour is it?" I called as I entered the candlelit inn, observing a small gathering at the bar.

"Late," called back a man's voice, scrappy and local.

"Have you a room?"

"Yeah, I've got a room."

I paid and signed in, watched by the gaggle at the bar, a curious quartet of regulars.

"Where you coming from, then?" asked one of them, a young man with a nascent beard.

"London."

"I thought so. Don't hear that accent much around here."

"I'm looking for a friend," I said, removing my coat and hat. "Perhaps you know him—Zachary Jackson."

They looked amongst each other, one slightly cracking a smile.

"No idea," said another of the company.

They were a motley sort, probably only a couple of years older than me. I was fifteen, but nobody ever believed that. I puffed my chest slightly and left them to their drinks. My room was on the chilly side, and the bed was not quite the king-sized promised, but I hadn't it in me to complain, the time by carriage since my last bed so sore in immediate memory—I had barely undressed before I fell asleep, leaving my case to be unpacked the next day.

Time escaped me entirely. My bones ached, a

dreadful humour overcoming them, and it was as if I was sleeping in that old carriage still. Something lulled me awake—I found myself groaning, sitting up, lighting a bedside candle. I felt immensely drained, the toll of travel finally sinking in.

As my senses came about, I heard something: high-pitched and tuneful at first, I aligned to the window to better listen. It was a song—a lady's voice, out there in the night. Perhaps she was walking alone. The melody was hard to pin, and myself not being a man of much musical knowledge past the silly rhymes of childhood, I could not yet say much whether it was major or minor. It was distant—must have been rather loud at the source. I looked across the moonlit park but saw not a soul. I went back to my bed and ensconced myself in the prickly sheets, and listened on—the longer I listened, the more the song started to unnerve me, for there seemed no breaks to breathe, it was simply one continuous string of notes—and the last thought I had before I passed back into sleep was the sense that the music was *submerged*.

My first destination was Mr Jackson's house. The local people of Toxteth were friendly at first, although upon hearing my accent seemed suddenly guarded—their directions to the street I required were absurdly vague. Eventually, I met a small group of Irish, and after some accent difficulties, their seeming leader said they would walk me to my location. The five of them, led by my amiable namesake William, were day-labourers seeking work, having travelled here to live with family who had left Ireland during the Potato Famine. They led me well to my destination—but upon seeing the abode, which was of course supposed to be Mr Jackson's home, I could not at first believe it. It was one of a row of small houses near the neighbouring town of Dingle, quite close indeed to the riverside, and it was in a state of disrepair: the windows were boarded up, the door cracked and peeling, weeds running through the small garden. I had expected a house equalling the splendour of Mr Jameson's house—could this really be the home of Mr Jackson?

I knocked, futilely, on the door. The address was correct, no doubt about it. After deliberating for a while, I was able to convince William and his friends to get the door ajar for me, in exchange for a small payment. They didn't want to stick around after that, despite Dingle being a quiet little place, and so I entered the house alone.

Inside it was dusty and rotten through with damp. It was meagrely furnished, and with little in the way of personality—indeed it looked like some of the boarding houses I had spent the last few years in. Only the bedroom contained anything of interest, for it seemed the desk had been ransacked, some blank sheets of crumpled paper and a few pieces of worthless, rusted jewellery lying atop it. The mirror had been smashed, and inside the wardrobe were moth-eaten articles of clothing, some of those worn usually by common men like me, as well as a selection of finer lady's clothing. Mr Jameson had not mentioned Mr Jackson having a wife—could this indeed have been Jackson's house? Had he simply moved prior and lost Jameson's address? No answers seemed right to me, and I felt quickly a rush of unease in the place, but before I left, I performed a swift but thorough search of the rest of the room.

There were several other scraps of paper littered about the place, a few under the bed. Most were too water-damaged to read, but one, written in an elegant, feminine hand, read:

hours in St Laurence Church
left in this life, soon to be one with

I took it with me, just in case, yet it gave me little to work with. What was I to do? Return to Jameson empty-handed and without a single lead to follow? Certainly not. I would follow up on the church later. First, I knocked upon the door of the house to the left. An older woman opened it and observing my fine clothing, frowned.

"What do you want, then? If you're looking for Arthur, he's not in."

"No, good lady, I'm here to enquire about the tenant next door," I said, pointing to the dishevelled house.

"Nobody's lived there for two years," she said.

"Well, who lived there two years ago?"

"Why do you want to know?"

"I'm searching for a friend—Mr Zachary Jackson. He's a gentleman."

"No gentleman lived around here."

I relayed his appearance—based on the painting in Jameson's house—but to no further avail. Before I left, a thought came to me.

"I heard singing last night, somewhere in the town."

The lady nodded grimly.

"You heard it too?"

"Yes. And you'd be best staying away from the Dingle if you hear it again," said the lady.

"Why's that, then?"

She smiled wryly.

"Jenny Greenteeth."

"Who in Heaven is that?"

"She lives down in the river. She preys on nosy young boys like you, who think they know better. *Down by the Mersey, Jenny Greenteeth sleeps, Mother of Rotten Reeds and Duckweed; if you hear her song after night, stay close to the light, or Jenny'll give you a deathly fright!*"

She laughed softly after humming the silly little rhyme. I had no time for her Spring-heeled Jack nonsense, and left without saying another word. On my walk back I identified St Laurence Church, resting somewhere between Toxteth and Dingle. The boundary between the two towns was vague—it seemed to me that it'd have been sensible to simply call it all Liverpool.

St Laurence Church was not an imposing sight, built in a Norman style yet clearly not an architectural artefact. It had a small graveyard that carried down to a larger field, where children played amongst the trees. Inside it was cold, I realised due to one of the stained glass windows being broken. I observed the damage, likely a thrown stone.

"The children," said a deep voice from behind me.

It was the minister, a man in his autumn years who stood tall and broad in his vestments, with overgrown white hair and a white beard flecked with once-bronze.

"There are some unruly youths in this town. They need guidance but reject it. I try to simply forgive them. My apologies; I am Father August, welcome to St Laurence."

I greeted the minister, introduced myself, and asked him whether he knew Mr Jackson.

"I knew the Mr Jackson you spoke of, yes. From London, like you. He left town two years ago, so you're rather late, I'm afraid."

Another dead end. I would have to set off back to London the next day, and tell Jameson of my failure. Before I left the church, I know not why, I asked the priest:

"What do you know of Jenny Greenteeth?"

The minister looked taken aback, but he regained his composure quickly.

"A fairy tale used by parents to scare children. They say she lives in the Mersey, and invites young men down to the banks with her song; that she takes the form of a beautiful but wet and river-muck speckled lady, but when her quarry gets close, they see her true form, one that is too horrific for words."

"A folk tale, as I thought. Yet I did hear singing last night."

"Yes, there is cause for the tale. The singing from

the banks, and the disappearance of three young men, some years back. There have been others that have claimed to see this spirit, yet no material evidence. Other disappearances have been linked to her—but they are easily put down to young men travelling, as is their wont—take your Mr Jackson, for example. It is all clearly mild hysteria, ultimately; God would not allow for such an abomination to exist."

I lay in my bed in the Phoenix Tavern, lightly dozing. Earlier, I'd had some drinks at the bar, and spoke again to Irish William and his friends. They were wary of the topic of Jenny Greenteeth—it seemed they really believed it. I got details about the first disappearances, and when the bankside singing first started—two years ago, thereabouts. Yet none of those who went missing at that time were Jackson, they were younger types, apparently around my age. Yet, the myth of Jenny Greenteeth was older than the singing and the disappearances—it dated back to antiquity. I steered the conversation back away from the singing water spirit, instead sharing bawdy tales with my new friends—with the men's names switched for women, of course—and forgetting my troubles with strong drink. Yet, as I dozed, I once again lost sense of time, and when I came about, still fully dressed, the bedside candle almost out of wax and wick, I could hear it: the submerged singing.

Definitely, now, I could sense that it sounded as if it was coming from *underwater*. It was entrancing, and I felt a pull like no other—I found myself in the gaslit streets of Toxteth, my shoes clacking and echoing on the mist-strewn cobbles, dragging myself—still drunk—towards Dingle. Not a soul passed me on the way, and the song did not get louder as I got closer, but maintained an exact volume, ethereal and troubling, drowned in duckweed and moss, with no breaks in the disquieting melody.

At first I stumbled and staggered, but the night air brought me around, a velvet-gloved slap to the face. I was no longer drawn to the sound as I had been, but yet continued on, a killing curiosity.

The Mersey was laden with fog, a penumbral shroud across a widow's brow. A light rain drizzled, its patter keeping time with my footsteps as I crossed past the house I had explored earlier, closer to the source of the music. The banks were covered in muddy grass and reeds that dipped into mossy rocks and grey sand, and I felt immediately water seep into my shoes. Yet, I had found what I obliquely sought: there in the water, waist-deep, softly danced a figure. Slow twirls and shifts, childish and innocent only as a lost girl can be. The moonlight shone upon her shoulders, dark hair coated with river slime— she was unclothed, her skin pale yet also covered in darker spots of turquoise algae—before I knew it, I was drawing closer to her, the murky water up to my knees, the reeds to my waist.

The figure's song came to an end: it sounded like the sigh of the ripples across the broken surface of the river. I knew then that I was, truly, a fool, despite knowing that Jenny Greenteeth, Spring-heeled Jack and all the rest were just daft stories. I hovered uncertainly as the figure approached. She did not reveal the full of her face, so I only saw it in eclipse, yet there was something familiar—distressingly familiar—about that visage, but my mind could not pin it, so hazy were my thoughts. It seemed an abnormally handsome face, and overall her body gave the impression of a girl just in her maturity, yet malnourished. Her arms and legs were thin and sinewy, her ribs visible through the skin that I began to realise was translucent—patterns shimmered beneath, a kaleidoscope of swirling duckweed.

There were only a handful of steps between us, yet there stopped her approach. An aching sound crept from her throat, gurgly and viscous, and I fell back with a start. The noise was inhuman: it was, to my afeared senses, the sound of a soul at unease, a conscious yet detached sorrow, a mourning croak and a death rattle. As I listened on, the sounds started to form syllables—and it was then I realised they were the same two sounds, repeated again and again: *churrr-chhh*.

I asked it what it wanted of me—I asked it to spare my life—I found myself wailing and hollering, the water having soaked me through, slime and pond moss now coating my clothes, hands and face—I found myself alone, shaking on the bank, looking out at the river where no entity stirred nor sang. With time I stood up and brushed some of the filth from my jacket and face. I knew not whether I was a lunatic, or else had truly just encountered a demon of the river—but it did not matter, for the word that the figure had uttered gave me a febrile clarity, a new destination. All the while on the walk back I laughed to myself, and sang a bit—I am an appalling vocalist—believing all of this to be a dream, and that in the morning I would awake and begin my empty-handed return to Mr Jameson.

St Laurence Church slept without a murmur. I stole inside and lit a candle, not knowing what I was to look for, walking up and down the pews, inspecting the pulpit—all seemed in order. What would a river spirit want from a house of God? I checked again the ground and found an odd black patch by one of the pews. In the candlelight it was hard to tell what it could have been—blood, sure. But why?

At the back of the church I found a door behind a royal blue curtain—I went through to find the minister's quarters. It being so late he was, of course, not here, so I was free to rummage around his personal effects. I spied academic texts, religious tomes, and browning bibles upon wooden shelves, and an open closet that contained vestments—still I wondered my purpose here, for nothing was noticeably unusual. I sought out the desk, which was busy with holy trinkets, crucifixes, and papers—the priest appeared a disorganised man. I began searching through the desk drawers and quickly discovered a bottle of cheap gin, which I took for my own.

In the second-to-bottom drawer were more papers, these written in a variety of different handwritings—skimming them, I realised they were written confessions: infidelity, assault, masturbation, abortion, molestation, rudeness, rumour-spreading... all kept together, for whatever reason. I became fascinated with the sheaf of scandals, and pulled them all out and started reading through them there upon the floorboards. As I skimmed the lascivious documents, sipping at the bottle of gin, an envelope fell out from the middle—it had a slight burn mark on the bottom-left corner but was otherwise intact, and blank of address or addressee. It was unsealed, so I opened it up and removed the letter inside, which I quickly and correctly identified as the same script as the scrap I had found in Jackson's supposed house.

The letter read:

My dearest Alexander,

I believe this will be the last letter I compose to you, sweetest friend. That which I am containing within these pages will sound as if my psyche has finally shattered, so if it is easier for you to consider these the delusions of a madwoman, so be it. Yes, madwoman: for you know as a child I preferred the name Amelia, rather than the brutish Zachary, and I have taken that name in earnest, and will hold it to the end of my life, which may not be far off. I wish I had told you earlier; I have been Amelia since first arriving in Toxteth those five years ago. I had hoped this small town would be subtle enough that I might pass around with ease, but that is not the case; a group of young uncouths have begun to make my life a living Hell, and I believe they mean to do me great harm. Of course, I cannot approach the law—my status as a woman here is tenuous enough, and

I fear they would likely side with my harassers; I know for certain my neighbours are no admirers of mine. I know I could leave; but if I cannot live here without reprieve, then where?! London, where my dear Fanny and Stella were so brutishly molested and disgraced? No. It seems there is nowhere for ones like me, and I refuse to return to that gentleman shell I hid within for so long. I will live openly or not at all.

But there is another matter, and this is where I may lose you. I have been down to the river, and as I have told you, I spend many hours walking the banks of the Mersey. Further down it becomes quite wild, and there I found Jenny Greenteeth. She was a waking myth, a childish tale come to life... a being of ancient power and wisdom. We spoke for days, and nights, when I would visit her home under the water... she saw my soul, and she knew that it was of the utmost feminine aura. Next week, I will join her under the water in dedication, and remain inside the Mersey forever.

You may remember our days in the theatre... of course you do... and how I played Amina. That was when I truly knew my destiny. I had been myself a sleepwalker, and now I cross the most reckless bridge to the beyond. I have been unable to sing here, and yet I must, I must. My song must be heard in all of its truth. Jenny, although unbearable to the normal human eye—sallow and twisted of form, oh, those oceanic eyes of shimmering endless black! those gnarled, cracked teeth so grimly green!—has divine musical skill... well, of course, not divine, but older than that... the euphonious chthonic piping of Gryndyllh... she will be my mother, my sister, my governess, my saviour...

I am frightened, Alexander. I am overtaken by darkness and cruelty. I believe my fate is sealed, yet still each night I make my prayers in the church, to ward off this darkness, but Hell, it is no good! The Mother of Rotten Reeds and Duckweed has me now; if God had wanted my essence then He would have born me in a body fit for my soul! Yet still, I am scared. I wish only that I had spoken of this to you earlier, or, that I could have seen you before it all became so convoluted. But alas... life is ever an unfulfilled beast, Alexander.

Please forgive me for such a short letter this time. I cannot bear to write these words, and I write them in the presence of God and His watchful priest. I love you, Alexander. May we somehow, somewhere, see each other again. I only hope there is still enough of myself to recognise you...

Yours in eternity,

Amelia Jackson

What was I to do with this? What was I to believe? I put my faith in the bottle, and finished the damned gin there and then, reading the letter again and again. Drunken stupor having embalmed me once more, I could barely stand when I heard a deep voice—shaky yet with resolve—bellow through from the church hall.

"Who goes there?"

The priest found me in his chamber. He was swaying slightly—drunk, like me.

"You. What are you doing here? Are you a common thief? I thought your accent was amiss."

"I'm no thief. How did you know I was here?"

Despite my inebriation, my voice was clear, and firm.

"Mrs Boden saw the door ajar from her window and had her son call for me. I had expected youths, yet it is you I find, Mr Watson," he glanced at the papers on the floor, "rummaging through the whole town's secrets. Blackmailer, eh?"

"I'm no thief nor a blackmailer."

"You are a thief—of gin, at least."

I held up the letter.

"What do you know about this?"

Father August's voice then cracked as he said, "That letter, there? What is it, exactly?"

"You knew Jackson. You said he'd left. You said he'd gone travelling."

"By the Father... I knew this moment would come, one day..."

I allowed him to pass by me and retrieve another bottle of gin hidden in a compartment in the open closet, a large bottle of finer quality. He set out two glasses and poured them, then indicated for me to take one, and sat down. I picked up the glass as he started speaking, his voice quivering.

"It was two years ago. Mr Jackson came here regularly. I knew he was a man, it was clear enough when you got close. It enraged me: *The woman shall not wear that which pertaineth unto a man, neither shall a man put on a woman's garment: for all that do so are abomination unto the Lord thy God.* He never confessed to it, and so his soul was dirty. Yet I allowed him in, for all men have a home at church, even if they are doomed to hellfire. I hoped he would, at last, confess, and put aside his sinful ways, for I knew him ultimately a gentleman of respectful lineage and good stock; yet, he never did. He was taunted frequently by a trio of youths from the town; they attacked him on a number of occasions. Their shows of violence got worse each time."

The father finished his glass and poured another one, whilst I nursed mine.

"The night it happened, Jackson was here late. He was hesitant, nervy; he was also writing that letter you hold now. We had never really spoken before; yet, that night, he asked me: *Father, could God ever forgive me?* and I said, *You must confess, my son.* He tittered to himself at that, and our conversation went no further. Soon after, the trio of youths arrived. They had found some liquor, and were quite drunk. They started throwing small rocks at Jackson. He ignored them, whilst I implored them to be civil in God's own house. Yet, in honesty, I took some pleasure at the time... seeing such a sinner receiving the clear message that he is living *wrong* and with evil. After one of the youths threw a particularly large stone, Jackson stood and turned to face them. I do not remember what he said, but it was a curse, I knew that... it was in a language I did not recognise, but the cruel tongue was dripping with Satan's hexes. The youths, enraged at the outburst, set upon the man. Although young, they were strapping lads, and before long Jackson was on the ground. I had stopped protesting. The youths kicked and stamped upon the cowering form. Soon, Jackson moved no more. His blood began to leak, and I covered the floor with cloth to stop the spread. The youths started to panic. I let them know they would be safe. That they had done God's work... we waited until night was deep and between us carried the body to the Mersey and cast it in naked. The clothes I later burned."

As I listened, my fist clenched. I saw Ada there instead of Jackson, set upon by fiends and without a soul to protect him. It took all I had to not slay the priest myself, right there.

"The letter I discovered when I returned. I thought them the words of a man mad with sin... I set to burn the letter, yet, I held back and kept it. All of the confessions found here should have been burned a long time ago. Yet I keep them as a record: I pardoned all those who confessed, and Jackson was the one soul I could not save. Soon after, the singing started drifting over the town from the river. Each of the youths went missing, just weeks apart. Then I found myself at the bank... I had to see for myself. I felt myself entranced by the song and wandered closer. In a moment of clarity, I started to recite the Our Father. The spell broken, I ran away. I returned here and prayed and drank all night. Since then, youths and young men have been disappearing.

Sometimes less regularly, sometimes more. I've read that letter one thousand and one times at least. What do I know? That God allows such abominations to exist upon this great grey earth? That Satan takes form through the evil of men, and sin is channelled through us and through our actions, or lack of action? The Lord does not answer me. Can a woman's soul be born trapped in a man's body? If he dies, will the female soul go on, consigned to wander the earth? Will it be drawn through with malice and vengeance? *I do not know.* I do not know! What I do know... is that I... cannot bear the weight of my inaction any longer. I have carried this far enough, and you have exposed me and listened to my confession. Now, whilst the fire is still with me, I must leave. I will leave this town. I must make my penance and pray that God delivers my soul safely to Heaven."

He stood up and fell back into his chair. The next attempt worked. He stumbled to the door, but turned before he departed.

"I am sorry for your friend. I am sorry that I did not save him; his soul, nor his life."

I spat on the ground and watched him go. I'd have liked to beat him senseless, kill him even, but I'd had enough of violence. After finishing the glass of gin, I left too, to follow the wayward priest.

I trailed him through the still-dark streets, walking softly to not alert him. He staggered an uneven line to Dingle and the shore. Standing on the bank, he bellowed:

"Jenny Greentooth! I am here."

Silence at first—then—the first note. The river spirit's song—no, not the same song, this was different... distinct in malevolent tones—rose, as she did, from the Mersey, both song and spirit coated in duckweed and turquoise algae. The priest and the figure in the water approached each other, the cruel, vengeful song ringing through the night.

The two figures were barely lit by the moon; as they came close to one another it was hard to distinguish them. I thought I sensed the female figure wrapping many arms like ragged slimy vines around the man, and pulling him down as if in seduction; all the while, the priest was chanting the Our Father. Their forms then mingled or merged—I could not tell in the light—and the priest cried out:

"God! Those eyes! *Those teeth!* What art thou! I cannot stand the sight! Lord, protect me—"

His voice was stifled as both figures sank into the water. Only bubbles and rising duckweed remained, and the final mournful notes of that vengeful song.

That was the end of it. I returned, somehow, to my room, and fell asleep once again fully dressed, still sodden through.

When I woke, I knew it all had been a dream—until, of course, I found Amelia Jackson's letter. I took a few drinks to steady myself, before realising I was feeling extremely sick. Regardless, I took the cart back to Liverpool, and, not feeling like spending another minute by the Mersey, hired the first carriage back to London. The journey was rotten, and by the time I reached London I was barely conscious at all, with a vicious fever—I awoke three days later in one of Mr Jameson's guest bedrooms, with his handsome, sad face watching over me.

Lady Jameson had passed away from consumption the night after I left; it broke me to tell the beautiful husband that his old friend, too, was no more. Before I said anything else, I kissed him, and let him weep. Later, I showed him the letter, and explained as best I could what had transpired. It was, of course, a lot to believe all at once, yet with the letter as evidence, and my word good—after assuring him I had not yet been struck with fever when the events took place—Jameson resolved with stern sorrow that he would leave London the next day, to find Amelia, to present himself to her at the banks of the Mersey and hope she remembered him. I tried all I could to sway him, but it was an impossible task.

He paid me one hundred pounds for my service, and thanked me dearly—but most of all, he spent a final night with me in that guest bedroom. Curled up in his strong arms, I knew what I would do next.

I bid farewell to Mr Jameson, holding back a few tears as his carriage set off. It was the last time I saw him—for I left London the same day, and never returned. I sent word for Ada to join me, and we departed for Scotland. Along the way, I asked Ada about her soul. Ada said she knew what she was, even if God had given her the wrong body. I held her tight. I would from then dedicate my life to making sure that if Ada's soul wanted to sing, then it would sing free—uncowed by Man or God.

AT THE END OF A PISTOL

C.C. ADAMS

"We each begin in innocence. We all become guilty." - Leonard F. Peltier

Norwood, South London
19:41, 27/05/1843

BACK AT HOME NOW, GEORGE OPENED the door and let Lizzie go in first, following in behind her. She made her way to the dining room, listlessly pulling out a chair before she sat at the table, eyes fixed on the wood. Seeing, but not seeing.

His movements careful as a mouse, George moved to a corner of the room, where he circled in front of her, but kept his distance. Folded his arms as he weighed his words.

"Well," he said, his tone false with joviality. "We'll have to do that again sometime."

No answer.

"I'll still have my work cut out for me. Father didn't do everything, but he still oversaw a lot of the operation. Someone has to keep an eye on the staff." George, long since adamant to outshine his father, had heavily invested his time in Winwood's to ensure that everyone in Norwood knew the finest tailors were in their midst.

Lizzie, her gaze vacant, idly dug a fingernail into the table. "Yes. Someone has to."

"It will take me a while before I can get things into proper working order, but I'm sure I'll get there. Existing staff already know what they have to do. Maybe I'll hire some more to take up the slack in the meantime. At least that way, when people see the business is still running like clockwork, they'll be encouraged to keep shopping, which will keep the money coming in, which in turn..." He drifted off, watching Lizzie scratch at the table's wood.

"We'll be able to make all the pantalettes you need."

Reverie broken, Lizzie looked up. "Huh?"

George folded his arms, lips pursed in amusement. "Pantalettes."

In spite of herself, her lip curled as she bit back a smile.

George craned his neck, a devilish smile now in place. "That's right. *Pantalettes.*"

Trembling as she fought to hold it in – then burst into a sniggering fit. George took his cue and circled back to her side, pulling a chair up beside her as he sat. He draped an arm around her shoulders as she leaned into him.

"See?" he said. "Pantalettes make everything alright." Lizzie's mouth formed an 'O' of mock indignation, but George cut her short by pulling her into him.

"George Winwood, you are…"

"Yes?" Eyebrows raised in amusement.

"You are …incorrigible."

He leaned forward in a small bow. "Of course. Because I try."

Growing sombre, he released his sister and eased back in his chair. "Lizzie, you must be starving by now, I'm sure. You barely touched your pie." And while The Horns had more than its fair share of avid gamblers like many a tavern, they were known to serve excellent pie. Chicken and rich pastry.

"I had enough."

"Now, now, Lizzie, we both know that's not true." It wasn't; George knew his sister's appetite nearly rivalled his own – certainly behind closed doors. Not that he was complaining. If he wasn't careful, those frock coats wouldn't button up on him.

He took her hand in his, and she flinched.

"Lizzie?"

Now her gaze grew fearful.

"Father's gone. But we're still here. Don't you forget that, okay?"

She grew teary, seeing the same grief in her brother's eyes.

"And we'll always have pantalettes – well, *you* will..."

"George!"

Her tears ran freely, over a weary smile.

"Laughter." George broke away, surreptitiously pulled a handkerchief from his coat pocket and dabbed at the corner of his eye. "I think we'll be needing some laughter in our lives soon."

Lizzie gave a tentative smile of relief. George was right. They had each other and, more importantly right now, they *needed* each other. What family would do was –

"I'm surprised we didn't see that Robin fellow."

Lizzie froze.

If I see either one of you again, I swear I'll bloody kill you.

"Lizzie?"

"Hmmm?"

"I was saying I was surprised we didn't see that Robin fellow."

"Oh. I, uh, hadn't noticed."

"Quite surprising, actually. I have it on good authority that he likes his gin. Not a big step up from beer in a time of crisis, eh?"

Lizzie drew back, and shot him a look of derision. "Why are you telling me this?"

A short laugh. "Because it's noteworthy. I must have seen that fellow every day in the run up to Father's funeral, and now there's no sign of him. I also hear tell that the man was a thief and a pickpocket. I dare say someone found out and scared him away. No wonder no one's seen the man –"

Abruptly, Lizzie stood up, her chair falling backward in the process – only to be caught deftly when George flung out a hand.

"Lizzie?" Chair still balanced in one outstretched hand, George looked up at her, his gaze wary. "Lizzie, are you alright?"

"I ... I..." Gaze flitting here and there, like a bird fluttering in a cage. "I think I need to lie down."

She left the room as George righted the chair, slowly, and incredulous. Headed upstairs, her footsteps ringing out smartly on the wood.

Shut the door behind her and braced her back against it, hyperventilating.

If I see either one of you again, I swear I'll bloody kill you.

She crossed to her bed and sat down as slowly as an old maid, next to her bedside chest. Beyond the bedroom window, the warm glow of a sunset, framed by green drapes cinched away from the window by golden ties. Casting Lizzie's memory back to another sunset.

Robin caught red-handed – empty-handed. She'd seen to that. She and George made sure Father was buried elsewhere. Robin, drunk and pathetic, lost for words.

Sighing, she bent down and reached for the bottom drawer of the little chest. Slid it open, the grating of wood ominous in the quiet, like the opening of a miniature coffin. Reached inside, until her fingers closed around something cool, metallic and hard.

Brought it out and laid the pistol on her lap.

Pepperbox, she mouthed, tracing the frame's engraving with her fingertip. It seemed like such a strange name for a pistol; a pepperbox. But there it was. Everyone had them, as a matter of personal safety.

That's not why you had it.

That's not why you used it.

Lovely handle – walnut or mahogany; rich, dark and polished wood. Metal screws through the handle. Curled floral engraving on the metal of the frame. 'Allen's Patent' on the handle. It was a beautiful little thing.

But that isn't why you used it.

Nausea rose in her like a shore-bound wave, and she pressed a hand to her mouth, swallowing, eyes closed.

"At least when you die, no one will ask where you're buried!"

Two of them: that drunkard Robin and his pathetic stooge James. Both men at the end of a pistol as she swung it between them.

She fired, hitting neither of them.

Neither man waited to give her a second chance and, already trapped in the grave, both dove into the empty coffin they'd unearthed. Screaming and squabbling as they closed the lid on themselves, before she fired a shot into the lid of the coffin.

"You listen here now, both of you. If I see either one of you again, I swear I'll bloody kill you."

Whispers from inside the coffin.

And then she proceeded to shovel the dirt back in.

Burying them.

Both men were most certainly dead.

"I didn't..."

None of the shots fired had hit either man.

But they were most certainly dead now.

Lizzie hefted the pistol, horrified when her finger slid through the trigger guard and across the trigger. Feeling it depress, even momentarily, was too much and she recoiled in horror. The pistol hit the floor with a thud.

Her heart pounding in her chest, compounding her nausea.

That sickness you feel? That's guilt.

I didn't mean to.

And yet, two men are dead because of you. That makes you a murderer.

I didn't mean to!

Murderer!

"I didn't –"

"Lizzie?" Beyond the bedroom door, George's voice, accompanied by the weight of his footsteps.

Hurriedly, Lizzie scooped up the pistol and stuffed it into the farthest reaches of the drawer, before shoving it shut.

A knock at the door. "Lizzie?"

She sat back on the bed, back straight, prim and proper, smoothing her dress. "Come in."

George came in, gently closing the door behind him. Concern clouded his features, his lips parted in hesitation. Then: "Are you alright?"

"I'm quite alright."

His footsteps slow and cautious, he made his way to the window, and stood at one side, watching the sunset. Hands behind his back, with one hand clasping the wrist of the other.

"George?"

With the sun having set further, George appeared more in shadow, although Lizzie noted that he hung his head. Whatever he was going to say wouldn't be easy.

"Lizzie," he began. "I don't want to sound like an old fusspot, but I do worry about you."

"I know you do," she said, through clenched teeth. "That's very sweet."

He turned away from the window, hands still behind his back. "Just remember that, even at a time like this ...well, life goes on. Something that Thomas Browning knows only too well."

"Thomas?"

"Oh, yes. I rather like the fellow. Comes from

a good family, and trustworthy. Granted, his head may be in a book more than it is in the real world, but there's something to be said for a man that willingly educates himself. I dare say he'll be most receptive of the joys that life has to offer, including that of a spirited woman. You might just bring out the best in each other, if you were to marry."

Thomas. Barely a man, but well-mannered and earnest. At least his humour extended past the likes of pantalettes.

George turned on his heel, stopping at the larger chest of drawers opposite the bed to regard the ornament on top. "What did you say this contraption was?"

Lizzie looked over her shoulder at him, his fingertip on the rim of the drum, rotating it back and forth. "That's a zoetrope."

"I see." He peered inside. Around the base of the drum, the strip of paper displayed a black-and-white sequence of prancing men, grinning as though juggling their own head with their neighbour was the funniest thing ever. George gave it a spin, the whirr of the drum breaking the silence. "And it makes these fellows look as if they're actually moving."

"That's right."

"Hmmm." He straightened, and folded his arms. "I think I remember this being called something else."

"Such as?"

A furtive glance before he leaned forward, his look conspiratorial. "The wheel of the devil," he whispered. He broke into a smile and then left the room, closing the door gently behind him.

Lizzie turned away from the door in indignation. *Wheel of the devil, indeed.* Pure and simple, the contraption was called a zoetrope, nothing else. As for *why* it was called a zoetrope, she didn't know and didn't care.

She sniffed in disdain – and caught a scent of earth.

Lizzie shook her head. The window was closed and when George stood by the window earlier, he hadn't opened it.

You're a murderer.

I never shot them.

Because your aim was so frightfully bad.

If I wanted to kill them, I could have.

But, you did. You buried those men.

...oh.

Slowly, Lizzie sat forward, focused on her hearing.

Whirring, from the other end of the room.

She looked, incredulous.

The zoetrope on the big chest of draws was still spinning; *had* been since George had first spun it. But that was minutes ago, and it didn't have the power to keep turning by itself; not for so long.

Easing herself off the bed, Lizzie went over to it. The drum still whirring, the sound conspicuous in the silence. Through the slits in the drum, animated black-and-white figures: a leering and suited man, gaily removing his head and passing it to his identical neighbour.

Wheel of the devil.

Cautiously, Lizzie raised a hand to the drum and pinched its rim – the drum lurched in her grip, such was its momentum.

But at last, it was still.

The grinning men inside the drum; indifferent.

Lizzie frowning at them.

Until, eventually, her attention was diverted by a nearby copy of *The Pickwick Papers*. Exquisite it was, too; bound in green Moroccan leather, with gilt titles and tooling to the spine. And so, she brought the book back to her side of the bed and read. Relaxed. Even joined her brother downstairs for a portion of supper before retiring to her room. Night, ushered in by an uneventful sunset, settled over the city, Norwood included. In the home of the Winwoods, like many others, all was still.

The downstairs rooms.

The staircase.

The upstairs rooms.

All shrouded in darkness.

In the Winwood home, cold air drifted along floors. Seeping through crevices between a door and its frame.

Lizzie, one arm across her stomach as she slept on her back, murmured.

Eyelids twitching.

Two men, standing in the grave beside an empty coffin: James, flushed beneath dirty blond hair, paunch straining at his shirt. Robin, cleaner, but more haggard. Stinking of gin.

"That's the right place for you! At least when you die, no one will ask where you're buried!"

Robin; a worthless layabout.

James; impressionable. The mindless sheep to Robin's wolf.

Both men fearful at the end of a pistol, both men diving into the coffin as she fired. A warning shot bit into the wood as they closed the lid on themselves. Screams became fearful moans drifting up from within the confines of the coffin.

"You listen here now, both of you. If I see either one of you again, I swear I'll bloody kill you."

Finally, she put her pistol away.

Shuffling and whispers rising from the grave.

"I'll bloody shut you up."

Reaching for the shovel, and throwing dirt back in to the hole.

No more Robin.

(murder)

No more James.

(murderer)

More dirt landing in the grave, piling in a mound on the coffin's lid until it began to whirr over the sides.

Wood gradually disappearing under shovelfuls of earth, obscuring the outlines of the coffin.

Whirr...

Whirr...

– and Lizzie's eyes snapped open in the darkness.

Brief disorientation in the transition from sleep to consciousness. Silhouettes resolving themselves in the gloom, the drapes framing the window, the chest beside her bed, the cabinet at the foot of the bed.

The zoetrope, still turning.

Whirring.

Stiffening, Lizzie looked to the door. Closed.

Looked back to the zoetrope. Whirring.

Goosebumps crawled across her skin in a violent shudder.

Eyes wide, she scanned the room. Not only was the door closed, but also nothing about it looked disturbed from when she came up earlier. A look at the window returned the same conclusion.

Rolling onto her side, she reached and fumbled for the bedside chest, fingers groping downward until she found the bottom drawer. Yanked it open and thrust her hand inside, rummaging around blind. Nothing but fabric; some smooth, some embroidered.

No.

Frantic now, her fingernails scraping the bottom of the drawer, loud enough to frighten her more. One nail almost bent backward. Still coming up with nothing but fabric.

Oh, no.

Not wanting to accept this, Lizzie slowly rolled back, bed linen dragging with her as she did so.

Across the room, the zoetrope was still whirring.

This can't be real.

Jaw clenched, Lizzie clutched tentative handfuls of bed linen and peeled it away from her body. Cool air settled on her like a mist as she swung her feet over the edge of the bed and sat up, getting to her feet. The zoetrope loomed closer as she approached it, each grinning man passing his head to his neighbour. Standing over it revealed nothing out of the ordinary apart from the fact it was still spinning; nothing else on the chest was out of place, there was no additional machinery that would account for the fact that it was still turning –

She flung out a hand grabbing it awkwardly, this time it resisted in her grip and buckled to one side. The rattling of it on the chest's wood made her yelp, she then tensed, petrified.

And silence returned to the room.

Bringing her other hand up, she gently righted it. Behind her, the figure lying on its back on the floor lay motionless. Dead, milky eyes stared from under a mop of shaggy blond hair in the direction of the dresser.

It occurred to Lizzie that the air was colder around the dresser – much colder. She folded her arms, clasping them to her sides under her armpits. The air felt not only cold, but ...*dank*. And the scent of earth had returned, vague and diffuse.

At last, she circled back to the bedside chest and knelt in front of it. Pulling out the drawer completely allowed for a full search of its contents, but the end result was the same.

Bleary-eyed, rummaging through the cupboards in the pantry, but still the same conclusion.

No pepperbox.

A restless night had led to a listless morning, short-changed by a lack of sleep. Lizzie pressed the heel of her palm to her forehead.

Things don't move by themselves.

They don't? You're forgetting the zoetrope.

Do not start –

A knock at the front door.

Grabbing fistfuls of her skirt, Lizzie marched to the door and flung it open – and the blond man in front of her flinched in response, before he regained his composure. Stiff, with his hands behind his back.

Momentarily, Lizzie drew a blank.

"Good day, Miss Lizzie." Young, lean, with neatly combed hair. Narrow-shouldered, blue eyes wide and eager. "I believe George made an appointment with me? For me?"

"Thomas."

Those shoulders relaxed, as a tentative smile tugged at one corner of the man's mouth. "That, I am." He brought a hand from behind his back, presenting a bouquet of red tulips. "These are for you. May I...?" Still with one hand behind his back.

Lizzie took them, inhaling their scent as she drew them close. The fact that Thomas was still standing with a hand behind his back seemed a little strange, a little too formal.

Like George.

The memory drifted back: *life goes on. Something that Thomas Browning knows only too well.*

She cradled the flowers like a newborn child. "They're lovely. Won't you come in?" she said, stepping aside in the doorway.

Lizzie led him into the dining room, regarding him from a distance. She wasn't sure how much older Thomas was (she was *sure* he was older, otherwise George wouldn't have recommended him at all), but something about him appeared nervous. Naïve, even. Still, he conducted himself with decency, which had to be worth something. Plus, he was ... *angelic*, and earnest.

"To what do I owe the honour of this visit?"

His smile faltering for a moment, Thomas cleared his throat, and Lizzie bit back a grin. "Yes, well. I wanted to see how you were since the funeral of your father. I do wish we could have been acquainted under better circumstances, but those unfortunately can't be changed. For that, I'm truly sorry."

Lizzie gave a wistful smile. Recent times hadn't been easy and although she had been somewhat withdrawn, it was refreshing to see that there were people who cared. Good people. Her gaze fell to his smile. His lips. "Thank you. That's very thoughtful of you."

His head bowed in appreciation. "I'm glad you think so." He took a tentative step forward. "Miss Lizzie, I hope you do not think me too forward, but I would very much like the pleasure of your company at a time more convenient to you."

"And why would that be, pray tell?"

"If I may be so bold, I would like to know more about you."

Lizzie's smile, beaming. "Again, I simply must ask: why?"

Thomas was grinning now, and more relaxed. "And in response, I must tell you: I'm enchanted by your beauty, and certainly by your humour. There's much in this life to be explored but, for the time being, my dream is to find a good woman."

Again, Lizzie drew a blank.

Lips parting, she fought for something to say and found nothing. Thomas, his gaze hopeful, scanning her face for any response, favourable or otherwise.

Lizzie was mute.

Good woman.

She exhaled.

Murderer.

What made it worse was that Thomas *did* bear some resemblance to James. She barely knew either man, only having met them in passing. But there were similarities; both young and boyish men. Thomas appeared to have more youth and less stomach, but James wasn't much older

when he died

when you killed him

murdered him

"Thomas," she began. "I fear I may not be able to give you the answer you desire."

"May I ask why?"

No more Robin.

No more James.

More dirt landing in the grave, piling in a mound on the coffin's lid until it began to drift over the sides.

Wood gradually disappearing under shovelfuls of earth, obscuring the outlines of the coffin.

Chest – and stomach – heaving, she raised her fingers to her mouth, pressing them against her lips. Thomas surged forward to her aid but she stopped him short with a forestalling hand. Then: "I fear I may not be the good woman you're looking for." Recovering, she met his gaze and gently handed him the tulips. "So I fear I cannot accept..."

James.

Standing in front of her on the grass, beside the grave.

Wide-eyed with fear, shaking his head, hands raised in surrender.

Her hold on the pistol shaky as she raised it, aiming at his chest.

Her grip tightened on the trigger

...and she thrust the flowers at Thomas. "Can't ... can't accept," she whispered.

Thomas held the tulips, looking at them in confusion. "I do understand that my timing and my phrasing may have missed the mark. But I want you to know that my intentions have not."

Standing in front of her on the grass, beside the grave.

Wide-eyed with fear, shaking his head, hands raised in surrender as he lowered himself to his knees.

"Well," he said. "I shall see myself out."

And so he did.

Leaving Lizzie dumbfounded, listening to the door close and returning silence to the house.

Two men were dead.

Buried alive.

Heat springing to her eyes now from imminent tears.

Lizzie turned her face to the ceiling and stifled a sob, making her way to the staircase. More than anything now, she wanted to lock herself away from the world and cry, weep, bawl; *anything* to rid of herself of the loathing and self-disgust. Her foot descending on the first riser, she slowed.

Stopped short.

Something registered on the floor at the range of her periphery; without turning her head, it looked like Thomas was lying on the floor.

Except she had seen Thomas leave, *heard* him leave. Her breath caught in her chest, the confines of her bodice gripping her like a vise.

From the floor, flat on its back, the figure watched her. Dead milky eyes under a shaggy mane of blond hair, its gaze intent on the staircase.

Under the confines of her clothes, Lizzie's skin began to crawl.

She allowed her full weight to come down on the first riser of the staircase.

It's not real, it's not real, it's not real...

Taking another step, repeating the process, not daring to turn her head, the same mantra repeated over and over. A terrible ache in her neck, daring Lizzie to turn her head as the topmost riser loomed into view. All the while, Lizzie ignoring the figure on the floor.

The room sat shrouded in darkness

Lizzie slept, one arm draped across her stomach, the other by her side, atop the bed sheet. Cool air ... that bordered on dank.

The sound came from nearby, soft and rhythmic, hardly enough to wake the deepest of sleepers. But Lizzie had not slept so well, and so that sound was soft and rhythmic and persistent, gently nudging Lizzie from the depths of her sleep.

Her eyelids twitched.

And again.

In the darkness her eyes opened, awareness tugging at the rest of her senses.

Something ...whirring.

Eyes widening, her gaze flicked to the zoetrope across the room. The drum was at rest, the grinning men inside holding their poses mid-prance.

Oh, no.

What was now alarming was that the zoetrope was motionless, but the whirring was soft and clear, from somewhere in the room. Linens rustled as Lizzie shifted on to her elbow to prop herself up and *here* she began to pinpoint the sound; somewhere behind her on the other side of the bed. Not only that, but the sound wasn't a whirr, but the muted squelch of ...chewing.

Eating.

What?

Stomach muscles tensing, Lizzie carefully rolled back from one side to the other and peered over the edge of the bed. With its back to her, one shadowy figure crouched over the unconscious body of another. From the vigorous bird-like bobbing of the head, it appeared to be kissing the fallen form.

And then it turned around, facing her.

Lizzie froze in shock.

The form unconscious on the floor was blond, stocky and male, milky eyes staring sightlessly into the distance. Skin hung from the side of the head in a ragged and bloody flap, exposing pulpy and glistening flesh beneath. Its devourer, now staring right at her with yellowed eyes, continued to chew, blood smeared across its nose, mouth and chin. On meeting her gaze, the figure stopped chewing.

Now Lizzie screamed.

Tearing back the bed sheets, she flung herself from the bed and yanked open the bedroom door. Barrelling downstairs, the thumping of her own footsteps scaring her even more until she clung to the bottom post of the banister like a shipwrecked survivor. Where was George – had he woken? Had he even returned from the factory yet? Oil lamps cast pools of light in an eerie glow, darkened corners all the more menacing, and Lizzie screwed her eyes shut.

Knocking at the front door, slow and hesitant – an insidious sound that drifted through the silence of the house. Nightclothes clinging to her in cold sweat, Lizzie gritted her teeth, a breath shuddering out of her. Whatever nightmare found its way into the house wouldn't just go away, but would come to her in malevolent deliberation.

Nonononono...

She opened her eyes. Saw the apparition in front of her.

Cloudy eyes trained on her face from under a mop of blond hair dusted with dirt – cold and earthy as if from a freshly-turned grave. Skin from the side of its head hung down as before, leaving a glistening ruin of dull and pink flesh from the ear and along the neck to the shirt collar soaked dark with juices. Through the figure, the outline of the hallway beyond, leading to the front door.

"I'm ..." Lizzie swallowed, her mouth dry. *James ... ohgodJames...* "I'm sorry."

Its gaze still fixed on her, it held up its hands as if in surrender.

And began to advance on her.

Not taking her eyes off the figure, Lizzie began to back away, her outstretched fingers groping in empty air until they found the table. Nails scratching along its surface as she continued her retreat, until her fingers found something cool and metallic that grated across the table's wood.

Breath hitching in realisation, she tightened her grip on its handle, one finger sliding across the trigger through the trigger guard.

Here?

The figure came to a halt a yard in front of her. At this distance, she could absorb all of the detail: the tang of sweat from the stains under the figure's armpits, the scent of open air, the smell of cemetery earth dusting the figure's hair and clothes. And a creeping odour of spoiled flesh.

Tears of fright began to leak from her eyes.

"I'm sorry," she whispered. "So ...so very sorry."

A louder knock as the front door blew in, slamming against the side of the house.

Its mouth opening in a silent snarl, the figure surged forward – and Lizzie swung up the pepperbox, firing.

At the end of the hallway, a blond figure teetered ...and then collapsed by the open door with a thud.

The bouquet of tulips on the floor beside an outstretched hand.

Her fingers loose with shock, the pistol slid unchecked from Lizzie's grasp, clattering on the floor. By the time she realised who lay in the doorway, both hand were clasped over her mouth as she backed away in grief. As she did so, movement registered at her periphery and she spun toward it, gasping.

The apparition, much closer now, indifferent to its mutilated flesh.

Shaggy-haired, with eyes as dull as old bones.

Dead.

Grinning.

A Living Cell

Rob Francis

I can't remember a darker or colder morning, even for December. Snow lies in drifts along the streets as Pryce and I make our way to the cemetery, but it's filthy and grey from its journey through the soot-filled London skies. My boots and trousers are wet, and my stomach hurts. My stomach always hurts.

"You've been to Cutgrave before, sir?" Pryce leads the way with the lantern as I tramp along as best I can, truncheon in hand. I always have it ready when it's dark and I'm in uniform. A lesson learnt the hard way.

We pass along Paternoster Row and come to the black iron gate of the little cemetery. Little by the standards of today, of course; at one time it would've been grand enough. The newer ones stand at the edge of the town: Kensal Green, Highgate, Abney Park. Cutgrave filled up years ago. It serves another purpose now. Plenty of folk come and go, but hardly any mourners.

The gate is open. No one bothers to lock it anymore, even at night.

It takes me a moment to realise that Pryce has asked a question; it is early, and last night's tincture still has a hold over me.

"Cutgrave? Aye, I've been through once or twice. A tumbledown place, as I recall. That old church stands at the western edge."

"Saint Hild's? That's right sir, it was Father Adams who found the lady this morning, on his way to open up."

"That's what he said, is it? On the way in, strolling through the graveyard? Not ministering to the fallen ladies in his own special way?"

Pryce shakes his head. "You've no faith, sir, none at all."

That's true enough, but I prefer not to concede it. I stay silent as we walk well-trod paths among the lichen-spattered gravestones. Most are modest but well-made. There is the occasional tomb, here and there a statue: a cherub floats atop a carved Latin Cross; a little further on there is a marble bird standing on one of the grander headstones, its wings outstretched, mouth open. On the left, outside the entrance to one of the older and larger crypts, an effigy of a robed and wild-haired woman holds a hand to the sky as if begging for an end to eternal torment. The locals must've had money enough, once upon a time.

I hawk noisily and cast some of the night's phlegm into the snow. My stomach kicks. I need to brew a cup of Imperial to clear my gut, but there's no time now.

"Here we are." Pryce taps me on the arm.

Ahead, Father Adams stands by the path under a small yew, his round red face creased in concern. Even from a distance, I can tell that he has been standing here for some time; his cassock is soaked to the knees in melted snow. He looks to have been weeping.

And no wonder, for at his feet lies a woman with her throat torn out. Her faded dress is intact but unhitched, one breast exposed, the rest of her body covered. Her hair is brown and darkened further by the snow, her face entirely washed of colour. A couple of steps away from her something lumpen and pale lies on the ground, a thin layer of slush partially covering it.

"Father Adams?" My voice is heavy in the cold air.

The priest nods. "Inspector Marshall." He glances at the truncheon nervously, as if expecting me to start wielding it with intent. I often have that effect on people; it's a residue of the military life. "A terrible thing to wake to on a winter's morning."

I shrug. "Woke to plenty worse in the Crimea." I don't mean to be a ratbag about it. I just can't help myself, especially around do-gooders.

Pryce commandeers the conversation, which is what he's best at.

"So, you were walking through on the way to Saint Hild's and came across this lady? From your home, which is...?"

"Over by Fitzroy Square."

"What time?"

"I always pass this way around six-thirty. Today would be no different."

"And she was just like this? The same position? You didn't move her or interfere with the body in any way?"

Father Adams couldn't look more offended if Pryce bescumbered his altar. "Of *course* not!"

I step in to contain the outrage, which is what *I'm* best at. This also gives Pryce the chance to examine the dead woman uninterrupted, while the priest's attention is focused on me.

"Now then Father, no-one's casting aspersions. Just trying to ascertain the facts. Get it straight in my mind, you see? So. You come across this lady and then carry on to the church?"

"Yes, to send my server boy, Albrecht, to the station. He can run much faster than me."

"I'll bet."

"Sorry?"

I ignore the priest and bend down to look at the pale object, brushing the snow carefully away. It's a model of a babe, exquisitely carved and swaddled in grey linen. I'm no expert on young children, but my guess is it's supposed to represent one that's only a few months old.

"Bloody funny doll." I lift it from the ground and am surprised to find that it's heavy, solid marble all the way through from the feel. I nod towards the woman. "I assume this must be hers, but... how? Something like this would be damn expensive, and she doesn't look the fancy type. And why lug around a stone baby like this? Even if you're playing dolls, it's a burden."

"Maybe she was a lunatic," says Pryce sadly. He claps his hands together as if cold, which means he's satisfied with what he's seen, and that we can move on.

"Most likely." I turn to Father Adams. "You don't recognise her?"

The priest shakes his head.

"Not a patron of your church?"

"I'm afraid not."

"Well, thanks, Father. We'll send the coroner to collect the body shortly. In the meantime, best get back to your flock. I'm sure they're lost without you." I hand the baby to Pryce. "You can carry this. And don't get any ideas!" I give him a wink, to the priest's bafflement. "Come on. I need two kinds of drink, and right now!"

I lead the way back to the gate.

Not far away from Cutgrave is The Brass Bell, which is the local meeting place for Peelers. I'm with the Metropolitan boys but I live in Camden, so I have an office at Eversholt Street Station where I keep most of my paperwork. I only go to Whitehall Place when I really must, or if Mayne, our withered turnip of a commissioner, needs to make himself feel more of a man by shouting at me. So, day or night, the Bell is where I can often be found.

A carriage sprays slush across my navy coat and trousers as we walk up Judd Street. I tap the heavy ash of the truncheon against my leg as we go, the dull pain a distraction from the stabbing in my gut. Pryce is quiet, and I can tell he's ruminating on the woman. The baby is cradled in his arms.

"What's your opinion, Pryce?"

Pryce purses his lips in a familiar gesture. I do it a lot myself. "A fallen woman, almost certainly, but not degenerate. The clothes were in a decent state of repair. The throat was torn out; not cut with a knife but ripped and hanging wide. So, a coarser tool, or even a hand if the killer was strong enough."

"Motive?"

He shrugs. "Opportunity. A savage, looking for entertainment. 'The savage in man is never quite eradicated', after all."

"Who said that, then?"

"Henry Thoreau. An American writer," he added in response to my blank expression. He's a real one for books and periodicals, is Pryce. Me, not so much. I'm a bit more vital than that.

We stand before the door of the Bell, and through the thick windows I can see Lucas Kolitsi sat at a small table, supping from a pint pot. "Time to put the word out," I say as I push the door open and enter the fetid interior of the pub. The parlour's as gloomy as an open grave at night, and just about as inviting. The wall-lamps are lit, but you'd hardly know it for the feeble light they give out.

Victor, the weasel-faced barman who seems a permanent fixture of the Bell, gives me a salute and I bark over, "Tea, Victor, and two ales."

Pryce goes to sit with Kolitsi, but I hang back, feigning interest in something I can see through the window but really trying to master the pain in my gut. Victor hands me a muddy cup of tea cooled with a little fresh milk and I gulp down as much as I can before stepping outside to vomit on the street. After that I feel a little better. Every morning, the same routine. Tea, then vomit, then the day begins.

I can feel Pryce's concerned gaze on me as soon as I step back inside, but I ignore it and cross to the table to sit by him and opposite Kolitsi. The man looks almost as ragged as me, his uniform unwashed and a thick rash of stubble across his cheeks and neck. He stinks of sweat and piss.

"Rough night?"

Victor places two pots of ale on the table and retreats to the safety of the bar. I slip the truncheon back into my belt and pull out my bottle of tincture, adding four drops to the ale. That should keep me going until evening. With a bit of luck, I might even manage an afternoon nap in the office.

Kolitsi nods. "Didn't make it home last night. I was 'ere 'til after midnight, then I was fetched to the

Museum on Great Russell Street, on account of—"
He stops as Pryce plonks the marble baby down on
the table so's he can pick up his drink. "Jesus, not
another bloody statue."

"Another one?"

"Not quite like this, but... yeah. I'm fetched to the
Museum on account of someone breaking in and
vandalising — that is to say, destroying — one of
the new exhibits, some statue that they got from
that mausoleum over in Asia Minor. Alley-carn-
something. You remember?"

I shrug. I've never been to the Museum. Never
felt the need. "What was the statue of?"

"Some woman. They told me the name. Starts
with a 'U'. Anyway, no idea how the blighter got in,
nor exactly how he did it, what with the night guard
being drunk on his arse."

"How do you know it was a man?" says Pryce. I
give him a little kick under the table.

Kolitsi looks at Pryce like he's an idiot. "There
was sweet eff-all left of the statue, son. Takes real
strength to smash apart something like that." His
face screws up in puzzlement. "Which is odd,
'cause there were hardly any pieces left on the floor,
just dust. And bits of a broken baby, like that one.
Where'd you get it?"

"Cutgrave," I say. "One of the strumpets — I
mean, one of the night workers," I glance at Pryce,
who looks slightly flushed in the amber light, "had
it wrapped up like this when she met her maker.
Priest found her on the way to work. We'll need
to put word out, see if any rumours are coming in

about who was in the area late last night. It was a savage business."

Pryce opens the linen so that we can see the babe more clearly. It is exquisitely carved, with impressive attention to detail. Even a philistine like me can see that. The eyes are open and have grooved pupils, not blank like you see on some statues. Tiny hairs have been etched into the scalp. It's also clearly supposed to be a boy.

Something about the effigy is bothering me, but I can't say what. Warmth is spreading through my gut, and I feel a little lightheaded. I drink more ale, grateful as always for the tincture.

"This is stolen, you mark my words." I point to Kolitsi. "Better get that out on the street as well. Any missing baby statues, we need to know. I don't suppose it could be from the Museum?"

Kolitsi shakes his head. "They said a woman and baby, that's all. Not two babies. Odd, though."

"Odd," we all agree. We drink in silence for a while, staring at the marble baby as if waiting for it to stir.

Outside, snow starts to fall once more.

Back at Camden station, I shut the office door and slump into the chair behind my desk. Pryce takes the other chair, relieved that once again the performance is over.

"Do you need to sleep, Father?"

"Maybe for a few moments, Kittie." Now the pain

has washed away, the world feels a lighter place, its burdens more bearable. Despite all the darkness. But I must rest to think clearly.

She's never complained, dear Kittie. The simple truth is, I need her around, and she's got just the right look for a young man if she keeps her hair short. So out there, it's Inspector Roger Marshall and Constable Edward Pryce. In here, it's just Father and Kittie. Though I think sometimes she prefers to be Pryce.

It was easy enough to get her recruited without fuss on my recommendation, once she was the right age. It's been just me and Kittie for a long time, since I came back from the war. Her mother, my sweet Cara, didn't even tell me she was expecting when I left. By the time I returned, Cara had almost wasted away from flux, and there was Kittie, four years old and the liveliest sprite you ever saw. I took on a governess, signed on with the Peelers – they were after military men back then — and worked my way up. I never told anyone I had a daughter. Never really told the other Peelers much at all. I don't get on so well with folks in general. But I'm good at catching scoundrels. And so is Kittie. Well — so is Pryce.

There's a bookshelf along the wall behind my desk, most of the volumes bought by Kittie. Studies on human nature, religion, law, science. Translations of Greek and Roman classics. Modern fiction: Dickens, Eliot, Browning. Even Darwin. Sometimes I thumb through them myself, on a slow day. If it's raining.

Kittie takes a book from the shelf and sits in the

cushioned chair in the corner. The volume's spine declares it to be Hesiod's *Theogony* and I consider asking why she's picked something so weighty for such a miserable day, but my head is already almost too heavy to hold up. I rest my forehead on my arms and drift off.

I stir a couple of times, as Kittie steps to the door to take reports. The only important one is from the coroner: a note to say that the Cutgrave woman has been identified as one Mabel Jameson, a local night worker who recently had a baby, which she tended to leave with one of the local girls when she had to work. Except for last night, as all the local girls were busy. Noted to have a tendency for hysteria. Cause of death was the torn throat, the weapon most likely a man's hand and brute strength.

Kittie starts to talk to me after the report comes in, but I can't keep my eyes open. When I finally wake enough to be fully aware of my surroundings, it is near dark outside. It's late afternoon and there's been hardly a mote of sunlight all day. I still have a few hours before the stomach pain returns. There is a freshly baked pie on the desk, which Kittie must have procured from one of the vendors on Seymour Street. She sits in her chair, watching me, *Theogony* open on her knees.

"Thanks Kittie," I say and set to work on the pie. It's beef and onion, with a rich gravy. I'm sure I'll regret it at some point, but for now it'll keep me going.

"You hear any of the coroner's report on the woman, Father?"

"Aye. Some." I chew and swallow. "Someone tore her throat out. Pryce was right again. And the hysteria — I'm guessing she thinks the little marble lad here is real, and the other ladies humour her. Probably lost the real child, and this is the substitute."

Kittie looks thoughtful. "But where did she get it from? I suppose it could have been stolen, but... And why would the other ladies say they weren't free to look after it last night, if it was just taking care of a statuette for a few hours?"

"Probably got fed up of the woman's nonsense."

"Maybe." She taps the page before her. "But what if—"

There's a sharp rap at the door and it opens before either of us can respond. Kittie leaps out of the chair, the book dropping to the floorboards. Kolitsi looks in, his cheeks freshly shaved and far more presentable than this morning, though a sheen of sweat covers his face.

"Disturbance, Inspector. Down on Harrison Street. You should come quick: you'll want to see this."

I grab my coat and hurry down the stairs, Pryce only a few steps behind.

It's snowing again as we hurry down Euston Road and to Harrison Street. My boots skid on the slush and scum, but I'm used to moving fast on wet paving and manage to keep my footing all the way to the three-storey town house that is clearly the scene of Kolitsi's disturbance. Outside the front door, two Peelers whom I recognise but am not familiar with stand over a bloodied shape that I quickly surmise to be a woman's body. They stand back as I approach.

"Inspector Marshall." One of the men, a burly fellow who I think is called Wright, gives me a wide-eyed salute for no reason at all. At his feet, a woman in what looks to be an expensive satin dress with an exquisitely detailed floral pattern is sprawled across the stone slabs of the street, eyes wide with shock, the side of her head resting on the ground clearly smashed open, from what I assume is the impact of a fall. I look up.

A third-storey window is broken, jagged teeth of glass outlined in the fading afternoon light.

"She was thrown, sir." Wright's voice trembles a little. "Another woman, so says the servant. An intruder."

I nod and motion Pryce to follow.

The interior of the house is impressive. Not huge, but well-appointed with expensive furniture clearly selected by someone with a taste for such things. I almost feel bad about tracking wet soot and other street filth into the house. Almost.

There is no-one in the entrance hall, but I can hear a woman weeping upstairs. I tramp the carpeted steps, Pryce alongside me. He's very quiet. Making his meticulous observations, I expect.

A door stands open on the top landing, a woman just inside sitting on a bed and sobbing into a handkerchief. I open my mouth but Pryce steps forward, slipping into the room ahead of me.

"Miss?" he says. "I'm constable Pryce, and

this is Inspector Marshall. Could you tell us what happened, if you're up to it? The sooner we know what's afoot, the sooner we can act."

I take in the room. A double bed, carefully made up, occupies one side of the chamber. On the other side stands a dressing table and mirror, and a large, wide cot in which a baby can be seen sleeping through the wooden bars along the side. Snow drifts in from the shattered window, turning invisible as it passes from the darkening sky into the well-lit room, before melting away completely.

The woman on the bed looks around, her eyes red, cheeks burnished pink from wiping away tears. Her greying hair is only half-pinned, the rest falling about her face and across one shoulder.

"I'm Applethorpe, the nanny." Her throat sounds raw, as if she's been screaming or shouting. "I came in, 'cause it was feeding time, sirs, and... there was a woman. In the room, standing over the cot. She was tall and wild-looking. Hair all bushed up and out, skin off-colour: grey or violet, like she was ill. Talking, she was. Standing over the cot and talking, but the words weren't like anything I've ever heard. And the *voice*. Like that of a man, but deeper. Worse." Her eyes widen and tears well up.

"What did you do?" Pryce speaks quietly and puts a gentle hand on her arm, just to bring her back from the edge for a moment.

"I shouted. The mistress, Mrs Tebbs, weren't far behind me anyway and she came running in. When she saw the wild woman, she went straight for her. The mistress wasn't scared, you see. New mothers can be ferocious. But the woman wasn't scared either. She just grabbed Mrs Tebbs and threw her through the window. Then she leaped out herself.

"What?" I chime in. "Jumped out of the window? From up here?"

"Yes. I ran to look down, but I only saw the mistress, lying there." Applethorpe starts to weep, then sob. "And the baby…"

I step to the cot and look in. The baby there is pale, and very still. I reach out a hand before realising that its skin is a familiar shade of marble. It is almost the same as the one back in the office. I tap its forehead lightly. Solid as stone.

"Jesus." Pryce comes over and we exchange a look. I cross to the window and look out. In the distance I can see the church tower of Saint Hild's, and further away the dome of the Museum's roof. I turn back to Pryce.

"Tell Wright to fetch the coroner, if he hasn't already. We'll take the baby back to the station. I need to think about this. If Kolitsi's still around, he can take Miss Applethorpe's statement."

"You're taking the baby?" The nanny looked aghast at the prospect.

"Aye, miss. I need to examine it. I think it might relate to another case we're looking into right now. Can't be helped."

"But what about the other one?"

"Other what?"

"The other baby. They're twins. Jeremy and

Julian. That's Julian. The woman took Jeremy with her."

Back at the station, my stomach is giving me hell once more. I take a few drops of tincture in a glass of wine and settle down to look at the two stone babies side by side on the desk. They are both marble, but they aren't identical. Different sizes, different positions. Both still in their swaddling clothes.

"I don't believe a woman is stealing babies and leaving stone ones behind. I just don't believe it. And how can she have jumped from the window and fled so easily? There is trickery here, Kittie."

She picks up the Cutgrave baby. "They really are superbly carved, Father. The tiny details... Damn!" Kittie plonks the baby down on the desk again and scowls at the broken marble pinkie in her hand. "Sorry, Father. It just broke off."

"Never mind, Kittie. Could have been worse. At least it wasn't an arm or a leg."

She peers at the tiny digit. "Huh."

"Kittie?"

"Strange, it seems almost like there are markings inside."

"Cracks, you mean? Fractures in the marble?"

"Looks more like... the outline of a fingerbone. But that's not possible."

I examine it myself. The markings do indeed resemble the outline of a bone, a little circle in the middle of the finger, the texture of the stone within the circle's boundary subtly different from that without.

Kittie fixes me with a fierce stare.

"Father. What if these *are* the babies?" Kittie grabs *Theogony* from the floor and begins leafing through it.

I shrug, then grunt as a spasm runs through my gut. It'll take a few minutes before the tincture starts to have an effect. "I don't understand. Speak plain, Kittie."

"What if the babes were turned to stone? All their living cells petrified. Like a fossil."

"Jesus, Kittie, what are you talking about? It's not possible, is it? Start making sense."

"It occurred to me this morning, but I dismissed it. 'Entities should not be multiplied without necessity', says Ockham, remember?"

I shrug, the meaning lost on me. She continues.

"Anyway. Fossils are found underground. But some of the ancient myths talk of living people turned to stone. Well, only one really: the gorgons, from the Greek legends. From here." She pats *Theogony*. "And other places, of course."

"Myths are myths, Kittie. Not to be given credence."

"But all myths and legends have *some* root in truth. You've heard of the gorgons, at least?"

I sigh, and ruminate for a moment. "We had a corporal out in the Crimea, he'd read a lot of books. Used to tell some of these sorts of tales, distract us from all the cold and misery. Medusa. Snakes for hair. Got her head lopped off. Two sisters."

"Yes. But as with all legends, the details vary. Three sisters, yes: Stheno, Euryale, Medusa. But some say only Medusa had snakes for hair. Some books say they all had wings, and the lower parts of snakes; others don't mention this. A few texts suggest that the sisters were immortal, apart from Medusa. Others are silent about immortality, or what it meant. But they all agree that the sisters could turn flesh to stone."

"You think a *gorgon* did this?"

"Not as such. A gorgon is just a way of demonising powerful women. Men have always feared powerful women, Father. Make them into terrible monsters and it becomes easier to justify limiting that power, for all women. I doubt the gorgons ever existed in the way the myths say. But maybe there was some truth in the idea of petrification. The power to turn things to stone."

I consider the idea for a moment. "If that were true, it might at least explain why the babes are still in their clothes. The clothes aren't alive, are they? Only the flesh has become stone."

It seems so outlandish. I wouldn't dare suggest it to anyone. But then, the whole thing makes no bloody sense, however I look at it.

Kittie purses her lips and gazes thoughtfully at the ceiling. "Kolitsi said there was a statue at the Museum. A woman, with a baby. Then the statue disappears, and the baby it held is left behind, broken. The statue came from the mausoleum excavated by Sir Newton. Halikarnassos. The gorgons were creatures of Hades. Fitting that they would be found — or represented, perhaps — in a giant tomb."

The tincture is warming me through, easing the spasms. I'm not sure I fully understand what Kittie means, but I concede that it might be possible. What do we really know about the world, after all? Look how fast it's changing. Look at the new things we're finding in the modern age. This is perhaps not so far-fetched. And Kittie is rarely wrong.

As I stare at the babies, I finally realise what was bothering me about the one we found at Cutgrave. And the other, now I come to see it.

"They have eyelashes, Kittie."

"What?"

"They have eyelashes. Tiny marble eyelashes, fine as any hair. Who in the name of Jesus can carve a set of *eyelashes* from marble?"

I resolve to get to the bottom of it.

I open the desk drawer and pull forth a small chisel that I keep handy in case I ever need to get in anywhere I wouldn't be welcome. And a small lump hammer.

"Hold it for me, Kittie." She holds the small statue's torso, pressing it down against the desk so that it won't slide when I hit it.

"Are you sure, Father?"

"You said yourself, if it's living matter turned to stone, it should still *look* like living matter inside.

Right? No-one can carve the inside of a statue. So. One strike and we'll know."

I place the sharp edge of the chisel against the baby's forehead. My stomach lurches.

"God forgive me, if it's true."

I bring the hammer down. The infant's head is cleaved in two, the uneven halves separating from the neck and rocking back and forth on the desk. And there, preserved in pristine detail, are the petrified fissures and convolutions of brain tissue, the eyes, the sinus cavities. The clear outlines of a tongue.

I rush to the window and vomit into the darkened street.

When I am able to talk, I turn to Kittie.

"Fetch Kolitsi."

Kolitsi seems to think he's in some trouble, despite my best efforts to reassure him. He keeps wiping sweat from his eyes and blinking nervously at the cloven baby on the desk. I should've covered it up, but it's too late now. I move to stand in front of it.

"Now then, Lucas. This business at the Museum. What details do you have? Be as specific as possible now, there's a good soul."

"It was a statue, of a woman. There was a baby too, but the curator says the baby got cracked in transit. When they were shipping it, y' see? They couldn't fix it, but were going to exhibit it like that anyway. Mother and baby, from the Mausoleum."

"And did they give you a name for the statue, the mother? You said it started with a 'U'?"

"Yeah, that's how the curator pronounced it, something like that." He tugs a ragged scrap of paper from his pocket. "I went again this afternoon, to follow up. I don't know how to say it properly, but 'ere you go. E-U-R-Y-A-L-E. Some Greek name. Or Latin."

Pryce stares at me, face pale.

"What?" says Kolitsi, suddenly afraid. "Have I done something wrong?"

"Nothing, Lucas. You've been a great help." I usher him to the door and clap him on the shoulder before shoving him through and closing it behind him. I turn back to Kittie.

"Euryale?"

"The far-leaper," she says, picking up *Theogony* and leafing through. "The fastest of the sisters. Capable of jumping to a great height..." She falters. "A terrible voice."

"Bloody hell." I look again at the bisected stone head on the desk. "So, for the sake of argument, let's say there *is* some truth in the myth. Euryale is a woman from ancient Greece — or wherever — who can turn people to stone and live forever. Somehow, she herself becomes stone, or looks like stone, and takes up residence — or maybe is imprisoned, or asleep — in the Mausoleum. She gets shipped back to England with her baby, but the baby breaks on the way. Then she wakes, and..."

"Goes to look for another baby. And they get turned to stone."

"Why are the babies turned to stone and not the mothers, though? Why did she have to kill the mothers with her own hands?"

Kittie purses her lips and stares at the office window and the darkness beyond. Her reflection stares back. "Maybe only children turn to stone. Or maybe she can choose who does and who doesn't. Or maybe only males are affected. Both babies are boys, after all. And in the legends, it was mainly men being petrified, I suppose."

There is a tap at the office door.

I drape a handkerchief over the baby. "Come in, Kolitsi."

Though it is not Kolitsi that enters, but a young lad on the verge of manhood and wearing a surplice. He looks cold, face red, chest heaving as he tries to catch his breath. Flecks of snow are melting in his black hair.

"They sent me up," he pants. "To see you. Inspector. I'm Albrecht. Father Adams says. To come to Cutgrave again. There's another. Baby."

I grab my truncheon and coat and head for the door, pausing for a moment to take a swig of tincture from the bottle on my desk; then another. I catch Kittie's eye and look away. I ignore the twinge in my stomach as we bowl down the stairs and out into the gaslit gloom once again.

Father Adams is easy to find, the light from his lantern visible through the overgrowth almost as soon as we make our way through Cutgrave's iron gate. Pryce and I avoid the paths and instead cut through the vegetation to save time, wet leaves and branches trailing over us as we push toward the glow.

The priest stands before one of the crypts we'd passed this morning, his face even redder and more creased now the day is nearing its end. He flinches as we burst through the bushes beneath an old yew.

"Father Adams!" I tap the truncheon against my thigh again, trying not to think about the prickling in my gut, which will soon turn to a fierce agony until the tincture takes effect. "What's afoot?"

He steps to one side to reveal the statue of the woman with wild hair that I'd spotted earlier in the day. But instead of reaching for the sky, she now has her arms folded before her. And enveloped in the fold is a small marble baby.

Father Adams blinks. "This statue. I don't remember seeing it before. And the baby... marble, just like the one we found this morning!"

Pryce steps forward. "Good God," he says. "This must be Jeremy."

The statue's eyes snap to Pryce's face and there is a sound like the earth tearing open. And then the stone woman leaps past me, her hand catching my shoulder and spinning me round so that I sprawl on the wet ground, snow and dirt in my mouth. The sound comes again, a roar like the rising tide. I look up. Where the statue was there is now only the baby, lying abandoned in the snow. And next to it, another pale statue, facing the tomb.

A marble figure dressed in a navy swallowtail coat and black boots. I can't bear to look, but I know.

Pryce. Kittie.

I turn away from the crypt.

The lamp drops to the floor and Father Adams runs, wailing, toward Saint Hild's. The woman pounces, reaching him in a few loping strides and grabbing his arm, twisting it hard behind his back so that the cracking of bone rings out in the still air. He screams. Just for a moment.

She bends over him and two blinding green sparks light up her eyes, brighter than any flame I have ever seen. Father Adams is silent and still. After a glance towards me, the gorgon takes the time to snap the priest apart, limb by limb, grinding his marble body to dust between her fingers. When only the head is left, she crushes it beneath her bare foot.

I stagger to my feet, body aching. Euryale waits beneath the yew, a dark shape amongst the leaves. My hand trembles as I grip the truncheon, but the thought of Kittie gives me strength.

I yell at the creature, formless noise with no meaning.

She moves so fast I can't believe it. I swing, but the club passes harmlessly as her fist punches into my stomach, doubling me over so that I see only a constellation of tiny stars against the muddy ground.

I vomit, the sour iron tang of blood strong in the air. For a moment I am gone, and when I open my eyes she is standing over me. She speaks, deep, guttural words in a language I don't understand.

I wonder why I am not turned to stone, or torn apart.

She bends close to me, her scent that of dust and sulphur. She places a hand on my gut and cocks her head to one side as if thinking. She doesn't appear grotesque, or horrific. She looks all too human, her features sculpted by pain. I have seen the same expression borne by the denizens of London; the ones life has treated too harshly.

For a moment she looks at me, and I think I can see pity in her eyes. Then she straightens. I turn painfully onto my front and crawl back to Kittie. If I'm to die, I want to be close to her. I reach her feet, still encased in black leather boots, and reach up to grab the white marble of her hand where it rests against her thigh. The baby is lying in the mud nearby. I pull it to me and hold it in the crook of one arm.

I am ready.

Euryale walks to me and plucks the baby from my arm. She smiles down at it, and I see in her face only affection. This is the face of a mother, not a monster, despite the terrible power she holds. She walks to stand beneath the yew tree and sits on an old stump there. After a few moments, she shrugs aside her robe to expose a breast and lifts the marble baby to it.

To my astonishment, the baby moves. Its pale

skin reddens to attain a warm pink hue. Jeremy opens his mouth to wail, but a moment later is suckling as if at his mother's teat. Euryale growls, but there is no menace in it.

My heart races at the realisation that the petrification can be reversed.

"Please," I say, as loud as I can. Tiredness is creeping up on me, and I am like to faint. "Please, this..." I pat Kittie's leg. "This is my daughter, she... she's my child, she's all I have."

The gorgon watches me, an odd expression on her face. Sadness, perhaps. Or sympathy. Or amusement. I wonder if she can understand me, or intuit my meaning.

"Inspector Marshall!"

Kolitsi's voice, carrying across the cemetery.

"No," I whisper, and with a great effort, pulling on Kittie's hand to help me, I rise.

Kolitsi turns the path and sees me standing before the crypt in the lantern light. "Inspector?"

"Go," I say.

He looks confused. "I heard there was trouble."

"Turn around and *walk away.*"

Euryale watches us from the shadows beneath the trees, a faint green glow in her eyes. The baby still feeds.

The world softens as the pain begins to fade, the laudanum finally doing its job. I harden my voice.

"Kolitsi, leave us be!"

He turns away, and I let go of Kittie's hand as the ground rises to meet me.

I don't leave the house anymore.

The winter is almost done, but I stay by the hearth in my drawing room, taking tea with a healthy dose of tincture and the occasional hard biscuit. Simple sustenance, things that are easy to digest.

Cancer, of course. Once they got me to the University College hospital the physicians were quick enough to diagnose it. Growing slowly but now quite advanced. I may make it through summer. Possibly. I received a decent pension from the force, for the remains of my time.

Sometimes I wish I'd been petrified by the gorgon after all. But that soon passes. Especially given what Pryce says.

The feeling of joy when I woke up and saw Kittie – Pryce – by the bed still resonates in me now. I don't know why the woman restored him. Something of the pleading in my voice perhaps. Or the pity I read on her face when she stood over me. We can't presume to understand the reasoning of such beings. So I tell myself.

When we came home, I asked Kittie about it. I worried it would upset her, but she was brave enough to tell me. Why did she turn to stone? Not just men after all, then?

She said biology didn't matter. Conviction was enough. On her part or the gorgon's, I don't know. Since then she's been only Edward Pryce, and I'm content with that. We both are.

What was it like, I asked? For those few minutes he was no more than a statue. Could he remember?

You're aware, he said. Transfixed, but aware. He felt me take his hand, when I thought I was to die. You are a living cell, he said, trapping everything you are inside.

That was hard, once I realised what it meant. The baby, I said. The one I took the chisel to...

Yes. He had tears in his eyes. Yes.

Pryce is still a Peeler. He'll make sergeant soon, I'm sure. Every time he's on patrol, and even after, he's searching for the gorgon. Euryale, the far-leaper. She's still out there somewhere, with little Jeremy. In the boneyards of London, or somewhere underground. I know it.

Julian rests on the windowsill, where he has a good view over the park. I've wrapped him in the most comfortable cloth I could find. I talk to him a lot, when I'm able. Pryce told the family that both babies were taken by the intruder, a lunatic, and that the marble babe was left behind. Just like at Cutgrave, earlier in the day. A madwoman, you see. No sane reason behind it. As evidence, the little statue must be kept by the Peelers. It's the best he could do. The truth is just too strange.

I hope Pryce finds her. If there is anyone in all of London who might be able to appeal to her and have Julian restored to the flesh, it's Edward Pryce. That's what I'm holding on for.

I tell Julian it won't be long now.

I hope it's the truth.

The Color of Paris in the Spring

Macy Harrison

MERE SECONDS AFTER SETTING FOOT INSIDE the house, I heard the tell-tale tapping of late summer rain pelting the windows. As the maid—some new girl whom I'd never seen before—helped me shuck off my traveling cloak, Mother appeared at the top of the stairs and exclaimed that I had not arrived a moment too soon.

"It isn't as if I would have melted for a little rain," I said. "I'm not made of sugar, you know."

"What, dear?" Mother stopped at the base of the stairs, a confused look on her face. "Oh. Has it begun raining? I hadn't noticed."

"Then whatever did you mean by saying I hadn't arrived a moment too soon?" I asked as we embraced.

"The decorators," she said, a fiery gleam in her eye. "They were late with everything, and I feared we would not finish before you returned. Indeed, they only delivered the drapes half of an hour ago. But, for all that, I do believe everything is finally squared away and ready for you."

"Mother," I said, trying not to groan. "You haven't redone the house again, have you? It hasn't been a year since the decorators were here last."

"You needn't moan," she said. "I've only done the bedrooms, as they were not fit for habitation, and I wanted you and Willie to have someplace nice to rest your heads when you returned home."

"You know he hates being called 'Willie,'" I said as she linked her arm through mine and steered me up the stairs. "Has he returned to school already?"

"He is my son, and I shall call him what I please. But to answer your question: yes. The new term has already begun. We are to visit him on Family Day next month, and you shall get to see him then."

As Mother led me up to the second floor, where our bedrooms were located, she asked a few cursory questions about my trip: How were my aunt and cousins? How did I find the Continent? Had I enjoyed Paris as much as she had at my age?

"Paris was lovely," I said in response to the last question. "I especially enjoyed seeing La Madeleine, and I had a fine time finally being able to make good use of all those French lessons."

"To be nineteen and strolling down the Champs-Elysées—is there anything more perfect than that?" she mused as we came to a stop outside my bedroom door. "When I decided on the décor, that was my inspiration, you know. Your trip. I wanted to capture the color of *Paris au printemps*."

With a flourish, she opened the door and ushered me inside.

The bedroom I had left three months prior had been, if not exactly fashionable, at least fitting for the house, parts of which dated to the early sixteenth century. I had liked my timbered walls and square, medievalesque furniture, and had, up to that point, successfully preserved the room from my mother's frequent redesigns. I suppose I should have expected that she would seize the opportunity of my being away to change it.

Upon setting foot in the room, I found myself assaulted by the most fashionably zealous shade of green imaginable. The walls, from floor to ceiling, had been papered in the color, which was broken only by the inclusion of small white-and-yellow lilies in the pattern. And Mother had not stopped with the walls. The draperies were likewise green, as was the wingback chair that now stood where my heavy chest of drawers—which had been original to the house—used to be.

I dare say even the bed linens would have been green—if there had been any bed linens. Mother must have made this observation a split second after I did, for she gasped and threw herself between me and the bed, as if there was something unseemly about it, and she did not want me to look.

"They forgot the linens," she cried. "How could

they have forgotten the linens, of all things? Did they not see the bedstead was bare?"

"It's quite alright," I said. "I shall be more than happy to have my old bedclothes."

"Out of the question," Mother said. "They do not match the new paper, and, besides, we do not have them any longer. I have already distributed them amongst the domestics."

Once more, I suppressed a groan.

"It is a good thing your brother has already returned to school," she continued. "You will take his bed for tonight, and tomorrow I shall make sure you have new linens."

"Could you choose some in a different shade than green?" Quickly, I added, "Not that I don't like the color. I only fear it would overwhelm the senses."

Her face fell. "You do not like it."

"I do," I insisted, though I spoke a lie. "Truly, I do. But I think a nice cream would offset the green very nicely—it would really showcase it—don't you agree? It is such a lovely color that it does deserve to be showcased."

"You are quite right," she said, her frown flipping back to a smile. "It is a very special color. It is the color of Paris in the spring."

More like the color of Parisian mildew, I thought, but it was a thought I wisely kept to myself.

Mother kept me up until the clock struck a half

hour until midnight. She wanted to hear all about my trip—what I ate, where I ate it, what famous places did I visit, and so on. She insisted I spare no detail.

I was happy to indulge her since Mother loved traveling, but rarely got to, as Father hated being away from Swallowtail House. I've often ascribed her love of interior design to this—unable to visit new lands, she instead settled for creating new rooms.

Father, for his part, retired promptly at nine o'clock, as per usual. He announced himself content to know I was home safe and had enjoyed my trip.

"Your mother may allow herself to indulge in such escapism," he said as he rose from his armchair, the evening post folded beneath his arm. "But I've no use for hearing about places I never intend to visit."

With that, he left us to our indulgences.

When Mother finally allowed me to retire, I automatically went to my bedroom and was halfway to my dressing table before I remembered I was to sleep in my brother's room that night.

In the daylight, this had not seemed like a very great thing. But deep in the belly of the night, I found that old apprehension welling up in my stomach. I was to sleep in the witch's room again.

At nineteen, I should have been long past believing in some silly story a cruel cousin had told to frighten me when we were children. I knew there were not really such things as witches, and that Rebecca Hanson had merely been an unfortunate victim of a less-enlightened society. But even so, as I went through my nightly ablutions, I kept hearing my cousin's voice taunting me:

Wicked, old Rebecca Hanson,
Lived upon the hill in Cranston;
Killed her husbands one by one;
Poisoned them, and when done,
Poisoned good the village well,
And opened up a gate to Hell.
When she burned, a promise gave,
That anyone, fool or brave,
Who woke her spirit from the fire,
Would die like her upon a pyre.

According to my cousin, one Arnold Phelan, my bedroom had once been Rebecca's witch's cabinet, which meant if I made too much noise in there, or left it a mess, her spirit would crawl out of Hell and burn me alive.

Good old Cousin Arnold. One wonders why they ever thought to toss him out of university.

At age five, the story had frightened me so much that I had outright refused to sleep in the room again. Father, ever the pragmatist, had attempted to set things straight by telling me the song was all wrong, that Rebecca had not been old, had, indeed, only been in her thirties, had only had one husband die, and had been hanged, not burned (I can still hear him proudly pronounce, "We English did not burn our witches, unlike the Continentals"). The part about the village well being poisoned was correct, but, as he pointed out, it had almost certainly been poisoned by naturally occurring toxins that had leached into the groundwater, not by Rebecca. Furthermore, her husband had died after drinking from that well; Rebecca likely had played no part in his death, either.

"The village thought her a witch because she dabbled in the sciences," Father further explained. "Which, in those days, meant fussing about with alchemy. It was an unwomanly pastime, to be sure, but hardly witchcraft. Witches do not exist, nor do ghosts. Simply because she was wrongfully hanged in the front garden does not mean her spirit intends to return to her old laboratory and burn alive the little girl who now resides there."

One wonders why his words did little to soothe me.

Unconvinced that Rebecca Hanson would not rise from Hell and get me, I, for all intents and purposes, forced my parents to switch my bedroom with Will's nursery. They did so on the condition that I never tell my brother about Rebecca Hanson. Which, as a responsible older sister, I of course did not. I left that task to Cousin Arnold.

As I settled into my brother's bed—he had not been spared the accursed green bedclothes—I tried to divert my thoughts elsewhere, away from Rebecca Hanson. This was soon done, for, once my eyes had adjusted to the dark, I found another facet of the room to fixate on: Mother's Paris Green. It was so saturated a hue that it seemed to glow even in the meager amount of moonlight that escaped through the drapes. The longer I stared at the paper, the brighter the color seemed to become, until I was convinced I shouldn't be able to sleep for so much visual stimulus.

I rolled over so that my back faced the window, but I could not escape the color, for even the pillowcases were Paris Green. It was beginning to give me a splitting headache. Rolling onto my back, I rubbed my forehead and eyes, but the pain would not subside.

Sighing in frustration, I propped up the pillows so that I could sit upright and I stared down the paper like it were an adversary. As I engaged in my one-sided staring contest, my mind, racked by exhaustion but unable to sleep, grew angry at my mother. Why did she have to keep changing the house? Why could she not leave my things alone? And why, for the love of everything good and decent, did she have to paper our bedrooms in such an awful color?

"Very well," I said to the paper. "I will allow you to win. Only let me sleep."

The paper did not respond.

I focused my sight on two particularly bright lilies next to each other in the pattern and tried not to move my eyes, as doing so made my headache worse. I focused on them so intently that my vision began to blur, and, at long last, my eyelids began to droop. Afraid that any change in my movements would cause sleep to once more flee, I continued staring at the two lilies as my eyelids grew heavier and heavier, and my vision blurrier and blurrier. It grew so blurry that, for a very brief moment, the lilies seemed to disappear entirely. Within a second, though, they had returned, glowing as brightly as ever.

My breath caught. My vision sharpened, and every trace of drowsiness fled. Wallpaper does not blink (does it?). The lilies were not lilies. They were eyes.

As I tried to keep my breathing even, I told myself not to be silly. The paper had not blinked. My tired mind had only imagined it.

But the longer I stared at the two white objects which may or may not have been lilies, the more they seemed like eyes. Though I almost could not bear to admit it to myself, they were far too round to be trumpet-shaped flowers. And they glowed far brighter than any of the other lilies in the pattern.

I do not know for how long I stared into those eyes—it felt like an hour, but it must have only been a couple of minutes. Gradually, I began to discern the silhouette of a head, and then of a body. It wasn't human-shaped—not exactly. The head was an odd, geometric form that tapered unnaturally to the neck, and the body was disproportionately short and wide. It was roughly child-sized but bore the proportions of no child I had ever seen. And those eyes. No human has eyes like that.

Frozen with fear, I could not think what to do other than to keep perfectly still and hope that whatever it was went away. As it was, I eventually got my wish—in the worst manner possible.

As I lay staring into the eyes, my body paralyzed with dread, I heard the sound of paper being ripped. I thought, at first, that the creature was tearing at the paper. But then I saw its silhouette start to twist, and it was then that I understood the true horror of what was occurring: the creature had not been standing in front of the paper—it was the paper, and was in the process of tearing itself free from the wall.

My heart in my throat, I dug my fingernails into the bedclothes and willed myself to move, but I could not. I could not do anything but watch in the faint moonlight as the wallpaper man tore first its head, then its arms, and then its body and legs free from the rest of the paper. With a shake of its flimsy head, it stepped down from the wall.

A moan escaped my throat. I was certain I was about to die. Whatever the wallpaper man was, it wasn't natural, and I had seen it escape. If nothing else, surely it would want to silence me for that reason.

Still staring into those glowing eyes, I watched the wallpaper man sidle across the floor, its gate surprisingly strong for one made of paper. I braced myself, waiting for it to round the corner of the bed and grab at me, perhaps wrap its paper arms around my throat and strangle the breath from me.

But it did not do that. It kept shuffling across the room until it reached the door, at which point it slid through the minuscule crack between the door and frame and disappeared into the house.

I sat nearly panting for a full minute before I regained control of myself and was able to move again. I grabbed for my matchbook and lit the bedside lamp, my hands shaking so badly that I nearly dropped the lit match on the bedclothes. Surveying the room in the lamplight, I saw what I had most feared I would see: directly across from the foot of the bed was a vaguely human-shaped hole torn from the paper.

In a frenzy, I leaped from the bed, the lamp in hand, and darted towards the door. My hand gripped the knob but did not turn it. The wallpaper man was out there, somewhere in the dark, dark house. Who was to say I wouldn't meet him if I left the room?

I had intended to flee to my parents' bedroom, but I realized that might not be the wisest course of action, not only because I didn't know where the wallpaper man was, but also because they wouldn't have believed me. What sane person would? Oh, certainly, I could show them the hole in the paper. But they were as likely to believe me the culprit as some supernatural being I could not even put a name to. They would think I had caught some strange disease on the Continent, some brain fever or other that made me a lunatic. And, by God, what if I had? True, I had the tear in the wallpaper as evidence, but if I could hallucinate a strange creature, then I could hallucinate a hole. If I was a lunatic, then I might have even done it myself, and didn't remember.

Stepping away from the door, I crept towards the tear in the paper, but could not bring myself to get close enough to examine it. Instead, I grabbed my dressing gown and shoved it in the crack beneath the door. Next, I took up some handkerchiefs from my brother's dressing table and wedged them, as best I could, between the door and the frame. Stepping back to survey my handiwork, I prayed that it would keep the thing out.

The maid would think me an odd duck when she came in the morning, but what was that to me when a strange creature had just torn itself from the wallpaper and made off into the house?

Father had proclaimed Rebecca Hanson an alchemist, not a witch, but I now knew better. I was certain the wallpaper man was her familiar, returned from the beyond for—I did not know what purpose. I did not know what had awoken it, either, unless Mother's decorators had caused commotion enough to literally wake the dead. It appeared Cousin Arthur's song rang truer than Father had led me to believe. I could only hope the last bit, the part about Rebecca burning me alive, was an exaggeration.

Crawling back into bed, I drew the ugly bedclothes up to my chin and tried to stop shaking. I would stay awake until morning, I pledged, to be sure the wallpaper man did not come back. In the morning, I would deal with it—whatever that entailed. All I had to do was stay awake until morning, and keep watch over the paper. Keep awake. Keep watch.

Despite this pledge, and despite the great shock I had just experienced, I did somehow manage at some point to fall asleep. If I dreamed, then I do not remember.

☠

The house bell woke me in the morning, and I came to with a start. The events of the prior night returned in a flash, and I couldn't believe I had fallen asleep. Sitting upright, I checked the wallpaper. The hole was gone. I could not even detect a tear.

"Can't be," I said to myself as I swung my legs out of the bed.

Though still apprehensive of the wallpaper, the daylight emboldened me enough to be able to approach it. I scrutinized the wall, my face inches from it, but I could not spy a single tear, nor even a single ripple or bubble in the paper. It appeared wholly intact.

I raised my hand, meaning to feel about for any upsets in the paper, but I could not quite bring myself to touch it. As I held my palm a mere inch from the wall, I imagined I could feel the menace radiating from it. It felt like holding one's hand up to a glass case that contains a deadly adder that wishes to strike.

It was in that position—my hand up to the paper, my body arched towards the wall—that the maid found me. As she entered the room, the handkerchiefs I'd stuffed in the door jam fluttered free, momentarily startling her. Pausing in the doorway, she looked from the pile of handkerchiefs to me, and I could tell she was fighting hard to keep from giving me a queer look.

"Was there a draft, miss?" she asked, stooping to tug my dressing gown free from beneath the door.

"Yes," I said, backing away from the paper. "That's all it was. A draft and nothing more."

It is amazing what a little daylight can accomplish. By the time I descended for breakfast, I had almost convinced myself the previous night's events had been nothing but a bad dream. A very odd, bad dream.

Entering the dining room, I found Mother already nibbling on a bit of toast. As I helped myself to the spread laid out on the sideboard, I asked what our itinerary for the day was, my intention being to discreetly inquire when we should be buying me new linens so that I could move back into my own bedroom.

"I'm afraid your father isn't feeling well," she said. "I think it best if we stay here today. In case he should need anything."

"He seemed perfectly well yesterday," I said, setting down my toast point. "What's happened?"

"He has a headache," she said, her tone dismissive, as if she didn't really believe him ill.

"A headache bad enough to keep him in bed?"

"I shouldn't worry," she said as she took up a spoon and gave her egg a delicate tap, shattering the shell. "I'm certain it's nothing more than a case of his having had a bit too much brandy and a few too many cigars at his club yesterday."

As I chewed on the edge of my toast, I could not help but think of the wallpaper man. Could he have been real? Could there be some connection between his appearance and my father's illness? It all seemed so unaccountable. So surreal. I did not know what to think beyond that I did not want to sleep in the witch's room another night. I considered how best to broach the subject with Mother.

"As we are to occupy ourselves here today," I began, "which, I assume, means we will not be ordering my new bed linens just yet, perhaps we could have Will's linens moved to my bed? It's only that I've been away so long, and should like to sleep in my own bedroom."

"Where is my head today?" she asked, scrunching up her face like she'd tasted a sour lemon. "That was the other thing I meant to tell you. It appears you shall have to make use of your brother's room a while longer."

I shall have to *what*?

"Has something happened?" I asked, my body going cold.

"There's been some sort of leak in your bedroom," she said. "It seems to have been quite severe, for the paper is utterly ruined. There are streaks running throughout it where the water washed the pigment away."

"I shan't mind a bit of ruined paper."

"That isn't the matter, Caroline," Mother said. "I can't have my daughter sleeping in a damp room, especially when it is likely to rain again tonight. You would catch your death."

I couldn't argue with that, especially when my reason for wanting out of Will's room was so outlandish. Mother must have noted the apprehension on my face, for she set down her egg spoon with a clank and shook her head.

"Do not tell me you are still frightened of that room," she said. "You are nineteen—a grown woman. There are no such things as witches, and, even if there were, your brother has slept in that room for fifteen years without incident. There is nothing the matter with that room."

"It isn't that," I said, thinking how best to voice my concerns without sounding insane. "It's only— did you not hear someone walking about last night? I'm certain I heard someone walking about well past when everyone ought to have been asleep."

"I slept soundly and heard nothing," Mother said. "If someone was about, then it was only a maid. Really, Caroline."

I said nothing in response, for what could I possibly say? I saw a creature rip itself from your hideous wallpaper and that is why I'm afraid of the room? I'd be in Bedlam in an instance.

I fretted about the room all that day. As an addition to my anxiety, shortly before dinner, I overheard mother tell the housekeeper to send word to our doctor to call the next morning. I knew it had to have something to do with Father, but she refused to tell me anything, saying only that she had called on the doctor as a precaution. I knew this was a lie, or at least a half-truth, for, just prior to this, I had passed by their bedroom and heard the sounds of someone being violently ill inside.

When evening fell, I attempted to convince Mother to stay up and play cards with me, but she declined, saying she was far too tired for having spent all the day looking after Father.

"He is quite ill, then?" I asked.

"I suspect he only ate something at his club that did not agree with him," Mother said. "Your father has a way of, how shall I say this, worrying himself and, for that matter, everyone around him, sick. I wouldn't worry.

"Unless, of course," she added, "what you really mean to say is that you wish to stay up because you're still being foolish about the room."

"Not at all," I said. "I'm not tired yet. That is all."

This was quite the lie. I was incredibly tired, but I was also incredibly wary of sleeping in that room. Having no other option, for I couldn't very well sleep in the parlor, I trudged up the stairs behind Mother and entered the witch's room.

I had no intention of sleeping, of course. Once the maid left, I relit the bedside lamp, propped myself up against the pillows, and took out my needlework kit. Anytime I felt myself begin to doze, I would prick my finger with one of the needles. This worked to keep me awake until after midnight, at which point I had to get out of bed and walk briskly back and forth across the room to fight off the drowsiness.

It was after one of these impromptu sprints that the fatigue well and truly hit me, and my head began to swim and pound with pain. Slumping back on the bed, I pressed my palms against my eyes until the headache began to subside. When it did, and I removed my hands and opened my eyes, I experienced the abject terror of realizing myself completely blind, for I could not see a thing.

I very nearly screamed, but then I caught a glimpse of moonlight and realized that I had not gone blind at all. Rather, my lamp had somehow gone out.

Heart racing with fear, I felt about the bedside table, desperate to find my matchbook and the lamp. The former I found readily; the latter had apparently disappeared. I swiped my hands back and forth across the table, but the lamp was not there anymore. As I had not heard it crash to the floor, that left only one explanation: someone had taken it.

Just as the full horror of this realization hit me, I heard the sound of the paper tearing.

I tore at the matchbook, my hands shaking so badly that I spilled the matches across my lap. Grasping at one, I tried to strike it, missed, tried again as the sound of ripping paper filled my ears. Unable to keep a low keen from escaping my throat, I struck the match once more, and finally it caught. Holding it up, I looked to the wall, fully expecting to see the wallpaper man ripping himself free. But that was not what I saw.

In the previous night's darkness, I had mistaken the being's costume for its body. But now, in the light, I saw that it was neither a creature, nor a man, but a woman in old style dress, with a ruff around her neck and a wide skirt. She appeared to be made entirely of Mother's green wallpaper.

The woman finished ripping her skirt from the wall and then turned to look at me, her eyes glowing white. As she inched closer to the foot of the bed, my match went.

As I fumbled to light a new one, I heard a voice speak to me, and it was as gravelly as the voice on a bad phonograph recording.

"Terra Mater begets all that can be created and recreated."

My match caught and I once more could gaze upon the woman made of wallpaper. It was impossible to discern any features for all the wrinkles and tears in her, but I knew there was only one person she could be.

"Rebecca Hanson," I whispered.

She pursed her paper lips and blew. Instantly my match went again.

"Projection be our ultimate goal. Through cupellation, the mundane may become the noble. Thusly we transmute arsenic into gold."

When I got my new match lit, I realized that she wasn't at the foot of my bed any longer. Frantically, I searched the dark corners of the room, but could not find her. Somehow, in the second between the end of her speech and my lighting the match, she had disappeared.

I threw myself out of bed and made for the door. Though more frightened of her than ever before, my greater fear was that she would do something to make Father worse. Though most of her speech had been utterly foreign to me, one word I'd had no trouble understanding: arsenic. She was poisoning my father.

I raced down the hall, my bare feet pounding the floor runner. When I reached my parents' bedroom, I didn't pause to knock—I tore open the door and ran inside.

The room was utterly dark, but I could hear her crinkling somewhere in that darkness. My heart beating so fast that I feared it would tear free of my chest, I struck a match and held it aloft.

She was in the room, alright. My light had caught her in the act of bending over my sleeping father. Mother was nowhere to be seen.

Unconcerned by my light, she carried on with her task. As she menaced over Father, she seemed to pulse green, the color growing brighter and brighter as if she were sucking it up like a sponge. Simultaneously, as she grew more vibrant, the wallpaper of my parents' bedroom grew dimmer, fading until it was almost white.

Rebecca bent her face close to Father's and opened her mouth. A waterfall of green liquid poured from her mouth into his.

I screamed. I screamed so loudly that it rattled the windows and tore my throat raw.

Rebecca vanished, but I kept screaming. I screamed until Mother raced into the room and began screaming herself.

"What are you doing?" she shouted. "What is wrong?"

I stopped screaming and gasped for breath. Pointing to the bed, I croaked, "Father. Check Father."

Mother ripped the matchbook from my hand and went to his bedside, where she lit the lamp. In its light, I saw that all the color had drained from her face.

"Joseph?" she asked softly as she shook Father's shoulder. "Joseph? Wake up, dear."

I fell back against the wall as she continued trying in vain to rouse him. If I had not been so focused on Father, I might have noted that the wallpaper on which I leaned was two shades lighter than it had been that morning.

"Caroline. Go and wake Mrs. Chalmers. Tell her to fetch the doctor at once."

"He's dead," I cried. "Rebecca Hanson killed him. She was a witch, Mother. She was a witch."

"What in heavens are you talking about?" Mother ran to me and shook my shoulders. "Stop this nonsense and go and wake Mrs. Chalmers."

"He's already dead," I continued. "What is the doctor going to accomplish?"

Mother stopped shaking me.

"I do not know," she said. "But it's the only thing I can think to do."

For the next few nights, Mother allowed me to sleep with her in the guest bedroom, which was where she had been sleeping the night Father died as a precaution against catching his illness. Thankfully, it was not papered in green.

She never asked me to elaborate on what I'd meant by naming Rebecca Hanson as Father's murderer, and I've never brought it up again. Considering the frenzy of that night, I doubt she even remembers I said it.

After the funeral, I prevailed upon her to remove all of the green wallpaper from the house. This was easily done, for not only was it inexplicably faded, but also the doctor suggested we remove it, as he feared Father's disease might yet cling to the paper. His official cause of death was cholera, even though it had come on suddenly and there were no other cases reported in the area. All the same, I let it be.

With Will still in school, it fell mostly to me to look after Mother in her widowhood, but I soon realized my attentions as a caregiver were not really needed. Tossing convention to the wind, she came out of her mourning a full four months early, her head full of schemes and ideas. She let me in on her grand plan only a few days after she'd put away her weeds.

"I've already talked things over with your brother," she told me, "and I've come to a decision: we are to let the house and get away from Cranston."

This news startled me so much that I let my sewing needle slip, and accidentally stabbed my thumb. As I wrapped it in a scrap of cloth, I asked whether she was sure that was a prudent thing to do.

"Will and I haven't even come out of mourning

yet," I argued. "Do you really think it would look alright to let the house and go off somewhere?"

"Pish," she said with a dismissive wave of her hand. "It isn't good for us to coop ourselves up in this musty old house. A spot of traveling would do us a world of good."

"You want us to travel?" I asked, incredulous.

"Only you and I, dear," she said. "Your brother must still attend school, after all."

"What ever has come over you?" I asked. "I don't think it would be seemly to go traveling when Father has been gone less than a year."

"You needn't be such a prude, dear," she said. "You enjoy traveling, and so do I. And it has been so long since I've left Cranston."

I sat on this for a moment. I didn't like the thought of doing something which might be viewed as coarse, or disrespectful to Father, but Mother did make a fine point. After all I'd witnessed in Swallowtail House, I was desperate to escape it.

"If I consent to this scheme," I began, "and I am not saying that I do, but, *if* I do, where exactly do you envision us going?"

"Why, Paris, of course," she said with a grin. "If we leave next month, then we should arrive just in time to see the first spring flowers bloom. As you know, my dear, I do so love Paris in the spring."

THE GOOD WORK

JAMES DORR

"Look," Wendy said. "D'you see 'em there, glowing?" Neither Coz or me could see anything, 'cept the usual muddled bootprints in the snow. But then, of course, we weren't girls like Wendy.

"An' there," she continued. The wind rose up outta Kensington Garden just as she spoke, and this time I almost thought I *could* see something. "See there?" she said. "Look, Coz, they're cloven. Like little hooves, they are."

I looked again, but this time, again, it was only bootprints. That and the prints of somebody's dog, maybe out for a walk -- they didn't have strays in London's West End. Not like the part we lived in. But Coz, he nodded, as if maybe he had the second sight too, even though Wendy said, often enough, that only girls got it. And most, like her, 'uld be losing it soon enough as well, soon's they grew to be women.

'Cept, of course, for the ones we was after, what used the gifts God give 'em for doing evil. The ones that was witches.

"Hey, Brendan, you coming?" Since we'd met Wendy, Coz was always calling me Brendan, my proper name, like we was going to church or something. Or back at the orphans' school. Now he was already darting between the wagons and carts on Bayswater Road, so I ran to catch up. And that's when I saw it.

"Look, Coz," I whispered, stooping down to pack a snowball once we was both on the other side. He looked where I looked, at the cat that was rubbing up against Wendy. I cocked my arm, ready, when Wendy glared back at us.

"No," she whispered.

Coz grabbed my arm till I dropped the snowball. "Don't you know what that is?" he asked.

I saw Wendy was smiling.

I tried to remember. "A f-f-familiar?"

Wendy came up to us. "Watch carefully where the cat's going," she said. "It *is* a familiar. A witch's familiar. And, if you haven't frightened it too much..."

I knew what she meant now. Coz had explained it all to me before, when the three of us first took up the Good Work. If only girls Wendy's age had the second sight -- could see the actual *signs* of witches

190

-- and even they, when they got older, would lose it, it was likely enough most grown-ups would no longer believe in witches. And yet they was still here to do their evil, even in cities as up to date as this, with horse omnibuses and steam trains and all the rest. Ships sailing out to all parts of the world. Yet milk still spoiled as soon as you'd get it. Men who'd been sober for years would get back the taste for gin, as if they'd never lost it, and beat their children. Or things even worse.

'Cause witches *killed* children too. Wendy told me that. Killed them and cooked them to use in their rituals -- like in the stories you used to get read to you when you was little. And Coz had it figured the coppers knew, too, 'cept they couldn't do nothing about it, what with the Council and all not believing. And not themselves having the second sight either.

So that left the children, like us, to hunt witches all by ourselves, and that's what Wendy meant. That, if you spotted a witch's familiar, that meant a witch had to be really close by, and even without the second sight, you could follow a cat -- like the one *I'd* spotted -- home to its witch's lair.

That was the first night. We'd followed the cat west on Bayswater Road up to Sussex Gardens, Wendy sometimes spying more of the glowing devils' prints when we'd lose sight of it, almost as bright, she said, as the gaslights that come on at dark to light up the wider streets. Jostled by crowds 'cause it still wasn't all that late, rushing to home to get their suppers. Us smelling the smells of hot meats and puddings then, till we finally come up to the Widow Blackburn's. We didn't know her name at first, of course. Only after Coz asked around. But that was the method, to find out everything you could find out about the one what you suspected of witching.

So Coz talked to tradesmen and such in the neighborhood over the next weeks, mindful of course that the longer we waited, what with the New Year coming and all that, the more powerful the widow would be. It works with all witches -- once Hallowe'en comes, it's their time of year, and they gets more powerful on up to their big mid-winter festival. Their "Saturnalia," as Wendy calls it -- she knows how to read and she says she got the name outta some book. But that's when they needs the children they've cooked up, to grind their bones into a powder like flour to bake the special breads they have for it.

Wendy read that too.

So that made it safer to do the Good Work in the summer mostly, when Wendy and Coz, being older than me, would go in the witches' lairs themselves, leaving me outside to watch out for demons or anything else that might come up to help them. Then, once they was done, we'd run back to our place, taking the darkest streets, back to the alleys that runs outta Holborn and Newgate. That's where we lived, in an old, tumbly building where Wendy and Coz had a room from an old man what Wendy knew. And Wendy would get me some gin and some water -- to help with my sleeping later on -- and throw me a wink, like, when she and Coz went in their special room and closed up the curtains.

Then just like with the witches' houses I'd wait and watch with my little knife in the hallway outside. And I'd drink my gin and I'd hear strange noises, like tiny little screams and things, what Wendy told me come from the evil the witches left behind.

Then, in the morning, we'd see the swag Wendy and Coz brought with them out from the witches' lairs, because there was a law -- Coz had explained that to me, too, how Wendy'd told him -- saying that if you caught a witch and were able to kill her, you got to keep all the stuff that she'd gained by doing her bad deeds. Except, because the law was real old, and what with so many people no longer believing in witches these days, you weren't supposed to tell anybody where you'd got it. Money and jewels and stuff -- things we could sell quick -- but all safe now from the witches' spells now that it was daytime.

But this time, anyway, Coz had said it was going to be different. What with the part of town we would be in -- a swells' part of town where the witch might have servants if we wasn't careful to pick their night off -- Wendy had said if I just stood outside, in my old coat and scarf, I might look outta place. Besides, Wendy said, I was getting older, and *sometime* I'd have to do inside work with them. And Coz had argued, but later they went in their curtained back room together and, even though we'd sold off all the last witch stuff we'd gotten, I woke up later and heard the little screams and thumps from where I lay rolled up in my blanket outside in the hallway.

And then I dreamed some -- and maybe I'd dreamed *that* -- but anyway I dreamed about the Good Work, and about Saturnalia. The witches' sabbath. The ground bones of children and flying and broomsticks. And witches making noise with the Devil. And then, next morning, Coz said it was settled, and I'd have to act brave and grown-up 'cause this time I was gonna help 'em to do in the Widow Blackburn.

So there we stood, hiding in the dark, out in the mews behind Widow Blackburn's, shivering in the winter cold. We was dressed up like carolers, what with it being less than a month before Christmas by now. It was Wendy's idea, that. That even though Coz's voice had gone froggy, like boy's voices do when they starts getting older -- sort of like girls and the second sight, Wendy says -- hers and mine was still high enough for door-to-door begging. 'Cept this time, of course, we wasn't going to just *any* houses, one by one up and down the streets, but to one house only. The Widow Blackburn's.

We waited, hidden, and watched for the servants -- only two servants, as Coz had found out -- to leave for their evening out. It seemed like hours, my eyes starting to smart from staring so long, when the door across the small back-garden finally opened. Two women came out in tattered cloaks, the elder a cook by Wendy's reckoning, the other most likely a maid-of-all-work, scarcely looking older than Wendy herself.

We shrank back behind the dustbins in the alley until they'd passed, Coz following somewhat to make sure they wasn't going to come back 'cause maybe they'd forgotten something, while Wendy and me stayed crouched where we were. "You see how the witch has the kitchen to herself now for doing her evil work," Wendy whispered. "What I heard is that she murdered her husband on just such a night as this, 'cause the Devil told her to do it."

I wished I was younger and didn't have to go in the house with them, all dark in back and rising up high like it might fall over at any minute and bury us under it. Especially when Wendy added, "She'll murder you too if you don't do what me and Coz tells you exactly. Any of us makes a mistake, we could *all* be killed." And yet I felt proud too. I *was* getting older. Old enough to help out with the Good Work, and not just wait outside. Maybe even old enough soon to go into the back room with Wendy and Coz and help de-witch the gear what we collected.

And Wendy knew, like she could read what was in my head. "Don't think," she whispered. "Remember, Coz an' me's done this before. Just stick close to me an' you'll do all right, Brendan."

Brendan, like we was in church or something.

But then, in a kind of way, we *was*. Like Coz explained -- *someone's* gotta fight evil 'cause, if not us, who'd be left to do it. I mean, if the witches was able to kill all the children like we knew they'd like to.

I felt Wendy's hand on my shoulder and watched as she winked at me, maybe thinking she'd give me courage, and then Coz was standing at my other side. "All right," he whispered. "The servants is gone now. I followed 'em all the way down to Hyde Park. And the widow's alone inside, just now going to the kitchen. I saw through the window. . . ."

Wendy put her finger to her lips. "Let's do it then," she hissed. She led Coz and me out of the alley, around to the front door, where we started singing -- Coz just pretending, because of his froggy voice. We started out with "God rest ye merry," and then did some "Greensleeves," and Wendy was real good like she'd practiced singing, or else had a real knack. While me, I was shivering, not just from the cold but more and more hoping that Coz was wrong, that the widow was gone for the evening too.

But then, slowly, the big front door opened.

I near to pissed my boots. There, in front of us, stood the witch, younger than I'd have thought -- maybe almost pretty by one way of thinking -- but still all dressed in black, wearing a kind of a shawl on her shoulders. Her hair kind of messed, too, and all red around the eyes -- I could see Coz was shivery as well, maybe taking sort of a half step back while Wendy stood her ground.

"Why children," the witch said. Her voice was sweet and high, not all gravelly like I'd expected -- Wendy had told me once that witches sometimes would fool you that way. "What lovely voices.

But isn't it late at night for children? You must be freezing!"

"Smile," Wendy whispered into my ear, so I just smiled and nodded while Coz, his voice cracking, said we were, and "thank you ma'am" and like that when she asked us inside. And then Wendy pushed me and held my hand and led us up the stairs behind Coz.

And then we were in the witch's parlor.

The door shut behind us!

"Now children," the witch -- Widow Blackburn -- said, "I'll bet you're hungry." She gave a little smile herself, but kind of tight-lipped like. "I've just been baking sugar biscuits, so why don't I get you some? Maybe some chocolate too. I'm making them for my Church Action group, but what's a half dozen or so more or less" -- she winked at us then, as if she was maybe hiding some secret -- "when I can just bake more?"

And then it hit me. *Her church group, indeed.* I nearly fell into the huge soft sofa the witch pointed out for us to sit on while she went to the kitchen. For a moment I thought I was already trapped -- that I'd sunk in the pillows and couldn't get up. But then Wendy squeezed my hand.

"Look," she whispered. She pointed to the big parlor mirror, draped all over in black crepe. "You know what that is?"

"She's a widow, ain't she?" I started to say -- I mean, I'd thought widows always had black stuff around. But Wendy shushed me.

"One way you can tell a witch is that they don't make reflections in mirrors. That's why it's covered up." Where we live, of course, there ain't many mirrors, them being expensive. But Wendy continued, still in a whisper. "As for those biscuits she says she's baking -- I don't think I'd eat them. . . ."

I *did* piss my boots then. It suddenly hit me. "Y-you mean that the f-f-flour. . . .?"

"Probably ground from the bones of her husband," Wendy whispered. "But maybe children, too. Coz, what d'you think? You see any children in the neighborhood when you was trailing the servants just now?"

I turned toward Coz and saw that his face was white, just like mine must have been. "I-I think we'd better get this over with," he whispered, standing up suddenly. Wendy and I got up too and followed him, creeping silently through the dining room, into the hall at the back of the house.

"Shhhh," Wendy whispered.

We all stopped, suddenly, me bumping into Wendy and Coz. We looked in the kitchen -- felt the blast of hot air in our faces.

The widow -- *the witch* -- had just pulled open the door of the huge woodstove's oven, big enough to cook a whole Christmas dinner all at one time. Her back was still toward us as Coz inched his way through the kitchen door, then reached for an iron pot. Wendy joined him, finding a butcher's knife, while I -- I confess it -- I remained, rooted, just where I was standing.

Just then Coz's pot clanked as he pulled it off

the shelf, raising it high. "Wh-what?" the widow said, turning in response, dropping the tray she had pulled from the oven.

"Now!" Wendy shouted, thrusting with her knife, stabbing it twice more, forcing the widow against the hot stove. I smelled cloth singeing as Coz brought his pot down.

The widow screamed, her face contorted, trying to push back away from the heat. The flesh of her hands searing. Even as Wendy continued stabbing.

"Again!" Wendy shrieked as Coz struck down with his pot a second time. This time I saw blood spurt from the widow's hair.

This time she didn't scream. Even though, a moment later, her shawl had caught fire.

"Now push!" Wendy whispered. She ripped the shawl off and pulled the widow's body down onto the oven door. She bent it so the arse end went inside first. "You help push too, Brendan."

It took me a moment before my muscles worked, then I ran up and helped push too, as hard as I could. But the widow was wedged tight.

I heard Wendy cursing. I wanted to turn my head away, or at least close my eyes, but I couldn't help myself. I watched her knife flash down, cutting into the widow's legs above the ankles. I nearly fell when the body twitched.

I heard Coz talking, as if from a distance. "Wendy -- God dam' it! The head. It's still stuck!"

"Yeah. Here, Coz." I heard something suddenly gurgle, saw the knife flash at the widow's throat, chopping away while Wendy cursed again under her breath. "Right. Like this. Help me twist it like this. Now!"

I heard a dull thump. A clattering as Wendy's knife dropped. Then a loud clang as the oven door swung closed.

"Shyte," Coz whispered. I heard water splashing, the wheeze of the pump at the kitchen basin, while I just stood, rooted, my eyes on the stove.

Then I felt his hand press my shoulder, but shaky-like. Like his voice.

"Brendan, c'mon," he said. "You done all right, Brendan. But c'mon, quick. While Wendy's still washing. We gotta see what we can take, then get outta here."

I followed blindly into the parlor, holding a sack as Coz, then Wendy, scooped stuff into it. Silver candlesticks, next to a book. It looked like a *Book of Common Prayer* -- I'd seen one in church once -- but in a witch's house? Money. Gold coins. A necklace. Jewelry. Then we were out through the kitchen door, quickly in case we'd been heard from the street -- or by one of the neighbors. Out to the alley behind the house when something brushed past me.

"Wait," Wendy whispered. She reached down and grabbed something -- pulled it up, howling.

The witch's familiar.

"Quick," she whispered. She scowled as if angry, but then she smiled. A strange kind of smile. She twisted the cat's head. "Coz, c'mon. Hurry. It must join its mistress."

I waited, half outside the kitchen door, as they went back inside. As Coz pulled the oven door open one last time.

I gagged at the stench, like meat that was burnt. That and the widow's burning clothes -- it twisted my stomach. I closed my eyes tight as I heard the door thump shut.

I wanted to throw up.

Then Wendy's hands gripped me, still slick with blood even though she'd washed them. Grasping my left arm as Coz took the right one. As Coz picked the sack up where I had dropped it.

"Brendan," he whispered. "Now back to Holborn. Best we be ready to split up soon. Make our own ways home. You understand, Brendan?"

I nodded dumbly, letting them help me outta the alley, towards Edgware Road. My britches all stiff where the piss had dried in 'em -- and maybe not just piss! Only now starting to hear again the city's noises, even at night, to notice again its own stenches and smells. The cold of the trodden snow. Out through more alleys to Baker and Wigmore where, finding my legs again, I let them loose me to find my own way back.

Behind, in the distance, I heard coppers' whistles.

I dreams more now, since I helped with the widow. I dreams the most when Coz and me and Wendy finds new witches and goes to destroy 'em, but then it's the Good Work and someone -- children

like us, long as Wendy's still got the second sight --
has got to do it. And those nights, just after we kills
them, Wendy brings me my gin *without* water.

Those nights, with any luck, I doesn't dream at
all. I just leaves Wendy and Coz to their work in the
room behind my hall. I just curls up and tries to
ignore the little screamings -- Wendy still says I ain't
old enough to help in the de-witching -- and thinks
about Coz and me, 'fore we met Wendy. Back in the
orphans' home, how we was best of friends. How we
escaped and ever after was always together.

'Cept then we found Wendy an' started the Good
Work an' sometimes, days at a time, I hardly sees
Coz at all. An' sometimes I dreams then, but dreams
of Wendy.

I sees how she walks. I sees how she holds her
hand in Coz's an' how, sometimes, she pushes her
lips on his. How then they go in their back room
together and, just before they closes the curtains,
she glances back an' gives me that knowing look.
Gives me that wink of hers -- that's when I dreams
worst.

'Cause sometimes, then, I begins to think the
ones we're killing ain't the real witches.

THE SUN WORSHIPER'S GHOST

DAVID LEE SUMMERS

THE MUMMY OF PRINCE NEFERAMUN OCCUPIED an armchair in Professor Augustus Harriman's study. Dinella Stanton, a spiritualist by trade, considered the mummy's closed eyes, sparse hair clinging tenaciously to a bald head, and thin fingers resting on its lap. If she didn't know better, she'd assume the mummy, dressed in a smoking jacket and trousers, was just a sleeping old man.

Dinella steeled her nerves, reached out and took the mummy's hand. The texture reminded her of cold sausages left to cool in bacon fat.

Less than a week before, Professor Harriman had embarked on an experiment. He acquired the mummy of Prince Neferamun, whose name meant "the good of the sun god," then rehydrated its skin with a mixture of salves and ointments. Once satisfied the mummy would not crumble to dust, he fitted it with a sophisticated clockwork mechanism to simulate lifelike movement. He then sought Dinella's services to reunite the simulacrum with the prince's spirit.

Professor Harriman cleared his throat. "I almost hesitate to raise the subject given how many of my esteemed colleagues see fit to belittle your work, but it seems something went wrong when you summoned Neferamun's spirit."

"Something is most certainly wrong." Dinella returned the mummy's hand to its lap. "I sense no life whatsoever from this ... creature." She reached into a pocket hidden in the folds of her skirts and retrieved a handkerchief and wiped her hands.

"I mean, a week ago." Harriman tugged on his unruly beard. "At first I thought Egyptian princes must be a bit ... peculiar, but then as I watched his behavior, I noticed clear patterns. He only seemed interested in hunting rodents and birds. He would sleep for many hours of the day. He would rub his head against my leg..."

Dinella's cheeks warmed. She should have admitted her suspicions at the time, but had been too embarrassed. At the séance where she attempted to summon the prince's spirit, there had been many personal items, including a cat's mummy. She had seen hints that she'd raised the wrong ancient spirit.

Harriman continued. "Like many in the species felis catus, our sun worshiper proved adept at hiding.

Three days ago, he hid so well that I did not find him until after his clockworks ran down. When I wound him up again, I observed no signs of consciousness."

"Of course." Dinella shrugged. "The spirit departed. That's what they do when the body stops operating."

Harriman frowned, then led Dinella to a small table nearby. The scientist's butler, Talbot, appeared a moment later with a tea service on a tray. He poured tea for Harriman and Dinella, then departed. Harriman leaned forward. "Would it be possible for you to make a second attempt at summoning the prince's spirit?"

Dinella picked up a sugar cube with a pair of tongs and placed it in her tea. "Is it so valuable to have the spirit of Neferamun's cat within the clockwork mummy?"

"I do not speak of the cat's spirit." The professor sampled the tea, then added a small dollop of cream and stirred, not meeting the spiritualist's gaze. "I am not a man prone to irrational fear, but last night something happened that chilled me to the bone. I awoke near midnight convinced someone sat on the edge of my bed. At first, I saw nothing, then my gaze drifted upward to where a person's head should be. For just a moment, I glimpsed a shadowed face glaring at me with malevolent intent. My skin broke out in gooseflesh."

The professor paused, then ran his fingers through his great mass of hair. "I turned to the nightstand, grabbed my spectacles and lit the oil lamp. Although the light revealed an empty room, it also revealed an indentation on my bed, where I thought I'd seen the figure. I sprang from to my feet and summoned Talbot, who arrived sometime later, sleep rumpled in his dressing gown and pyjamas. I could not convince myself that he had been the intruder. I dismissed him, then returned to my bed and blew out the lamp.

"As I began to doze off, a cold, slaughterhouse draft wafted through my bedroom. I started to sit up, but something pressed me down onto the bed. The more I struggled, the more force was applied. The force passed the barrier of my skin, probing, searching. It seized my heart. A chill spread from the center of my chest throughout my body. It squeezed as though it wanted to snuff out my very life." The professor's voice hitched. "I could not move, could not call for help no matter how much I tried."

Dinella sipped her tea to chase away an involuntary shiver. "What happened next?"

Harriman shrugged. "As best as I can tell, it didn't quite have the strength to do what it intended. With a jerk, it released me. Although I couldn't see it, I sensed it stormed from the room. It left me alone and chilled. Eventually I climbed from the bed and retrieved more blankets. It seemed to take an hour before I could get warm. An hour before my heart stopped racing. At last, I fell into an exhausted slumber."

Dinella set the teacup down. "You suspect this presence was the real Prince Neferamun?"

The professor folded his hands in his lap and looked down. "I have never encountered a sensation like that before. It was power that would not be denied. I cannot say it's the prince's spirit with absolute certainty, but I don't know what else it would have been."

The spiritualist arched an eyebrow. "It's possible you just encountered some other malevolent spirit inhabiting this house."

"I've lived in this house for over two decades." Harriman snorted a laugh. "If there were malevolent spirits here, I would have thought I'd have encountered one before now."

"It could be the recent séance made you more perceptive of the spirits…"

"…or it could really be the spirit of Prince Neferamun."

"Or it could be another spirit associated with the prince. Royalty often has an entourage." Dinella took another sip of her tea. "The only way to know for certain would be to hold another séance."

"Could we do it now?"

Dinella glanced over at the clock. "It is still rather early in the afternoon. Night is better for summoning spirits … also I am a spiritualist by trade."

The professor took her meaning. "Name your price." He seemed to perk up now that the matter at hand had been settled. "In the meantime, I hope you will join me for supper while we await nightfall."

After a lovely dinner, Talbot cleared the dining table, then brought a candle. Harriman collected several artifacts that belonged to Prince Neferamun. These included a curved headrest supported by a carving of the god Shu, a game board that resembled an oblong chess set, and some amulets which had been discovered in the mummy's original wrappings.

Dinella noticed that Harriman did not bring the cat-shaped sarcophagus found in Neferamun's tomb.

The professor lit the candle in the center of the table, then seated himself. Dinella took his hand, then steeled her nerves and took the mummy's ointment-slicked appendage. Harriman took the mummy's other hand. She concentrated, then spoke in somber tones.

"Prince Neferamun, are you here?"

Silence.

"We reach out through time and space to summon the prince whose empty shell sits with us at the table. We wish to commune with the prince and hear the wisdom he would grace us with."

The flame flickered and the fine hairs on Dinella's forearms stood on end. A presence stood near.

"Neferamun, we invite you to join the circle, come to me. Let me be your conduit. Speak through me."

Professor Harriman yelped out a strangled cry. His hand spasmed and he nearly broke the circle. Dinella turned to face him. As she did, a presence slammed into her. She gasped at what she first believed to be a violation except the mind she sensed seemed more confused than violent. Questions roiled through her thoughts, but no words formed on her vocal chords no matter how much she tried. Whatever spirit possessed her was new to her. She sensed a haughtiness and a self-importance. She sensed vast, accumulated knowledge. All of this meshed with her impression of an ancient Egyptian prince.

With slow deliberation, she broke the circle and stood up. She moved behind the mummy and placed her hands on its head. A yellow aura formed around her arms and encompassed the mummy's head.

Her knees weakened. Talbot appeared at her side and supported her. She managed not to fall into a faint, and soon recovered her balance.

The mummy's mouth fell open and an eerie groan emerged. Dinella hoped she hadn't discharged the spirit too soon. She believed ancient spirits needed time with a medium to learn language and be able to speak.

Dinella turned her attention to Professor Harriman. He sat, dazed. After a moment, a smug grin appeared on his features. "Well that seems to have gone very well, indeed."

"Did it?" Dinella's brow furrowed.

"Oh, I think this was a most successful experiment." Harriman turned to Talbot. "Would you please see Miss Stanton home?"

"Right away, sir." Talbot looked almost as confused as Dinella felt. Even so, he indicated Dinella should follow. She looked from Harriman to the mummy.

Its mouth flapped up and down as unintelligible sounds emerged.

"Wouldn't you like me to stay? Try to interpret..."

Harriman shook his head. "Thank you, but I believe this is a most delicate phase in the experiment. I should have time alone with ... the prince."

Dinella wanted to stand up straight and insist on her right to stay. After all, who was the expert on spirits here? Then again, she was no longer a proper guest. She was the paid employee, as the notes in her handbag would attest. With a sigh, she turned and followed Talbot from the dining room.

Two days later, Dinella reviewed her appointment book in the privacy of her bed-sitting room in Sloane Garden House. Work as a spiritual advisor provided good but infrequent pay for a single woman. Sloane Garden House proved modest but comfortable accommodation and was situated near the homes of her best paying clients. When she needed extra income, she helped in the shops on the ground floor.

A knock at the door startled her. She rose and answered. The landlady, Mrs. Green, handed her a card. "A tradesman is calling on you. He's waiting in the dining room."

Dinella took the card and noticed Professor Harriman's name. The professor, with his long hair and beard did not always take the best care of his attire, so she supposed he could be mistaken for a tradesman by a person who didn't know him. "I'll follow you down."

They walked downstairs into the dining room. There sat not Professor Harriman, but Talbot, his butler. Instead of wearing fine clothes, he wore a tweed jacket and rough trousers. A bowler hat sat on the table. No wonder Mrs. Green called him a tradesman.

The landlady disappeared around the corner into her office, but left the door ajar. Unlike the boarding houses run by Christian societies, Sloane Garden House did not attempt to chaperone unmarried women, but the staff did watch for men who might attempt to proffer unwanted attentions on the residents. Dinella appreciated that.

Talbot stood. "Thank you for seeing me, Miss Stanton. I hope I'm not imposing on you, but I wondered if it would be possible for you to come see the professor. Something has gone horribly wrong."

Dinella narrowed her gaze. "What would that be?"

"It would be easier to show you than tell you." Talbot rubbed his hands together in clear agitation. "Would it be too forward of me to ask you to come with me to see the professor?"

Dinella considered her appointment book. She didn't have anything on her schedule for a few hours. "Of course, Talbot. Let me get my coat and hat. I'll meet you on the outside steps." She went upstairs to retrieve the items she mentioned. The séance two nights before had seemed wrong. Perhaps an old, malevolent spirit did occupy the professor's house and that's who she channeled into the mummy.

Outside, she discovered Talbot had summoned a hansom cab. He helped her onto the seat and they departed. Instead of going toward the professor's house in Marylebone, they went east and crossed the Thames. Dinella turned to face Talbot. "Aren't we going to the professor's house?"

Again, Talbot wrung his hands. "I'm afraid we've been evicted, Miss Stanton."

"Evicted?" Dinella's eyes widened. "How did that happen?"

"It'll make more sense if I allow the professor to explain. Fortunately, my sister's husband was willing to take us in until we can sort out this unfortunate situation."

The hansom cab pulled up in front of a new, modest house in Brixton. Talbot led the way inside. Dinella followed him down a hall and into a back bedroom. There, instead of Professor Harriman, sat Prince Neferamun's mummy.

The mummy turned and faced Dinella with glowing, golden eyes. "Miss Stanton," it said in a voice that reminded her of hinges that required oiling, "thank you for accompanying Talbot. To my great shock and shame, I have not only been evicted from my lodgings but from my very body."

Dinella put her hand to her chest, then narrowed her gaze at the mummy. "Is that you, Professor Harriman?"

"It is," said the mummy. "The séance of two nights

ago was a tremendous success. You summoned the spirit of Prince Neferamun. However, he never entered your mind. Instead, he forced his way into my body and threw me out. I think he must have pushed me into your mind. I remember looking around the table and seeing myself along with the mummy. With no control over the motion, I stood and walked to the mummy. A moment later, I found myself in this body." He indicated his current form. "I tried to speak, to protest the wrong which had been committed upon me, but I did not know how to control the vocal mechanism I had created. It took a day in order to learn to speak."

Dinella put her hand on the wall to steady herself. Talbot appeared at her side a moment later with a chair and helped her sit. "Where is the prince?" She asked the question even though she already suspected the answer.

"The prince has taken control of the professor's body, ma'am," said Talbot. "He then kicked us out of the house and has assumed the professor's duties at the British Museum."

"This body is sufficiently complex, the clockworks run down every six hours. Talbot must wind them regularly or else I will die as surely as Neferamun's cat." The professor's squeaky voice sounded so sad, not like the robust man she had come to know. "We were able to take a supply of the salves I created to keep the skin of this form hydrated, but every part of the body must be attended to regularly, or there is a risk of the skin flaking or even parts falling off."

"Without an income, the professor cannot make more of his ointments," said Talbot.

"I have never felt so fragile, so helpless. Although we never know how long our bodies will last, I fear this one will expire much sooner than my mortal body."

Dinella pursed her lips, thinking it served the professor right. She never liked this reanimated corpse.

The squeaky voice interrupted Dinella's thoughts. "Is there any way you can restore me to my body?"

Dinella considered the problem. "First, we must get Prince Neferamun to flee the body he possesses. Given his strong will, I doubt he'll leave of his own accord and he may not be able to at this point."

"He evicted the professor from his body," said Talbot. "Surely there must be a way to get a spirit to flee a human."

"There is one certain way." Dinella swallowed, hesitating to speak the obvious. "If the body dies, the spirit will flee. It's what spirits do at death."

The light in the mummy's eyes seemed to brighten. The professor faced Talbot. "Do you remember the technique of cardiopulmonary resuscitation that I showed you?"

Talbot gritted his teeth. "Developed by those Kraut doctors?" The manservant nodded. "I remember it, but I would hate to rely on it."

"I fear we must." The mummy sat silent for a moment, the clockworks clicking and whirring as the professor formulated a plan. "Yes, I think an extract of belladonna delivered directly to the heart to stop it. Then Neferamun should flee my body. After that, an extract of manchineel as an antidote, but the heart won't start on its own. Talbot, you will need to use the resuscitation technique."

Sweat beaded the manservant's brow, but he nodded. "If that's what it'll take to defeat that villain, then yes, I will do my very best."

"This is very different from a séance, Professor Harriman," cautioned Dinella. "I don't know if I can extract your living spirit from the mummy and return it to your body."

"Do you know anyone better able to attempt this?"

Dinella frowned and considered that. For a moment, she thought she must be making clockwork noises similar to the professor in his mummy form. At last, she shook her head. "If I can't do this, no one can."

"I will need time to prepare the poison and the antidote," mused Harriman. "Fortunately, I have some credit with my suppliers and they know Talbot. Are you available for this ... experiment ... tomorrow afternoon?"

Dinella gave a curt nod. She felt an obligation to try to help the professor after all that had transpired. She appreciated that she would have some time to prepare. She could attend to her séance that evening, meditate and, God-willing, get a few hours' sleep. "I'll be ready."

They made a plan for the next afternoon, then

Talbot summoned a hansom cab and escorted Dinella back to Sloane Garden House.

The next afternoon, Dinella sent her card around to Professor Harriman's house. She received a reply an hour later, saying the professor would receive her at 7 o'clock. Dinella forwarded the information to Talbot by way of a messenger.

Shortly before the appointed hour, Dinella hailed a cab, which conveyed her to the professor's house. She climbed the steps to the door and hoped Talbot and the real professor would be on the scene and hiding as they expected to be. She knocked, and a dark-haired, bronze-skinned boy just into his teens answered. "Please enter," he said in clear, but accented English. She guessed the boy was Egyptian, though she had no idea how he came to be in London or how Prince Neferamun hired him on such short notice.

The boy led Dinella into the sitting room. She gasped in spite of herself at the sight of Professor Harriman's body. Prince Neferamun had shaved the professor's head and face, except for the portion of his beard attached to his chin. This, the prince had oiled and tied with a thong, so it hung in a neat line. He looked the very image of ancient Egyptian royalty. He wore trousers and a smoking jacket. A fez topped his bald head.

She gave a curtsey in spite of herself and almost said "Prince Neferamun" but caught herself in time and said, "Pr...ofessor Harriman, I'm pleased to see you looking well."

The prince in the professor's body bowed and indicated that Dinella should be seated. "I'm sorry I asked you to leave so suddenly the other night. Events at the séance transpired so quickly. I found myself ... disoriented."

"Seánces can have that effect." Dinella narrowed her gaze. "I have conducted many over the years, but I have never known a departed spirit powerful enough to force a living person from their body."

Prince Neferamun chuckled to himself as he returned to his chair. "So, you figured out what I had done?"

"Your choice of coiffeur was a significant clue." Dinella shrugged. "The professor spent too many years growing his mane of hair to cut it all off so casually."

He shrugged and smiled. "I know, but I could not stand that tangled mass. It seems the professor's colleagues at the museum think the new appearance is much more in keeping with a gentleman of letters."

Dinella leaned forward. "When the professor hosted the..." she struggled to find a euphemism for 'mummy unwrapping party', "...the unveiling of your mortal body and asked me to summon your spirit, I thought I had failed when I summoned the spirit of your cat."

"Ah, my beloved Mau." The prince's features took on a wistful look. "He was a faithful companion in life and in the afterlife and he never left my side.

There was no way you could summon me without summoning him."

"I had not encountered an animal's spirit before." Dinella shook her head. "I had no idea they could be so strong."

"Most animals are not so strong, but the goddess Bastet has always favored her own."

"How did you take over the professor's body?" Dinella hated to be so forward, but she did want this answer before the real professor and Talbot arrived.

The prince sat back and steepled his hands. He resembled a professor ready to deliver a lecture. "There are countless planes of reality which only a spiritual body may access. When we're born, our spirit is anchored to our physical body. The séance, as you call it, loosens that bond and allows you to see, if imperfectly, into those other planes and find spirits as they wander. Mau and I returned together. In our wanderings, we developed a rapport. We both wanted to see if a return to a mortal body was possible. I watched you call Mau and place him in the clockwork horror that used to be my body. Although a fascinating exercise, I knew I didn't want to be in that body. Its usefulness ended at death. No matter how clever the professor was at automating the corpse, it's still a machine and subject to man's control."

Dinella furrowed her brow. "If you could travel countless planes as a spirit, why would you want to come back to a mortal body?"

"Traveling the spiritual planes is fascinating. I have seen worlds you cannot imagine. I have learned things no human has ever conceived." The prince held his hands out to his side. "I thought it would be fascinating to apply what I know now to physical existence, improve the world. Besides..." Neferamun removed the fez and stood. "When I looked in on your séance, I realized I missed certain pleasures." He took a step toward Dinella.

She stood from the chair and backed away.

Neferamun stalked toward her, not unlike a cat stalking prey.

Dinella's eyes darted from side to side, seeking escape. Had the professor and Talbot been delayed? Had something happened that kept them from being there at all?

The prince sprang upon her and pushed her against the wall. He forced his mouth to hers, his hot breath and tongue gagging her. His hand grasped her bottom, making her curse the lack of a sensible bustle. She pounded the professor's shoulders, which only made Neferamun laugh. He grabbed a handful of cloth and yanked, tearing her skirt. He whipped her around and held her hands behind her back while bending her over an arm chair. Tears of anger and frustration sprang from Dinella's eyes, making Neferamun laugh even harder. His hand grasped the top of her bloomers.

"No!" The voice reminded Dinella of fingers scraping down a slate. Never before had she heard a more welcome sound.

Neferamun froze.

In the doorway behind the prince stood the prince's clockwork-automated, mummified body.

Talbot dashed forward from behind the mummy. He held a syringe in his hands. He tried to thrust it into Professor Harriman's possessed body. The prince knocked the syringe aside, then fell back into a fighting stance.

Talbot lunged forward, grabbed the prince's wrists, and tried to wrestle him to the ground. The prince, though, seemed to be the more experienced fighter. He kneed Talbot in the groin, then head-butted him. Blood oozed from Talbot's nose and his grip faltered. The prince shoved Talbot to the ground.

As they struggled, Dinella went for the syringe. Her legs caught in the ruins of her skirt and she tumbled to the ground. She reached down and tore the remains of the skirt away and dashed for the syringe.

She turned around and faced the men on the ground. Neferamun had his hands around Talbot's throat. She hesitated. Though the needle seemed dreadfully long and sturdy, she knew if she hit bone, it could snap and all would be lost. If they failed today, the prince would be more careful in the future. They might not get a second chance to extract him from the professor's body.

Talbot's skin had taken on a blue tint and his eyelids fluttered. She lifted the syringe. Just then, Neferamun leapt to his feet, whirled around, and grabbed Dinella's arm. Before he could do more, the clockwork mummy sprang forward and knocked Neferamun to the ground. The prince struggled to move the heavy, clockwork mummy. "Now, Dinella," squeaked the mummy.

Dinella leapt forward and plunged the syringe between two ribs in the professor's human body. The prince fell limp. The mummy pushed itself back into a kneeling position. Dinella looked around. Had Neferamun killed Talbot?

Dinella put her hand on Harriman's shaved head. She sensed the prince's spirit had departed.

"We need the second syringe," croaked the mummy. Harriman pointed to Talbot. She dashed over and checked his pockets. She found it, then rushed back to Harriman's body. She plunged the needle into his chest. The body's eyelids fluttered and for a moment, she feared Neferamun still possessed the body, even though she no longer sensed his spirit.

"What do I do now?" asked Dinella.

"You need to restart the heart." Harriman struggled to get the words out. "You need to push on the chest ... hard ... many times ... keep going until there's a pulse. You'll be pushing the heart. If you are successful, you'll restart it."

Dinella gritted her teeth and straddled the body that so recently had tried to violate hers. She put one hand on top of the other on Harriman's chest and pushed, then pushed again.

"Harder," urged the mummy. "Keep pushing."

She did her best, but she could only push so hard. The clockwork mummy, already on its knees, keeled over on its side. Just then, Talbot coughed and sputtered. He looked around, and took in the scene. "Allow me, Miss," he croaked.

Dinella leapt to her feet. Talbot took her place, then put his hands on Harriman's chest and began to push repeatedly. She cringed as bones cracked. She dashed to the mummy, afraid it was too late. The mummy's eyes no longer glimmered. She put her hands on its head anyway. "Spirit of Professor Harriman, come into me before the clockworks die. Come into me. It's time to return home." Blood rushed to her cheeks as she realized the intimacy of the words. Still, she needed the spirit to obey, or it would follow Prince Neferamun into other planes of existence. She forced herself to push away the shame and repeated the words. A flicker of spiritual energy tickled her consciousness. She urged it forward and felt it drizzle into her.

She turned and grasped Harriman's bald head. The professor's golden aura flowed down her arms, a little stronger now, into his own body.

Professor Augustus Harriman gasped, then made a horrible gurgling sound. Talbot hopped off his employer. The professor turned over onto his arms and legs, vomited, then passed out. Dinella tried to stand, but her head swam and everything went black.

Dinella awoke sometime later. She found herself on a bed somewhere in the professor's home. She sat up and looked around. Her skirt lay over a chair, mended. She stood and put it on then went out to the hallway. Talbot appeared a few minutes later. "Ah, Miss Stanton. You're awake. Good." His voice was still hoarse.

"How is Professor Harriman?"

"He is himself again, thanks to you, but he is not well." It sounded like speaking was an effort for the butler. "The combination of belladonna and manchineel has left him quite ill, plus I'm afraid I broke bones when I restarted his heart. He'll be indisposed for several weeks, but he'll be allowed to live out his days in his own body."

"That's good to know." Dinella followed Talbot downstairs and into the sitting room. There, she noticed a clock on a mantelpiece. It said the time was just after eight, but she noticed light coming in through the windows. "Did I sleep through the night?"

"You did. It's now morning. May I prepare you breakfast?"

"Thank you, but I'm not really hungry." She didn't want to put Talbot to unnecessary trouble. Also, the sight of the professor vomiting on the floor lingered in the back of her mind. "I think I'll walk home and get breakfast there. The fresh air will do me good."

"Allow me to get your hat and coat."

He returned a moment later. Only then did she notice he had donned his usual finery. A high, starched collar didn't quite hide the bruises on his neck. She flashed him a brave smile, then allowed him to escort her to the door.

As she walked down the stairs, she glanced back into the shadows. For just a moment, she thought she sensed something, lurking and waiting. She wondered what had become of the boy the prince had hired. Could it be him? She saw no one in the shadows.

She shook off the feeling and turned toward home. Just then, a cold breath, like the smell of rotten meat, wafted by her nose and something pressed against her hip. She stifled a scream and ran.

BLOOD TIES

KAREN J CARLISLE

HIGH TIDE LAPPED THE STEAMSHIP'S HULL. Lamplight flared in the evening fog, making it difficult to manoeuvre through the throng of well-wishers waving off their loved ones.

The ramp knocked against the wooden deck as Jack Findlay boarded the steamship. It was touted as the fastest ship to journey London to Adelaide. The faster, the better. He tugged his collar up against the evening chill. He was used to the city, and the anonymity of its dark alleys and winding Underground.

He glanced at the water swelling beneath the ramp. He wasn't fond of open water. Less so when he was imprisoned in a metal coffin bobbing across said open water. People became too familiar in such confined spaces.

"Good evening, sir." The steward nodded in greeting. His white-gloved fingers curled around the handle of Jack's leather valise.

The metal joints on Jack's mechanical hand clicked inside his own glove as he tugged it away from the steward.

"No," he grumbled.

The steward snapped to attention and avoided Jack's glare.

Jack cleared his throat. "It's my..." He held the valise against his chest. "Tools of my profession."

Jack stared at the steward and smiled. He'd discovered people found it disturbing to look him in the eye.

"My apologies, Mr...?" The steward took a step back, still avoiding direct eye contact.

Jack wanted to reply: *I am Jack Findlay, the notorious Ripper.* He was proud of who he was, what he'd achieved. He was so close to completing his research. To be sent abroad just when things were getting interesting...

He clenched his teeth and tugged his left coat cuff down over his glove. He couldn't give his own name; the authorities were most likely looking for Jack Findlay. He required an alias - one that would engender trust.

He smiled. "Dr. Collins," he replied, "retired police surgeon."

"Welcome aboard, Doctor Collins. I'm Mr. Cox, here to ensure you enjoy your journey with us."

The ship's horn howled through the fog.

The chatter of excited passengers engulfed him, as they milled around the edge of the deck and leaned over the ship's rail. Squawking children darted through the confusion of starched suits and skirts festooned with bows and ruffled passementerie.

Jack sneered. It was all too disorderly.

The ship's engines rumbled below his feet. Deck lamps flickered gently in the breeze. The paddle wheel housing cast a shadow across the deck.

Jack sidestepped the crush and gravitated towards the security of the darkness, away from the waving passengers. Sails slapped against their masts as the wind picked up.

The ship's horn mourned slowly, as if it knew of his plans for the voyage.

A light tube crackled on the wall near the cabin door. Its pale blue light reflected in the polished brass fittings and danced on the wood-panelled walls.

A bottle of champagne and a full crystal champagne flute, bubbles still popping at the surface, stood on the table next to a padded leather settee.

Jack ignored the invitation; there would be time to celebrate after his work was complete. He removed his bowler and dusted droplets of moisture from the red feather sewn into the hatband. He would miss England; he'd found great sport there.

A cool breeze lifted the curtains, revealing the etched glass of the open porthole. There was a faint splash. And another. The ship's engine thrummed under his feet. A rush of bubbles broke the surface of the champagne. The splashes became rhythmic, like the tick-tock of a clock.

Jack peered through the porthole as the steamship made its way out of the harbour. London was adrift in the night fog.

He placed his hat on the table by the untouched champagne and surveyed the cabin suite's sitting room. A green padded leather settee stood next to the table along the closest wall. A small dining table, with a pressed, lace-edged linen cloth, and matching chairs sat in the centre of the room. Candelabras were positioned at each end of a side table on the far wall. Jack's steamer trunk sat, still unopened, just inside the doorway to the adjoining room.

Knocking noises emanated from the other side of the wall.

Jack's mechanical hand twitched; its gears whirred. He snatched up his new walking cane and waited.

A ginger-haired man in a dark grey suit emerged from the sleeping quarters.

Jack's muscles relaxed. He tugged off his left glove and flexed the joints of the metal fingers.

"You've arrived, sir?" Evans wiped dark smudges from his hands with a rag.

"The cabin door locks?" Jack slipped off the remaining glove.

"All changed, sir," replied Evans. "The new latchkey is on the table by the bed."

"And my laboratory?"

"I don't think much of your employer's mechanics." Evans clicked his tongue. "I've had to add our own Stability Rectifier to modify the stabilising platform."

Jack strode into the private sleeping quarters.

The bed had been relocated to one side. In its place was a raised platform suspended in a low, metal cradle. On it were a workbench and carved wooden chair. A large wooden trunk, bound with padlocked metal straps, stood under the window.

Jack smiled; his employers had kept their bargain.

"Shall I set up the equipment, sir?" asked Evans.

Jack shook his head. "I prefer to do it myself."

"Very well. I'll unpack your clothes, sir." Evans shoved the cleaning rag into his pocket.

Jack laid his right hand on Evan's forearm and studied the traces of oil ingrained around Evans' fingernails.

"Wash your hands first," he said.

"Of course, sir."

Jack waited until the door to the sitting room clicked shut, then pushed a small button at the top of his walking cane. Its head rose slowly, revealing a hidden compartment. He retrieved the trunk key from its hiding place, unlocked the padlocks and eased open the front of the trunk.

A series of drawers lined each side. A rectangular object, wrapped in waterproof cloth, fitted snugly into a niche at the bottom.

He opened one of the drawers. It caught on the runners. Something rattled inside. He eased the drawer out all the way.

It was lined with padded leather, with indentations shaped to fit glass tubes and flasks. One tube had dislodged from its recess.

He ran a flesh finger along the glass and turned it slowly. It seemed intact. He checked each in turn. They'd all survived. He slid out the next drawer and examined its contents: various clamps and suspension rods. All intact. Evans had done an excellent job at securing his equipment.

Jack held his breath as he removed a small wooden box from the bottom drawer and placed it on the workbench. Inside was a square, metal device, with a brass plate screwed to the top and a crank on one side, and a switch on the other.

He unscrewed the plate, unlatched the lid and inspected the contents: a series of cogs and pulleys attached to the central rod, piercing the metal plate. The workings seemed to be undamaged.

He let out a long, slow breath and cranked the handle four times. The cogs quivered and whirred. Thin metal link-chains turned. The central rod turned slowly.

His eyes widened. Well done, Evans; the mixing mechanical would free up his time for more important tasks. He settled in the chair and watched.

The rod turned round and round, mesmerising him with its smooth movement.

A knock on the adjoining door broke his concentration.

"Excuse me, sir." Evans opened the door. "Your dinner suit, sir."

Jack checked his pocket watch; he'd been staring at the contraption for twenty-three minutes.

"How long before the device needs resetting?" he asked.

"Fifteen minutes per revolution," replied Evans.

"And the maximum limit?"

"Two hours, sir."

Jack raised an eyebrow; Evans was proving to be a very worthwhile investment. He flipped the switch on the side of the device. The cogs froze mid-turn. The links of the metal chain clicked in place.

"Is everything satisfactory?" asked Evans.

Jack nodded.

"Will you need me for anything else, sir?"

"That will be all, Evans." Jack glanced at the wrapped box nestled in its niche at the bottom of the trunk. He just needed to collect fresh samples once they were at sea.

Small clouds of steam issued from the bottom of oval service trolleys, as they trundled across the carpet. Waiters directed them toward the occupied dining tables, removed used soup bowls and replaced them with silver cloche-covered platters. Drinks waiters filed past the tables with bottles of wine and champagne.

A pianist played a soft melody on the opposite side of the room.

Jack sat at a corner table, with his back to the wall. The full moon was barely visible through the rain droplets dribbling down the windows on the opposite wall. Hints of green and red flickered in the leadlight surround. A tube light crackled behind him, casting shadows across the crisp, white tablecloth and glinting off his silver-headed walking cane leaning against the red wallpaper, always within reach.

A young gentleman, dressed in an expensive dinner suit, sat at a nearby table, and fussed over an elegant, older woman; the man's gaze lingered on the diamond choker circling her throat.

A well-dressed couple sat at the table closest to Jack.

"The lights are faulty in our cabin." The gentleman scowled as the waiter poured his wine. "And the ones in the corridor keep fizzling out."

"I'm sorry, sir," replied their waiter. "I'll have the engineer see to it, sir. Your cabin number?"

"Mr. and Mrs. Ivers. Cabin 12B."

"I'll inform the steward you require a lamp, sir."

The waiter bowed his head and excused himself.

Mr. Ivers unfolded his napkin.

"How am I expected to see the contents of my

dressing room?" Mrs. Ivers sipped her wine. "I shall have dinner in our cabin until it's fixed."

"You always look immaculate, my dear." Mr. Ivers patted his wife's gloved hand.

As if on cue, the tube lights buzzed and dimmed.

"Mark my words, Edith, this new-fangled technology won't last the voyage." He dropped his napkin on his lap.

The headwaiter paused by Jack's table. "The Captain would like to extend his welcome, Doctor Collins."

Jack smiled.

Wine glasses clinked. The ship swayed. A food trolley rolled into a table near the Dining Room entrance.

The headwaiter glanced up. More passengers had arrived for dinner. A striking woman in a magnificent emerald gown stood at the front of the crowd. She watched the drinks waiter fumble along the side of the mechanical's motor, as he struggled to extricate the trolley from the table.

She smiled and lifted her fan to her lips.

The headwaiter excused himself and strode towards the entrance.

"I do apologise for the inconvenience, Lady Ambrose. Let me escort you to your table." He retrieved a candelabra from the piano, led her past Jack, and placed the candelabra on her table.

"French champagne for Lady Ambrose." He waved the drinks waiter closer.

Flickering candlelight caught auburn highlights

in her dark hair, as she swept her silk skirts to one side and settled into her chair.

Jack stared into her pale eyes. Those eyes... They reminded him of...

He took a deep breath.

Another time. Another life.

Lady Ambrose looked in his direction and smiled. Her eyes glinted green. Green, like...

Jack lifted his steaming teacup to his lips. Catherine was gone. And he was bound for a new life in the Colonies. He swallowed the liquid, scalding his tongue. He deserved it.

Lady Ambrose's gaze flickered over the room and settled on the young, well-dressed man at a nearby table.

"Who's that?" she whispered to the headwaiter.

"Lord Hubert Sebastian," he replied.

She licked her lips, eyed him over the top of her glass and slowly sipped her champagne.

Jack swallowed another mouthful of tea and set his cup down. She was so like Catherine. He longed to stay, to hold onto the memory.

Perhaps he should order dessert? Any excuse to linger longer.

His mechanical hand twitched. He had work to do; he had to collect his first sample before the first-class passengers retired for the evening, and the staff swarmed over the ship to prepare for the morning activities.

He finished his meal, dabbed his moustache with his napkin and retrieved his cane.

Flickering light spilled down the staircase and into First Class. Jack paused on the lower step and peered along the empty passage into the darkness.

He grinned. Evans had done his job; the tube lighting was extinguished. He was proving an excellent choice for an assistant.

Jack pulled his top hat low and turned up his jacket collar. If he was observed, he would claim he was going for a stroll on the deck.

He fished out a small disc from his pocket and tapped the device. It sprang open, unfolding into a funnel shape. He placed it on the first cabin door, and listened.

Silence.

He made his way along the passage, listening at each cabin door until he heard a faint noise from within. Something scraped inside.

He required only one subject and no witnesses. He adjusted the listening device and waited for any sign of conversation.

No voices.

Footsteps moved toward the cabin door.

Jack snapped shut the listening device, slipped it into his coat pocket, and spun on his heel to face the cabin door on the opposite side of the passage.

His mechanical hand gripped the head of his walking cane. The other wrapped around the doorknob.

The other cabin door clicked open behind him.

Jack pretended to close his adopted door, and turned to face the potential subject: a young woman, slender, sensibly dressed and, most importantly, she seemed in excellent health.

She slipped the door key into her apron pocket and hesitated.

"I'm sorry, sir." She lowered her gaze.

"No need." Jack slipped his right hand into his pocket. His fingers brushed against the cigarillo case in his pocket. He smiled, extracted the case and flicked it open.

"Don't tell the wife you saw me. I promised I'd given up." He tapped out a cigarillo. "You don't have any matches, do you?"

He popped it in his mouth and waited. It was a risky move but worth a try; being the first night on board, it was unlikely anyone would recognise their fellow passengers yet.

The young woman reached into her apron pocket and retrieved a box of matches. She struck one, stepped closer and held it to Jack's cigarillo.

Not close enough.

His mechanical hand twitched.

He sucked in a deep breath, filling his lungs with smoke and glanced over her shoulder into the darkness. He couldn't risk anyone wandering down from dinner. It wouldn't do to alert the crew so soon in the voyage.

He needed privacy. He clenched his fingers.

Patience.

He slowly exhaled.

The maid's eyelids flickered. She inhaled and eyed the other cigarillos in the silver case.

Jack took another breath and smiled. He recognised the look of a fellow addict. He'd seen it staring back at him in the mirror. But his addiction wasn't for tobacco.

"Would you like one?" he asked.

"Well..." The maid glanced along the passage. "The Parsons have only just gone to dinner," she whispered.

"Then I won't tell," he whispered back. "I was on my way to the Promenade Deck for some fresh air. Would you care to join me?"

She bit her lip.

Just another nudge and he'd have her. He shook his cigarillo case. Her breaths quickened.

"I promise we'll be finished before they return from dinner," he said.

She nodded. "Just a quick one."

The nearby cabins were still in darkness. Moonlight cast long shadows across the deck; perfect for clandestine rendezvous and nefarious acts. The paddle wheel chugged rhythmically, splashing water against the hull. The rigging slapped softly on the masts.

A gentle breeze tugged at Jack's jacket, as he escorted the maid toward the wheel housing.

"What if the Parsons return early?" She scanned the darkened cabin windows along the deck.

Jack unhooked the safety rope from the rail and stepped aside. Steps led down, along the paddle wheel housing, to an observation platform.

She paused at the top of the steps. "Are we allowed down there?" she asked.

So close.

Jack dug his fingers into his palm. His heart thumped.

Patience.

"I must apologise. I never did ask your name," he said.

"Mary," she replied.

"I knew a Mary once."

"A girlfriend?"

"A gentleman doesn't tell."

She hesitated.

"I'm not that kind of girl," she said.

"I'm not that kind of gentleman," he replied.

Mary smiled.

Almost there. He puffed on his cigarillo and let the vapour envelop them.

"It could be the only adventure you get to have on the voyage." He tapped the case and offered her a cigarillo. "And I won't tell the Parsons."

She grinned, took the cigarillo and descended the stairs.

Jack removed his top hat and walking cane, secured them in a nearby lifeboat, and followed. The wind whipped along the edges of the platform.

He could taste the salt as the sea spray settled on his shoulders.

"You can taste the sea!" Mary's words whipped away in the wind squall as she leaned out over the rail and sucked on her cigarillo. Its orange glow pinpointed her position in the dark.

Jack snatched the cigarillo from his own lips and flicked it across the deck. He slipped the glove off his mechanical hand, swapped it for a handkerchief from his pocket, and wrapped it around his fingers. He stepped forward, towards the flickering orange light of the cigarillo end, and slipped the makeshift garrotte around Mary's neck.

Her cigarillo plummeted into the water. She clawed at the material. A scream gurgled in her throat as she squirmed and twisted to face him.

Jack stared into her eyes: wide open, pupils flaring at him in accusation. His heart skipped. He grunted and tightened the handkerchief between his metal fingers.

Mary wriggled and gasped for air.

He nuzzled his cheek against her neck. The smell of lavender and tobacco tantalised his nostrils.

"Hush," he whispered. "You should be grateful. You'll help save thousands."

Her scream was silent. Her eyelids twitched. She stopped struggling. A convulsion rippled through her body.

Jack released the pressure on the handkerchief. Her head lulled forward. His heart raced. He cradled the body in his arms and listened. A faint warm breath tickled his skin. It was ragged, but it was there.

He lowered the body onto the deck, unrolled a leather pouch and removed a large-needled syringe. After years of experience, he worked swiftly in the shadows. When the collection was complete, and the blood samples secured, he eyed the pale corpse now pocked with exsanguination marks.

Jack covered his jacket with the maid's apron, and squatted by the body. With a flick of his wrist, a seven inch blade slid from its sheath hidden in his mechanical arm. There must be no evidence left of his work. He sliced along her arms to conceal the puncture wounds. The skin was still warm. Blood flicked from his blade as he cut the torso.

Faint light flickered across the waves. He glanced back toward the deck. A few cabin lights winked at him.

He rose to his feet. Blood pooled and glistened on the platform; its sharp, metallic smell, mixed with salt caught on the wind. He wiped a wet fleck from his cheek and frowned. He'd been too enthusiastic.

He rolled the body over the rail, wiped his blade and snapped it back into its sheath, then removed the bloodied apron and tossed it into the wind. It fluttered, caught in the wheel and plunged into the sea where the body had fallen.

Jack watched the turning wheel and smiled. It would conceal his work nicely.

The cabin door rattled. A muffled voice came from the passage outside.

"Doctor Collins?"

Jack rolled over in his bed. His right hand snatched up the harness of his prosthetic arm. He shoved it onto the stump of his left forearm and snapped the clasps in place. Gears ticked inside the prosthetic. The metal finger joints whirred in response.

Another knock.

Jack glanced at the porthole. The curtains fluttered in the breeze. Light barely illuminated the material. He rummaged in his jacket pocket for his watch, and flipped it open; over an hour until breakfast.

He growled and grabbed his dressing robe off the hook by the bed.

"Evans, I left orders not to be disturbed."

He strode past his workbench, cranked the handle of the Centrifugal Cellular Separating Device.

A third knock. Louder this time.

"Sir?"

Jack dragged on his robe, strode into the suite's Sitting Room and yanked open the cabin door.

"Evans, you better have a damn g—"

The steward lowered his hand.

"Yes, Mr Cox?"

"I apologise for the early hour, Doctor Collins," replied the steward, "but the Captain needs to speak with you, urgently."

Jack sucked in a quick breath. They'd found the maid's body sooner than expected. He wrapped his robe around his naked torso, knotted the sash and jerked the robe's sleeve down over his un-gloved mechanical hand.

A breeze tickled the hairs on the back of his neck. His metal wrist twitched. The laboratory! He'd left the adjoining door open.

He resisted the urge to unsheathe the blade and rid himself of this nuisance. He moved to block Cox's view and stared directly into his eyes. Cox averted his gaze, settling it on the untouched, full champagne glass sitting on the table next to the settee- in the opposite direction of the laboratory door.

Jack's lip curled. They always looked away.

"May I inquire as to the nature of his business?" Jack clasped his hands behind his back.

"I'm sorry, sir. I was just ordered to bring you to the Captain." Cox hesitated, still unable to look Jack in the eye. "It *is* urgent, sir."

"I am permitted to dress." It was a statement, not a question; he wanted to watch the man squirm.

"Of course, sir." Cox's gaze remained fixed on the champagne glass. "I'll wait outside, sir."

Jack locked the cabin and followed Cox's eyeline to his private quarters. The door opened inward, blocking the view of his makeshift laboratory. He leaned on the wall and let out a slow breath. Fortune had favoured him, yet again. One day it would run out.

☠

Cox ushered Jack to the Medical quarters at the rear of the First Class passengers' cabins. The large cabin was pristine and sparsely furnished. A metal-framed partition, with a gathered linen curtain, divided the room, obscuring the back of the cabin.

A middle-aged, dark-haired man, dressed in black with a beige apron and wire-rimmed spectacles perched on his forehead, bent over a small microscope. He stared into the eyepieces and frowned.

Cox tapped on the door frame.

"Excuse me, Doctor Bucknall. The police surgeon is here."

The physician straightened up, wiped his hands on his apron, then slipped his spectacles back onto his nose.

"Ah, Doctor Collins." He proffered his hand. "I'm Doctor Bucknall."

Jack eyed his un-gloved hand and nodded in greeting. "I was told the Captain had urgent business."

"Ah, yes. Apologies. It's all terribly unexpected," said Bucknall. "He will be here shortly." He picked up a syringe, tapped its barrel and rose from his chair.

Jack's fingers twitched. He'd left his blade behind in his cabin. He clenched his teeth.

"Follow me," said Bucknall.

Jack eyed the syringe. The physician led him towards the temporary partition, and pushed it to one side.

Two cot beds lined the cabin walls, a closed door between them. The bed on the left was occupied by an ashen-faced gentleman. Jack recognised him as Mr. Ivers, who had complained about the tube lighting. His starched collar had been removed; flecks of blood marred the neckband. His shirt was unbuttoned. One sleeve was rolled up to reveal his pale arm. A blood-spattered enamelled dish and rags sat on a trolley next to the bed.

"What's wrong with the gentleman?" asked Jack.

"He's quarantined," replied Bucknall, "with possible flu. Best not get too close." He swabbed the man's arm and jabbed the needle into the skin.

The patient moaned quietly, ignoring their presence.

"What are you giving him?" asked Jack.

"Mercury Cure and Colloid Silver," replied Bucknall.

"Mercury cure for the influenza?"

"*Possible* influenza. We don't know what ails him, and I have to be sure. We can't afford it to spread to the other passengers."

Bucknall removed the needle. Silvered droplets dripped onto the linen sheets.

Jack grimaced. "May I examine the patient?"

Bucknall nodded and retreated from the bed.

Jack examined the man. The skin around the injection site was bluish grey. Ivers' fingers trembled. Jack pinched the patient's skin. No reaction. He inspected his eyes. The pupils were dilated.

Jack clenched his mechanical fingers; he

loathed incompetence. Already the tell-tale signs of overdose were there: numbness and tremors. He'd seen it before, when working in the Royal London Hospital. Whitechapel was rife with charlatans using the Mercury Cure for anything and everything. But Ivers hadn't shown any obvious signs of mercury poisoning at dinner last night; mercury poisoning required high doses or long exposure. How could Bucknall have missed them?

Jack inspected the labels of the medicine bottle on the trolley: Colloidal Silver, Mercury. Five times the usual dose. The quack; he was the sort that gave doctors a dubious reputation.

"Is this what you're giving him?" asked Jack. Bucknall nodded.

"How long have you been a ship's doctor?" asked Jack.

"Twenty-six years."

"Did you check he wasn't taking the Mercury Cure for anything else?"

Bucknall didn't answer.

Cox cleared his throat, and hovered near the partition.

"Excuse me, Doctors, but the Captain insisted you begin immediately."

"Yes, yes." Bucknall turned his back on his patient and unlocked the far door.

Jack raised an eyebrow.

Bucknall wrinkled his nose as he ushered Jack into the unlit cabin.

Jack smelled it too; the unmistakable stench of recent death. He knew it well.

The light tube crackled. Its sickly blue light illuminated the cabin. A body, wrapped in a dark-stained linen sheet, lay packed with ice in a metal tub.

"Good morning, Captain." Cox retreated to the other side of the partition.

Jack's shoulders stiffened. It had all been a ruse; even a ship's doctor, dealing only with bellyaches and over-indulgence of alcohol could not possibly be so incompetent. The bastards knew how to play the game. He thrummed his gloved fingers on his palm. How did they suspect him so soon? He'd been careful. And he *didn't* make mistakes.

He clenched his fist. He was surrounded; too many to defeat without his blade. He surveyed the makeshift morgue. No windows. Only the one exit. No escape. Even if he could, he was trapped on a steamship, in the middle of the Atlantic. His heart raced. He longed for the anonymity of London's endless foggy warrens.

Jack took a deep, calming breath and turned to greet the Captain.

The Captain was a well-dressed gentleman, with greying hair. He carried his white cap under one arm, and extended his other hand in greeting.

"Welcome, Doctor Collins. Captain Cates, at your service. I do apologise for the ungodly hour, but I'd like to have this unfortunate incident sorted before luncheon, if possible."

"Unfortunate incident?" Jack mentally calculated

his chances of dispatching all three men, and escaping unnoticed.

"We can't allow the passengers to learn of a suspicious death," replied the Captain. "It could cause panic." He nodded in the direction of the ship's doctor. "And Bucknall here is unsure if it *is* a suspicious death."

Bucknall unwrapped the linen cloth and folded it back to reveal the maid's face. Purple bruises blemished her pale skin.

"You've worked as a police surgeon," said Captain Cates. "I am officially requesting your assistance. I need to know if this poor lass took her own life, or if I have a murderer on my ship."

"We're fortunate to have someone more experienced in these matters." Bucknall lowered his voice. "This is beyond my expertise, I'm afraid."

Jack blinked. His fingers relaxed. His borrowed identity had an unexpected advantage. He listed the post mortem examination procedures he'd learned at University, in his head. It had been several years since he'd performed cutting procedures 'by the book.'

"May I assist?" asked Bucknall.

Jack gritted his teeth. He preferred to work alone, but there was no plausible reason he could give to exclude the ship's doctor. This time his work would have to look more... polite.

"I'll fetch my instruments," he said.

The body of Mary - last name still unknown - was unremarkable, except for the bruising around the temples, a longitudinal incision along the left wrist and forearm. Deep wounds cut throughout her torso, and a jagged laceration encircled her neck almost obscuring the strangulation bruises.

Doctor Bucknall hovered behind him, notebook in hand.

"Open the skylight," Jack said.

He slipped on an apron, rolled up his sleeves and leaned over the body to examine the hands. The nails were torn, fingers bruised. He checked under the nails. Any incriminating evidence had been washed away. Excellent.

Next he examined the head. The face was swollen. Clouded corneas stared back at him. Red flecks scarred the sclera.

Jack eyed his unwanted assistant. The man's face was pale, his attention fixated on the larger wounds in the abdomen. Jack smiled. He was certain Bucknall wouldn't notice the eyes, nor the swollen tongue.

"No indications of a struggle." He closed the eyelids and stepped back. "Bruising to the face and torso are consistent with damage from the paddle wheel."

Bucknall scribbled down the lie in his notebook.

Jack pulled back the collar of the bodice and pressed the epidermis. He'd have preferred the body to remain in the water longer...

Bucknall stared blankly at the corpse; the man

seemed oblivious to Jack's findings and willing to accept anything reported.

Jack was in control. Still, he couldn't be too careful; people forgot themselves at sea. Bucknall was proof of that. He took a deep breath and focused. He would not succumb to the lure of the sea.

"Where was the body found?" he asked.

Bucknall snapped his attention away from the corpse. "In the water, near the paddle wheel housing."

"That's consistent with the skin texture." Jack prodded the epidermis. "See? I'd say the body had been in the water only a few hours."

Bucknall's cheeks bulged. He stepped back and jotted in his notebook.

"How long has it been since you examined a body?" asked Jack.

"September 1880," replied Bucknall. "Heart attack. Died in his sleep."

Jack relaxed. There was little chance Bucknall would scrutinise his procedure.

"Let's get a closer look at those injuries, shall we?"

Bucknall turned his head.

Jack smirked. He unbuttoned the bodice and peeled away the fabric. Several deep wounds slashed the abdomen and torso. He closed his eyes. His muscle memory marked each one: a few inches from the left was a jagged tear, cutting through the tissue. Four more cuts downward. He opened his eyes.

"Paddle wheel, you say?"

Bucknall nodded his head. "Yes."

"That would be consistent with these injuries." Another lie. "I think, the lungs first."

He cracked open the ribcage and pushed the knife into the thorax.

Bucknall winced. "I'll get the trolley." He scurried from the room.

The grey lungs squelched as they were removed. Jack squeezed. Black liquid dribbled from the tissue. There was no pulmonary oedema.

Bucknall wheeled a trolley into the room.

Jack plopped the lung into one of the enamelled dishes on it. He shook his head.

"No water in the lung?" asked Bucknall.

Jack froze. Perhaps the man wasn't as incompetent he seemed.

"She must have died before she entered the water," he said.

"Suicide then?" Bucknall eyed the long incisions along the left wrist, avoiding the dissected torso open between them.

"It appears so." An untruth was more believable if backed up with facts. "The poor girl was obviously distressed and took her own life. She bled out before she entered the water, and was dragged under the wheel."

"But there would have been more blood on the observation platform." Bucknall frowned.

"The water washed it away."

The creases in Bucknall's forehead faded. He nodded slowly.

Jack removed the remaining organs, placed them

in dishes on the trolley and examined each one in turn, keeping up the pretence.

Bucknall scribbled more notes.

Metal squeaked in the other room. A quick movement caught the corner of Jack's eye. His head jerked in its direction.

"What was that?"

"I didn't hear—"

"I thought you locked the door." Jack's knife clattered onto the metal trolley.

He pushed past Bucknall, and elbowed aside the temporary partition. The cabin door was open.

There was a faint rustle. A flash of red. He dashed to the doorway and peered along the passageway. It was empty.

Jack thumped the door frame with his mechanical hand; metal cogs whirred in protest. His instincts rarely betrayed him.

He clicked the door shut and surveyed the cabin. The medicines were locked away. The instruments seemed to be in order. Nothing had been meddled with.

The gentleman patient moaned. His collar had been pulled askew. Blood trickled down his neck from an unhealed puncture mark of a large gauge needle.

Jack frowned. He pulled the collar back further to examine the wound more closely. There was not one, but two puncture marks. Jack sucked in a sharp breath. Catherine used to devour Penny Dreadful novels, with their stories of creatures that fed on blood. He shook his head.

Vampyres didn't exist.

💀

Waiters paced after the mechanical food and drink trolleys as they progressed through the Dining Room. The lights buzzed fitfully. They'd been malfunctioning all day, as if mourning the maid's death.

Piano music wafted across the tables, riding the warm Mediterranean breeze trickling through the open windows. Steam rose from the music machine, drifted into the draught and dissipated over the closest tables.

Jack sat in his corner, sipped his water and skimmed the menu: hare soup, fried fillet of fish, Poulet a la Marento, followed by a generous list of roasts and vegetables. He peered over the menu card and eyed the familiar diners, who occupied their designated seats.

Mrs. Ivers sat at her nearby table, picking at her food. She'd dined alone since her husband had been isolated in quarantine. Still, she kept up appearances, with not a hair out of place; obviously the steward had found her alternative lighting. The waiters delivered notes of condolence from gawping diners unwilling to approach her for fear of contagion.

Lord Sebastian and his mother had been relocated to a table on the other side of Jack, away from potential contamination. Every night, the young Lord fawned over his mother, while eyeing the young ladies - married or not - over the rim of his continually-refilled wine glass.

With a loud pop, the tube lights by the entrance fizzled out. Darkness cascaded across the room.

The whir of the trolleys ceased. A metal utensil clattered on a china plate.

"Must I dine in the dark?" Mrs. Ivers' voice broke the silence.

There was a scuffle, not too far away.

Jack's blade sang quietly as it slipped into his palm.

"Will they never fix those things!" Mrs. Ivers growled. "This is what happens when one relies on these new-fangled gadgets. The Queen would never stand for it."

Waiters appeared in the entrance, and ferried lit candelabra to the tables. The warm candlelight cast a shadow across Jack's menu.

The sweet fragrance of rose caressed his nostrils. Black, silk-gloved fingers curled over the top of the menu card, and slipped it from his hand.

"I took the liberty of ordering for us both." The voice was silky, the words almost sung, rather than spoken.

Jack glanced up. Lady Ambrose, an elegant woman with an alluring smile and piercing green eyes, swept up her crimson skirts and leaned forward, presenting her décolletage as she slid into the chair beside him.

A food trolley trundled up to their table. The

Head Waiter laid their plates before them: roast beef - rare and moist - and baked potatoes. He presented the Lady Ambrose with a bottle of red wine. She nodded. He filled her glass and turned to face Jack.

Jack shook his head and slipped his hand over his wine glass.

"Would you prefer tea, sir?" asked the Head Waiter.

Jack nodded.

Lady Ambrose raised an eyebrow.

The Head Waiter waved over the drinks trolley, poured a fresh cup of tea and excused himself.

Lady Ambrose tugged the buttons at the wrists of her silk gloves and peeled them off her hands. A wave of perfume embraced Jack.

"How very British," she said. "You don't drink wine?"

"Alcohol dulls the mind." He pressed his blade back into its sheath.

"Only if one over-indulges." Dark auburn curls cascaded over her alabaster shoulders.

She smiled. A perfect smile. Perfect lips. Perfect eyes. Jack's heart skipped. She reminded him of...

"Have we met before?" He stirred his tea, careful not to touch the sides of his cup.

"You're very forward, sir." Her voice; if he closed his eyes, he could imagine...

He took a deep breath. Catherine was dead. By his own hand. Dead and buried. For science.

"Forgive me." He couldn't tear his gaze away

from those eyes. He forced a blink. "You remind me of someone."

"A lover?" She sipped her wine slowly and gazed at him. No, past him.

He followed her gaze to the, admittedly handsome, young Lord dining with his mother.

"It was a long time ago." Jack dissected his roast beef, scraping his fork on the china plate.

Lady Ambrose's attention snapped back to Jack.

"That's a shame." She took a deep breath. "A man in his prime." She sipped the wine; her tongue licked an errant drop from her lips.

"Me, or Lord Sebastian?" he asked.

"A man may enjoy a tasty morsel, may he not?" Lady Ambrose replied. "But if a Lady is peckish, she is condemned." She grinned. "I prefer a full meal, accompanied by a more mature wine."

A smile twitched over Jack's lips. Her tongue was quick. Just like dear Catherine.

Her green eyes flashed in the candlelight. Intriguing. Intelligent.

He drew a slow breath. It'd been a long time since he'd enjoyed female company. He shifted in his chair and stretched his fingers. Perhaps he should enjoy the delights of the voyage? Once he arrived in the Colonies, work would consume him.

Lady Ambrose poked at her roast beef with her fork. Its juice had seeped into the potato.

"Is the beef not to your liking?" he asked.

She pushed the vegetables to one side.

"If you are unwell, I may be able to assist." He laid his cutlery on his plate. "I am a doctor."

"I thought you had that smell about you." She leaned forward. Her breast rose and fell quickly. "Didn't you attend to the girl, who—" She paused.

Jack's mechanical hand twitched under the table. The other passengers seemed oblivious to the maid's fate. The captain seemed content with Jack's reported findings. He'd thought he was safe.

She lowered her voice to a whisper: "Such a tragedy."

He nodded.

His trouser hem fluttered. Something touched his ankle and slowly brushed along his calf.

"It's been a long time since I had..." her eyelids fluttered, "a thorough examination."

Jack's pulse quickened.

He slipped his right hand across the table towards her.

Lady Ambrose leaned forward; she smelled of roses and honey. She placed her hand on his. Her hand was cold.

"Perhaps we could...?" She sighed, obviously well-versed in displaying her attributes to their best advantage. "Perhaps you could escort me back to my cabin? It's not far, and the lighting has malfunctioned."

Jack glanced around the dining room. Lord Sebastian grinned and nodded in his direction. It would be unseemly to be seen visiting her cabin.

Society, even on holiday, could be ruthless. And he, despite his sins, was still a gentleman.

"Perhaps my cabin?" he whispered.

"Yes." She squeezed his hand.

"In that case, I *am* honoured, Lady Ambrose." He rose from his chair and offered her his arm.

"Please, call me Charlotte," she whispered as she slipped her arm around his. "Thank you, Doctor Collins."

"My friends call me Jack."

The light tube in Jack's cabin crackled and dimmed. It appeared the entire ship was in danger of technological failure. Jack lit the lamp on the side table.

Charlotte surveyed the sitting room, her gaze pausing on the unopened bottle of champagne and clean champagne flutes on the table by the settee.

"I thought you didn't drink, Jack?" The corner of her lip curled.

He returned the smile.

"I believe I said it dulls the brain," he replied.

Charlotte opened the bottle, filled two glasses and offered one to Jack.

She circled the room, glass in hand, and halted near the open door leading to the bedroom.

Jack's mechanical hand twitched. The blade clicked in its sheath. His polite smile dropped. He hadn't intended on inviting anyone into his sanctuary. He silently cursed. He'd left an experiment running whilst he had dinner.

He stepped in front of the door, blocking her view.

"I hadn't expected company," he said.

She clicked her tongue. "I assure you, I am not easily shocked."

Jack slipped his hand around her waist, intending to sweep her away from his makeshift laboratory.

She kissed him on the cheek and unpinned her curls. Her hair caressed his neck, enveloping him in the aroma of honey and fine wine. He closed his eyes and breathed in the intoxicating perfume.

Charlotte clasped his hand with strong fingers, spun out of his embrace and glided through the doorway. Jack growled under his breath, yanked the glove off his mechanical hand and strode after her. He could not afford to have his work exposed or his samples corrupted.

Instead of a scream, Charlotte smiled. Jack hesitated, the blade tip resting on his fingertip, ready to strike.

"I thought you were a police surgeon?" she said.

"How did you—?" Jack frowned. "I never mentioned my occupation."

"The steward knows everything." She giggled. "I don't seduce just *anyone*, my dear Jack."

"I thought I was seducing you." Jack closed the door behind him; it would help muffle the scream.

She laughed; this time it was no girlish giggle.

"That is what women like men to believe." She

placed her champagne glass on the workbench. "It's less complicated that way." She slipped off her long gloves, rolled them up and placed them next to her glass.

"Are you an experimental chemist?" She circled the workbench, halted on the opposite side, and examined the array of glass vials suspended from metal rods. Above it was a pear-shaped glass funnel, its dripper still containing remnants of a red liquid. She sniffed the vial below it, containing dark clumps, suspended in yellow liquid.

Jack hesitated.

She stiffened; her eyes widened.

No scream? Jack's heart raced.

"I specialise in haematology," he said. "That's the study of—"

"Blood." Her pupils flared.

"How did you know?"

"My dear, departed husband was a scientist. As was I." She turned to examine the row of research books on the table under the window and ran her finger along the spine of a book. "I have a fascination for men of science."

She glanced at his mechanical hand and smiled.

"I see your work pays well." She returned her attention to the blood-filled vial.

"Is this why you're travelling halfway around the world?" she asked.

Jack nodded. "Australia is more liberal in its attitude to research."

"And the Queen has less control?" she whispered.

"It is advantag—"

He felt the touch of her soft, cool skin on his hand. His fingers twitched. How had she moved so fast? His brain buzzed. He shook his head.

She extracted the full champagne glass from his hand and placed it on the table next to the bed.

"May I ask, what takes you to the southern regions of Australia?" Jack let his muscles relax.

"I've been sent to expand the family business." She slipped her fingers between his and stroked his mechanical hand. "Tell me, is it painful?"

Jack opened his mouth to reply.

"Shhh." She pressed her finger against his lips. "It has been a long time since my husband died."

As she kissed him, she slid her hand under his dinner jacket and rested her hand on his chest, over his heart.

Jack closed his eyes, and savoured pleasant memories, pushing away visions of Catherine lying in her own blood. Whitechapel was across the ocean, in the past. He'd paid a high price. He deserved a little compensation.

"What's wrong?" she asked.

"Oh, just memories."

"Of what?" she asked.

"One doesn't compare lovers."

"Why not?" She giggled. Her cold lips kissed his neck. She slipped off his dinner jacket and tossed it on the floor. She sniffed his neck.

"You smell of—" She hissed and pushed him away.

Pain seared up his right arm. Jack's eyes snapped open. He wrenched his metal hand free from her grip. He flicked the blade free and thrust it into her chest.

She stared into his eyes. The corner of Jack's lip curled as his gaze locked onto hers. No one could withstand what they found there. Her eyes widened. There was fear.

Sharp eyeteeth protruded onto her lower lip. Her black eyes burned. Jack's heart skipped.

She stepped back and eased the blade from her torso. Her bodice was ripped, but there was little blood.

"What are you?" he whispered.

"Some call us strigoi. Others: Vampyre. To you, I am death."

Jack's mind raced. *Vampyre?* Impossible! They didn't exist.

He shook his head. It wouldn't be long before she remembered he was only human. He had to prove he was worth more alive; everyone had their price. What could he offer her? What had Catherine's books said? 'Vampyres feed on fresh blood.' But, his blood samples were stale.

Fresh blood? His smile returned. As a doctor, he had access to the quarantine quarters.

She circled towards the door, holding his blade in her hand. Her gaze shifted downward on his neck. Her eyelids fluttered.

"I should rip your throat out," she growled.

"And what after that?" His voice remained calm. "How would you explain my death?"

She scoffed. "The Captain will do anything I tell him. He's as weak as the ship's doctor."

Her eyes narrowed.

Jack felt her inside his head, rummaging around, rattling locks, looking for a way in. He had to concentrate.

The metal joints of his hand clicked as he raised it between them.

Get out of my head!

She winced. "How—?"

Jack's heartbeat slowed. She couldn't control him, and that scared her.

"I understand what you are, and I'm not afraid," he whispered. "We can help each other. You control Bucknall; he won't question my authority. I can quarantine as many patients as you need. I, in turn, get all the samples I need to continue my work until we reach Australia."

She edged closer. There was still fire in her eyes.

"You're a scientist - or were one. Surely, you can understand the logic of it." Jack held his ground. He understood the struggle of intellect over desire. "But I need to know I can trust you."

She paused. The fire in her eyes cooled. Jack lowered his hand.

"I am not a savage. I can control myself!" She grinned. Her eyeteeth dented her lips. "Most of the time." Her eyes glinted green in the lamplight.

Jack took a deep breath. "Then we have a deal?"

She nodded and dropped onto the edge of the bed.

"I must feed."

Jack didn't move. It could be a ruse to catch him off guard.

"I promise I won't attack you." Her eyelids drooped. The fire in her eyes was gone. She offered him the hilt of his knife. She bared her teeth; the extended eyeteeth had retracted.

Jack inched forward and took the knife.

"You know my weakness," whispered Charlotte. "Can I trust you to keep to your bargain?"

Jack placed the knife on the table by the bed, next to his champagne glass. He extended his right hand towards her and helped her to her feet.

"Dear Humphry understood me too, Jack." She leaned her head on his shoulder.

"I prescribe a visit to the medical quarters."

"But Mr. Ivers' blood is tainted." Her shoulders slumped.

"I believe his wife visits her husband every evening, after dinner."

She managed a faint smile, as if to show him that her teeth were still retracted, then closed her mouth and kissed his wrist. "Oh, we shall have such sport together, young Jack."

He patted her hand; the skin was ice cold.

"Eat first, then play," he whispered.

Jack had dreamed of Catherine, risen from the grave, beautiful and willing. He stretched his arms and opened his eyes. Sunlight glared across the rumpled sheets on the floor and streamed across his face. He raised his right hand to shield his face from the light and flipped over onto the opposite side of the bed, out of the direct sunlight, and pushed himself up onto his elbows and surveyed the room.

Charlotte was gone. He was alone.

On the bedside table, next to Jack's still-full champagne flute was a perfectly calligraphed note:

I keep my promises. I look forward to dinner tonight. Eat, then play.

Lottie.

Jack slid to the side of the bed and examined himself in a hand mirror. There were two small bruises on his shoulder; the skin was unbroken. He examined the rest of his skin. There were no puncture marks. She'd kept her word.

He dropped the mirror on the bed and laughed. He had a new playmate, who understood all his desires, and supported his experiments. Something Catherine could never have done.

He pulled on a clean pair of trousers, attached his prosthetic arm and reached for his blood-stained knife. A rivulet of thick blood rolled along the groove of the blade. It had not yet coagulated.

Jack checked his pocket watch: eight hours. He raised an eyebrow.

He balanced the blade, so as not to lose the precious sample, and drained it into a clean vial, then transferred drops onto a glass slide. Flakes of dried blood from his previous sample were added to the slide. He placed it under the microscope.

Charlotte's blood engulfed the dried flecks and mixed with the red blood cells. He waited. The mixed sample didn't re-coagulate.

Jack leaned back in his chair and let out a long, slow breath.

"Bloody hell." Was this the answer? Had he found a way to create an all-purpose donor for blood transfusions?

His heart raced. Perhaps he could ask Lottie for more samples? Or would that destroy their pact? He eyed the vial of her blood. He had enough for now. It could wait. There was almost two months before the voyage ended. Two months of pleasure. Two months before he had to make a final decision.

Jack wiped his blade and snapped it into its sheath. He slipped on a fresh linen shirt, apologising silently to Catherine as he folded Charlotte's note and slid it into the pocket, next to his heart.

He tied his cravat high on his neck and rolled up his shirt sleeves. He had some experimenting to do before dinner.

Jack surveyed the commandeered crew quarters, lined with over a dozen occupied bunk beds, adequate 'quarantine' quarters for those deemed to be suffering from influenza.

Once the word of a possible outbreak had spread, the Captain had demanded affected passengers be isolated, and put Jack in charge of quarantine. He had avoided the crew quarters since. The threat of infection kept nosy visitors away.

The past eight weeks had been both exhilarating and exhausting. Quarantine had provided a convenient source for experimental samples. He'd already isolated three different blood types, confirming his initial theory.

Jack slid the needle into Mrs. Ivers' arm. Her skin was thin and pale and dehydrated. She twitched on the crew's bunk bed. Her eyes stared past him, fixating on whatever alternate reality Charlotte had concocted. He drew back the plunger. Blood filled the barrel.

"Sleep, Mrs. Ivers," he whispered. "It's just a dream."

Mrs. Ivers closed her eyes.

Jack transferred the blood sample into a glass tube and stoppered it. It clinked as it joined the other vials in his bag.

Lady Charlotte Ambrose drifted into the cabin and clicked the door shut behind her. She was a vision in scarlet silk and lace.

Jack's heart raced.

"I felt a little peckish." She unpinned her bonnet, placed it on the table in front of him and drifted along the row of beds.

Jack closed his bag and followed her.

"I feel like..." Charlotte hovered near Mrs. Ivers' body and sniffed. Her eyes widened, her pupils dilated. "Was she part of today's collection?"

Jack nodded.

Charlotte leaned closer. Mrs. Ivers stirred and opened her eyes.

"She has such sweet blood for one with such a sharp tongue, unlike her husband." She glanced at Jack and smiled. Her smile twisted as her eyeteeth elongated. "Excellent choice, my love."

"Time to dance." She ran her fingers through Mrs. Ivers' blonde locks.

Mrs. Ivers rose slowly, held out her hand and smiled. Charlotte took it, reeled her in and wrapped her arm around Mrs. Ivers' uncorseted body. They swayed for a moment; a bizarre ritual, but one Jack had come to enjoy, almost as much as he did Lottie.

They floated, skirts entwined. Charlotte twirled her 'partner' between them. Their silk skirts rustled and brushed against Jack's hand.

Charlotte stared into his eyes, as if trying to reach the darkness in his soul.

His head thumped. Everyone craved something; some lusted after power, some chemical addictions, others: love. Blood tied them together; a bond stronger than mere love. It was their mutual addiction. They both craved it. She to survive, he to help others survive.

A smile flickered over Charlotte's lips. Her teeth

pressed against Mrs. Ivers' wrist and pushed slowly through the skin.

Jack dug his fingers into his palms, as she pierced the flesh. He could hear the blood rushing into her mouth.

Mrs. Ivers moaned. Blood seeped from the wound. Charlotte's tongue flicked across Mrs. Ivers' wrist. Charlotte's eyes rolled back. She latched onto the wrist and sucked with more vigour.

Jack envied her control. One day he would master such self-control. He would not reprise the mistake he made with the maid.

The cabin door rattled. A knock followed.

"Doctor Collins?"

"It's the blasted doctor," hissed Jack.

Charlotte glanced up briefly, her eyes unfocused, then returned to her feast.

Jack rolled down his shirt sleeves and approached the door.

"What do you want, Doctor Bucknall?" he asked.

"We're two days from port. The Captain wants an update. The Port Adelaide authorities won't allow us to dock with an influenza epidemic on board."

Jack turned to face Charlotte. He knew better than to interrupt her.

She growled, unlatched herself, and released her grip. Mrs. Ivers slumped onto her bunk.

"Let the beastly man in."

Jack swallowed. "Are you sure?" he whispered.

She licked an errant drop of blood from her lips and nodded.

He turned the key in the lock and opened the door.

"Locking the door now, Doctor Collins?" Bucknall blustered into the cabin. "Any news on a cure yet?"

He strode past Charlotte, towards a single bed near Jack's desk.

"How is Lady Sebastian? Any improvement? Her son has been asking after her."

Charlotte's eyelashes fluttered at the name. Something stirred in Jack's gut. Something new. He gritted his teeth. Was this what jealousy felt like?

"Perhaps he should visit her occasionally?" said Lottie. "I could do with some dessert."

"Shhh, he'll hear you," whispered Jack.

She laughed, entwined her fingers in his and draped herself over Jack's shoulder. A heady aroma of rose engulfed him.

"What was that, Doctor Collins?" Bucknall looked at Jack, and seemed to ignore Charlotte.

"Nothing," replied Jack.

"His mind is weak." Lottie extricated her fingers and moved closer to Bucknall. "He can't hear or see me until I tell him he can." Charlotte twirled in front of him. She would be the death of him.

"Are you feeling all right, Doctor Collins? You haven't succumbed to the flu, have you?" asked Bucknall.

Jack shook his head. "Two days until port?" he asked. Charlotte shadowed Bucknall as he returned to face Jack.

"Plenty of time to finish up here." She leaned past Bucknall and kissed Jack on the ear.

His heart pounded. He swallowed, trying not to react.

"Tell the Captain the experimental inoculation has been successful," he continued. "The patients are recovering. We should be able to dock safely."

"He'll be pleased to hear of your progress." Bucknall placed his doctor's bag on the desk. "One body is enough to declare to the authorities."

"Pardon?" Jack jerked his attention back to the ship's doctor.

"The suicide."

"I thought the body was buried at sea?"

"No, she's packed away in the ice house. The Captain didn't want anyone to get wind of it and upset the First Class passengers."

Jack swallowed. A real police surgeon would reveal his lie; a trained eye would spot the wounds were not self-inflicted, nor the results of a paddle wheel.

His gaze darted in Charlotte's direction, hovering behind Bucknall.

"What's wrong?" She frowned.

"I can't allow the body to be re-examined," he replied, ignoring Bucknall's presence. "She didn't commit suicide."

Bucknall glared at him. "What are you talking about, man?"

"Sloppy, Jack," she hissed. "If they investigate one body, they'll want to inspect them all."

She snatched up Bucknall's arm and pinned him against the end of the nearest (bunk) bed post, and sank her fangs into his neck. The bed thudded against the wall as she drank. He struggled.

Charlotte pushed harder on his forearms, until his hands paled. His fingers twitched.

"Lottie?" Jack gently placed his hand on her arm.

She growled - a deep, guttural sound, like a rabid dog not willing to share its spoils - and glared at him. Her eyes burned red, piercing through his. Her face contorted in both ecstasy and animal hunger.

Jack caught his breath. The stench of sickly sweet roses clawed at his eyes, invaded his nostrils and rifled through his memories. He sneered. It was the smell of betrayal.

He retreated.

She thrust her fangs deeper into Bucknall's neck. The bed scraped. She flicked her head. Skin ripped. She closed her eyes and rutted his neck, pushing deeper until blood burst from the jagged wound. Her tongue lashed out, sucking loudly as it gathered the escaping blood.

Bucknall's body convulsed. Charlotte moaned, and embraced the movement.

Jack flinched. In two days they would be free to leave the ship, free to start new lives, without fear of retribution for their sins. But how long until she lost control with him? He needed to strike before she turned on him.

He fingered the tip of his blade. Steel would not save him. He searched his memory for the tales

Catherine had whispered to him in the dark. A stake through the heart? Silver? He backed into the table. His hand groped for Bucknall's bag for the silver nitrate.

Lady Ambrose sighed and extracted herself from the doctor's pale body. It crumpled onto the floor and stared at Jack with sunken eyes.

She wiped the corner of her mouth.

"Who'd have thought the fool would taste so delicious?" She skipped to Jack and kissed him on the mouth. A long, lingering kiss. Her auburn curls choked him with the smell of stale roses.

"New perfume?" he asked.

"Yes, do you like it?"

"It reminds me of..."

"Another past love?" She giggled. "We are made for each other, Jack."

She stared at him, with desire in her eyes. You're next, they whispered. His muscles stiffened. He peeled her arms off him and moved to examine Bucknall's lifeless body. Deep gashes tore across the throat.

"What's wrong, Jack?"

"How can I explain another death?"

"The stupid man died of influenza. You can't work your miracles on everyone." She twirled and laughed. "He *was* careless; too many years tending to bruised egos. They'll need to burn the body, of course." She was by his ear now, whispering. The stench of betrayal followed her. "Which fortunately will destroy any signs to the contrary."

"Will he become... like you?" he asked.

"Heavens, no! I wouldn't want to be stuck with *him* for all eternity." She perched on the edge of the table. "It's all about the blood, isn't it?" She eyed Jack. "You only become one of us if you drink my blood."

Blood. The fresh blood samples... And her blood; uncongealed blood. It was as if lightning cracked through his brain. He glanced at the microscope. The blood riddle. If only he could...

Jack slid onto his chair.

He removed the slide from the microscope and placed it with his other samples. If he was to continue his experiment he would need more of her blood. He couldn't destroy her. He'd already sacrificed one love to science. Perhaps there was another way?

"An enquiring mind, even in adversity." She leaned over the table. "Did I tell you my first husband was a scientist?" She giggled. "I do love a man of intelligence. Always thinking, always planning."

Jack froze. Did she know?

She kissed him on the head.

"A beautiful brain." She leaned back over the table and stared into his eyes, her pupils now mere specks of black. "You're fascinating, Jack. I can never tell what you're thinking." She pushed his chair away from the table, lifted her skirts and plopped herself on his lap. "What are you thinking, Jack?"

He relaxed.

"Curiosity is good for the mind," he whispered.

She wobbled. Her head fell onto his chest.

"I thought feeding made you stronger?" he asked.

"Always the scientist." She closed her eyes and nuzzled his chest. "Eat, then play," she cooed.

"Later." An idea was forming in his mind.

She rose to her feet, shoved him away and stumbled back to an empty bed. Jack caught his breath; she was still too strong.

Jack rummaged through Bucknall's bag. The bottle of silver nitrate was nearly empty; Bucknall had wasted it on Mr. Ivers. He examined all the bottles, including a used bottle of Laudanum. The fool had been self-medicating.

Jack checked his pocket watch. The dinner gong would sound soon. He needed more time to think.

"You should change for dinner," he said.

"I love to watch you eat." Her speech was slurred. "And besides, Lord Sebastian might be there."

"Window shopping?" There was that stirring in his gut again. He ignored it. "For a little dessert?"

Her eyes widened.

"I knew you understood me." She clicked her tongue. "Better not. Too much of a good thing. I need to keep my head clear for the rest of the voyage."

She closed her eyes and fell onto the bed, arms outstretched as if intoxicated. Now was his opportunity to kill her before she killed him. He hesitated. Keeping her 'alive' would ensure a continuous supply of base blood samples to continue his work.

She lay on the bed, waiting for him as she'd done many times before. Wanting. Trusting. Apparently harmless. He remembered their first night: his untouched champagne by the bed, and hers on the workbench.

Jack grinned. Alcohol? Could it be that easy? But, she drank wine every night at dinner. His smile slipped. Not alcohol. Bottles rattled as he moved Bucknall's bag. The Laudanum? Perhaps it worked on vampyre physiology just as it did on humans? If he concentrated it? Added in something more? He needed just enough to keep her under control until they left the steamship.

He lifted Bucknall's body off the floor; at least there wasn't too much blood. He'd get Evans to remove it to the ice house. He'd inform the Captain of the doctor's unfortunate demise, at dinner.

Jack smiled. His plan was almost complete.

The gong sounded along the hall. And with it, the final piece of Jack's plan clattered into place.

It took only one day. An 'accidental' meeting in the Smoking Room. A bit of charm and truckle was all that was needed to befriend the handsome Lord Sebastian, the object of Lady Ambrose's wandering eye. That, and an expensive bottle of hundred-year old port, two Russian cigars and the promise of a personal, and private, introduction to Lady Charlotte Ambrose, one of the richest women on the ship.

The suggestion that his mother planned to disinherit him due to his promiscuous behaviour, prodded him even further towards this fate.

Alcohol and Laudanum-laced Absinthe had loosened the young Lord's tongue. He boasted he'd enjoyed every willing female on the ship. He seemed more intent on amusing himself than ensuring his mother's well-being. He was bored playing the dutiful son and heir.

Jack ushered Lord Sebastian along the passage, ducking the Lord's gesticulating hand as he swatted green pixies. Jack grinned. Lady Ambrose would cringe in horror when she finally met the buffoon. He doubted even Sebastian's handsome face and enthusiasm could compensate for lack of intelligence.

But Jack knew all too well lust's hold could override rational decisions. Twice now, he'd felt its pull. The first had not ended well. He would not let it happen again.

He nudged the clueless Lord towards his cabin door and opened it.

The late afternoon sun streamed across the sitting room. He still had time to set his trap. He led Sebastian through the sitting room to the bedroom, leaned his walking stick against the chair, and removed Sebastian's jacket.

Sebastian unbuttoned his shirt and collapsed on the bed.

"Ah, champagne!" The bottle scraped along the bedside table.

Jack frowned. How much could the man drink and still function? Jack grabbed the bottle.

"You can celebrate later," he said. The fool deserved his fate.

The main cabin door clicked. The tube light fizzled out in the sitting room.

Jack removed his dinner gloves.

"Jack?" Charlotte's sweet voice rolled over his skin and grated like crystallised honey.

He dug his nails into his palm; he must remain in control.

"Wait here, Hubert," he said. "Remember how rich she is."

Sebastian relinquished the bottle, fell back onto the bed and grinned.

The trap was set.

Jack closed the curtains and stepped back into the sitting room. Charlotte wrapped her arms around him and kissed him on the neck. Her hair tickled his nose. He held his breath and nibbled her ear; their traditional greeting.

"I've got a gift for you," he whispered.

"A gift?" She tugged at his shirt buttons.

"Not here. In the bedroom."

"I love surprises." She grinned and dragged him around the shadowed edges of the cabin and into the bedroom.

Lord Sebastian had already removed his shirt.

She gasped. "How can I resist such a tasty morsel?"

Jack's gut squirmed.

She kissed Jack hard, and licked his lips.

His heart raced. He'd made the correct decision. It was a matter of self-preservation.

He closed his eyes and kissed her back.

"We're perfect for each other," she whispered in his ear.

Jack let her hand slip from his. He'd miss her.

He retreated to the padded armchair near his workbench.

She leaped on the bed and ran her hands over Sebastian's now-naked chest. He undid her bodice.

Jack resisted the urge to drag her off the bed.

"It's unseemly to play with one's food, in company." She waggled her finger and flung her leg over Sebastian's torso.

The fool grinned inanely. He was either still mesmerised by green fairies, or her persuasive mental charms had already taken hold.

She sniffed his neck. "He smells divine."

Her eyes blazed. Her fangs protruded below her lips. She grinned and launched herself at Sebastian's neck. He moaned. This time there were no dainty sips; squelching, sucking noises filled Jack's ears. The trap was sprung.

He puffed on his cigarillo, and waited for her to sate herself.

Blood gurgled in her throat. She growled and lunged again.

Jack tried to ignore their gyrating bodies. An arm snaked out of the fray.

Jack flicked his wrist. The blade rang as it left its sheath. Nothing would ruin his plan. Sebastian would not leave the room alive. She must drink every drop.

Her clawed hand lashed out and caught Sebastian's pale wrist and wrenched it back onto the bed.

Every muscle in Jack's body tensed. He'd calculated the amount of Laudanum to add to the

Absinthe, based on her recovery time after she'd gorged on Bucknall - and doubled it. It hadn't mattered if it was a lethal dose; the man would be dead before morning anyway. Jack shifted in his chair. He prayed it would be enough to sedate her.

Sebastian's feet twitched. He whimpered; a pleasant sound.

Jack inhaled a deep breath of tobacco smoke to steady his nerves, averted his eyes and thought of his ultimate prize: the vampyre's transmuted blood would unlock the answer to successful blood transfusion.

She pushed harder, her head swaying with her victim's movements. The body convulsed. The champagne bottle rattled on the table and smashed onto the floor. She snarled, flung back her head and rocked back onto her haunches. Her eyes blazed red in the darkened room.

Jack swallowed. Perhaps he'd miscalculated. He grasped his walking cane: ash wood tipped with a silver spike. White oak would have been better. It wouldn't kill her, but it could slow her down.

"Jack?" Her voice was no longer melodic, but the rasp of a hoarse daemon. "I need you, Jack." She sniffed the air and stretched a shapely leg out towards the floor.

Blood dribbled from the corner of her mouth, trickled down her neck, and between her breasts.

"Join me," she whispered. "Be with me forever." She slit her wrist with a sharp talon.

Jack's stomach clenched. Bile filled his mouth.

She wobbled.

He held his breath.

She fell forward onto her elbows and giggled.

Jack let his breath escape slowly.

She rolled onto the bed, next to the drained corpse and wiggled her fingers at the ceiling.

"Hello," she cooed at the air. "Want to join me for dinner?"

Jack took a last puff of restorative smoke and crushed his cigarillo into a Petrie dish. He rose slowly. Glass crunched under his boots as he approached the bed.

"Shh," she murmured. "Someone's come to play."

Jack clutched his silver-headed cane and circled the bed.

"I think I broke your present." She reached out towards him and ran her fingers up his inside leg; the talons were gone, as were her fangs. "Have you come to rescue me, Jack?"

Jack extracted her fingers. Her hand fell into her lap. Her eyelids fluttered.

"Time to rest," he said. "We dock tomorrow, at noon. There are forms to sign before we arrive."

He retrieved papers from his workbench, pressed an ink-filled pen into her hand and indicated where to sign. She scribbled on the paper.

"Did we have fun?" She smiled.

"Oh, yes." He folded up the papers and tucked them in his pocket.

"Good." She buried her head into the blood-spattered pillow.

Jack checked her pulse, out of habit. Non-existent.

That proved nothing; he had no idea if her sort had one. He slipped his fingers between hers and squeezed. Nothing. He peeled open an eyelid. Green eyes stared back at him, the pinpoint pupils fixed. She didn't stir.

Jack moved quickly. He didn't know how long he had. He tapped his cane on the wall closest to the passageway.

A key rattled in the door lock. Evans entered, pushing a medical gurney with a large sack on it. He locked the door behind him.

"Is it done, sir?" he asked.

"For now," replied Jack. "But we must hurry."

Together they swaddled the comatose Lady Ambrose in a sheet, and wrapped the bundle in sturdy chains. Evans slipped on several padlocks and handed Jack the keys. Jack slipped them into his pocket, next to the signed Power of Attorney, and checked his watch. Almost time for first sitting. He had to be there, to be seen in public. He needed witnesses.

Evans rolled her shrouded body onto the gurney and followed Jack into the bedroom, where the emaciated corpse still lay on his bed. The throat had been ripped, the edges ragged and pale. There wasn't much blood left to clean up. Jack had seen worse; he'd done worse.

"Take them both to the ice house. I'll inform the Captain of the deaths. Poor Lady Ambrose, to be taken so...young." He shook his head. "And Lord Sebastian: one dalliance too many. In his exhausted state, the infection took hold quickly." He tapped a fresh cigarillo out of its silver case.

"Put Lady Ambrose in the maid's coffin, box it up and pack well with ice. It should help muffle any sound if she should wake early. The maid will join Bucknall, Lord Sebastian, and the rest of the influenza victims to be cremated on arrival."

"You'll need these." He handed Evans the paperwork. "This allows me to take charge of the suicide's coffin to deliver to the authorities. The Captain was all too grateful I would take charge. He has a schedule to maintain. Unfortunately, both the report, and the body, will be mislaid."

Evans nodded and kicked the gurney into life. Cogs whirred. Small balls of steam puffed across the floor.

Jack returned to the bedroom, caught up the edge of the bedclothes with the spiked end of his walking cane, and flipped them over the corpse. He screwed the silver cap back onto the end of his cane and rested it against the armchair.

"I want everything cleared up before I return from dinner."

"Yes, sir."

Jack donned his dinner jacket and examined himself in the mirror. He wiped a speck of blood from his cheek.

His voyage had been unexpectedly rewarding. Tomorrow he would arrive in Australia ready to begin his final, and most promising, experiments.

THE ARTIST'S HANDS

RENEE M.P.T. KRAY

THE SKETCH WAS SIMPLE, ESPECIALLY COMPARED to the sort of portrait that Sabine was known for. For the hundredth time Francis rubbed his hand against the image, smearing charcoal under his fingertips as he examined the signature at the bottom of the page: two handprints in bright red paint, with the sigil from her family ring - a cat with a serpent in its mouth - pressed between the thumbprints in crimson wax. It was certainly Sabine's calling card, a mark that Francis had seen a hundred times before, and while it had filled him with disgust and rage and annoyance in times past, this was the first time he'd ever felt a tinge of fear.

The whole thing was insanity.

Francis poured himself a respectably small amount of brandy, wincing slightly as he swallowed it and then exhaling as the burn turned into a warm cloak blanketing his insides.

Now is not the time to become hysterical. Maintain control. Maintain order. Francis had learned when he was still very young that it was order, not love or religion or monarchs, that made the world go around. He had spent his judiciary career making sure that those who were disorderly were put in their proper place, and the people behind the unnatural piece of parchment on his desk certainly needed assistance in remembering where they belonged.

Just one of her crazy followers, he told himself yet again. *They need to learn a lesson.*

Francis thumped the glass down on his desk and turned to the fire. His maid had built it just as darkness was falling, and he'd kept it alive through the watches of the night. He had only a few hours until dawn… if he was going to go, it had to be now.

He threw the paper into the open mouth of the fire, watching as the edges caught and curled towards the image that so many other people had already seen and were all whispering about. For one second more Francis saw the smiling portrait of a woman. Her curled brown hair and thick, almost masculine eyebrows above an upticked smile presented the Sabine that he had always known, but she was elevated and beautiful, almost unearthly.

Then flames rolled over the sketch and she was gone.

Francis pulled his cloak from his closet and checked to ensure that the gloves inside it were not the soft white ones he wore while walking to court.

He didn't intend to be soiling his hands tonight, but one could never quite tell what would happen on an errand like this. Walking quietly so as not to alert the maids, Francis slipped through his house and let himself out the front door. Streetlamps flickered a pale orange against the cobblestones, probably not bright enough for anyone to recognize him, but he couldn't risk taking that chance and turned down an alleyway like a common criminal. It was awful; if the courtroom was his castle then these streets were normally his kingdom, a place for the good folk of the town to tip their hats to him and wish their devoted judge a good day.

And if Sabine would have just kept quiet, it could have stayed that way, Francis thought as he emerged out the back of the alleyway and cut off into the adjacent forest. Everything had been going so well for him when his career first started. Francis knew that the only way to correct the masses was to make examples of criminals, no matter how petty their transgressions, and so he had ruled with an iron hand that could not be swayed by tears or supplications. He was well respected for being a judge who wasn't afraid to put criminals in their place, and the common folk praised him for keeping their streets safe.

But then had come Sabine, a woman with insanity boiling in her veins like rot under the crust of a loaf. Unmarried, outspoken, and pursuing the overly passionate career of an artist, Sabine vexed and horrified Francis by turns. She'd begun by quietly spreading discord about his decisions, asking if he wasn't being too harsh and taking his role too far. Then he sentenced a young woman to death for repeated theft, and Sabine had begun a full fledged attack against him. She started painting images of the criminals he'd had hanged in smiling, simple poses that highlighted their humanity, and she started telling anyone who would listen that some of these supposed criminals were not so different from law-abiding citizens and did not deserve death. Jail, perhaps, but not death. Francis had ordered her to stop, had arranged for her to be arrested, and had publicly shamed her, but Sabine always continued.

"Art reflects the truth," she had said at their last public meeting. "And the truth will not be stopped simply because you order it to be so."

Preposterous. Truth was what he decided, not what Sabine reported.

Francis looked over his shoulder to make sure that no one was following him, though of course no one was. No one came to this part of the forest, where the ground was so treacherous that you could easily trip and dash your head on a branch, or fall into the sharp ravine that opened silently in the darkness to swallow people who didn't know it was there. Sabine had been incredulous when he'd brought her here on the night before last and she must have known that this whole affair was bad news. But he had agreed to listen to her arguments if they were completely alone, and for a chance at victory she'd been willing to let go of logic and follow emotion, an easy thing for women.

"You need to stop this slander, Sabine," he'd

warned as they stood on the edge of the ravine. She had stared forlornly at him, her eyes deep and cold in the night sky. Perhaps she had already read her death in his face, because her reply was calm and resigned.

"Maybe you can stop me today, but there will always be a reckoning for people like you."

"We'll see."

The initial push hadn't killed her, though she'd certainly fallen from a great enough height to do the business.

Francis carefully slid down the rocky precipice where only a day before Sabine's skin had torn on branches and her blood had spattered over mossy stones. And when she had risen with the wavering lilt of smoke off an extinguished candle, he'd slid down to meet her just like he was doing now. She'd tried to fight off the rope that he'd brought as a precaution, but when her neck collapsed with a wet pop he'd known her reign of defamation was over.

Francis stopped at the bottom of the ravine and looked up. He was still alone under the blanket of darkness, exactly as he had been the last time he'd been here. So how had the damning image of Sabine as one of her martyr figures been nailed on the courtroom door the morning after her death, signed with Sabine's hands and ring?

Francis snapped on his black gloves, then allowed his memory to instruct his feet: forward three paces, turn right at the bent pine. Leaning down, he pulled away thick brambles that clouded the base of an old oak tree and swore as thorns poked through his gloves. Finally he tugged them back enough to see if she was still there, resting where he'd stored her body in lieu of digging a grave.

She was. Sabine was still recognizable, though something had nibbled away her left nostril since he'd last seen her. Her skin was almost purple against her yellow dress, which was a simple high-necked frock with long sleeves and a floor length hem, exactly the sort of plain thing that most respectable women would not be caught dead in outside of the home. The white fabric around her neck was torn back to show dark bruises alongside the reddish rope burn, like a heinous necklace set with ugly stones, and her face was swollen with cracked lips. It was really quite disgusting. Francis gagged and turned his eyes from her disfigured head to what he had come to see: her hands.

They were as stiff as the rest of her, lying flat on either side of her body. Francis reached forward and then recoiled, the thought of touching dead flesh making his fingers curl despite the protective gloves. He had brought a shovel last time that he hadn't had to use thanks to the brambles, and he'd left it with her so as to not raise suspicion on the walk back. Now he seized it and used the metal end to flip Sabine's left hand.

Crimson paint was dried along the palm.

Francis's stomach rolled uneasily inside him. Had the paint been there the night before? He was almost certain it hadn't. He looked around again, positive now that someone had seen them the previous evening. It was the only explanation, because it wasn't as if the corpse would have been able to cover her own hands in paint and sign that picture. To even entertain such a thought would be to abandon order altogether.

Sabine had always been clever. She must have had one of her little students follow them at a safe distance, observe what happened, and then pick up her task to defame Francis now that they had real dirt to hold over his head. He had known that Sabine was obsessed, but to willingly give herself to death just to bring him down was extreme, even for her. Francis couldn't help but feel a little impressed, not to mention flattered. But Sabine wasn't the only clever one.

Francis stood up and positioned the tip of the shovel at the base of Sabine's hand, right where the wrist met the arm. Blue veins were still visible beneath the skin, a unique criss-cross pattern connecting flesh to flesh. For a moment his mind revolted at even considering the possibility of pressing down and separating that hand from its master, but he struggled for mastery and reminded himself of the mad defamations of character that would continue if he did not put an end to this right now. Sabine's friends were apparently not brave enough to retrieve her body or they would have already done so. If he took away her signature, she would be forever silenced.

Francis breathed deeply, and then he leaned all his weight on the shovel.

The snap was loud and cold in the silence of the forest, and the second one was even worse. The hands were now lying belly up like two giant dead spiders, and Francis shuddered as he knelt down and took the first monstrosity by its little finger. The weight of it in his hand seemed heavier than it should have been and he quickly shoved the revolting thing into a pocket of his cloak. He had to stretch to reach the one with the ring, but finally he was able to put that into his other pocket.

Francis quickly replaced the shovel on the ground beside Sabine and backed away, leaving her as well hidden as before. When whoever was behind today's picture came to forge her signature again they would find it mighty difficult. Triumph soared in his chest as he pictured her followers gravely approaching her resting place with some newly drawn image, expecting to imprint the blessing of their master upon it, only to discover that she was silenced yet again. They might be able to put their own handprints in red paint, but they would certainly not be able to replicate the signet.

"Let's see you illustrate your truths now," he said. As was to be expected, Sabine gave no response.

Francis was diligently aware of his surroundings as he struggled back up the hill, watching for any sign of an observer. But there were no telltale shadows or subtle footfalls behind him, not even the uncanny feeling that eyes were on him as he retraced his steps back through town. The only thing that made this walk different from any other time he'd strolled up to his own front door was the weight in his pockets, pulling his cloak down and bumping against his thighs with each step. But despite the added weight, Francis felt lighter than he had when he'd left the house, and as he turned onto his street he was downright jolly. It was the same tranquility that settled in his bones when he sent a murderer to the gallows or a guilty man to jail. Order had been transgressed upon, and he had used his god-given right to put it back in order again.

Snickt. Francis paused at the sudden sound of the footstep, thin and sharp against the silence of the morning. Only an hour beforehand he would have panicked at the thought of being followed, but his spirits were high now that he had accomplished his task. Order was on his side, order was his mistress, and he was untouchable. Besides, it was close enough to dawn that someone could conceivably be out and about. Francis turned around, his hand raised to greet whoever was behind him.

It was a woman emerging from the morning fog in a pale tattered dress and muddy cloak. The warm greeting on Francis' lips turned cold at the sight of the unseemly girl, who had doubtlessly been out on street corners all night long. This was the very type of miscreant from whom he was trying so hard to protect his people.

And now there was no Sabine to stop him.

"Excuse me, ma'am," he said sternly. "Where are you coming from?"

His voice echoed in the silence, but the woman gave no sign that she had heard. She walked quickly with her face towards the ground, not acknowledging Francis even though she was headed in his direction. Francis was about to repeat himself, maybe threaten the girl with jail for the day to see if that would catch her attention, when he stopped.

Something was wrong.

The woman wasn't just walking in his direction, she was coming directly for him. Her steps were not the usual dainty stride of a lady but the quick, determined march of someone who had spotted something they desired. Francis took a step back, suddenly unsure as the woman approached. Dark hair spilled out from the base of her hood and bounced over her shoulders as she walked, and he realized that her high necked dress, which he had at first thought was a gentle cream color, was actually bright yellow.

Not possible, he thought, panic suddenly swelling in his brain like a growth. *Not possible. She's dead.*

"Hey! Stop!" he said out loud. His voice broke against the last word and sweat broke out over the back of his neck. "Identify yourself!"

The woman did no such thing. She picked up the pace, her arms swinging at her sides, and though Francis couldn't be sure in the dim light, he thought he saw a flash of white bone in red flesh where the hands should have been.

Should have been, but weren't.

Fear filled his chest and Francis turned and bolted down the street, heading for his own front door in a panic. He easily outpaced the girl and by the time he reached his house, unlocked it, and slammed the door behind himself, she was nowhere in sight.

Calm down, he instructed himself. *It was just a*

miscreant. His hands were shaking and he put them into his pockets to try to steady them, but he had forgotten what was in there. He yelped as his fingers touched the cold flesh and he ripped the cloak off and threw it on the ground.

For a moment he did nothing but let himself breathe in and out, his throat hard and ragged with fear. It was a street walker, nothing more. There was no other explanation, the natural order of things dictated that it was so. Francis tried to laugh at his own folly, but the sound wheezed against his dry throat like a boat scraping a sandy beach.

Maybe it was just one of her followers trying to scare you, he counseled himself. *She dressed up like Sabine and was waiting for you, and you imagined the hands in your confusion.* He knew even as he thought it that the answer was not quite satisfactory - after all, how could they have known that he was going to the grave, followed without him noticing, and gotten the exact dress that Sabine had died in - but at least it was possible. Francis shook himself and went to his window, determined to pull back the curtains and let the morning sun dispel his fear, but as soon as he parted the fabric his heart broke into a panic.

She was standing in the street, silently watching his door as if she had been waiting for him to see her. The hood still covered most of her face, but he could make out harsh bruises around her neck, a swollen and cracked lip, and one single eye that was blood red, as if every vessel in it had burst. Yet despite its ruin, that eye was looking directly at him.

Francis ripped the curtains shut, too afraid to

even look at her hands. He struggled desperately to remind himself that it was a trick, but no words came to his mind.

Tump. Tump. Tump. Three knocks at the door, slow and heavy, the blow of someone who didn't have knuckles with which to make a light rasp.

"Stay back!" he screamed, no longer caring if the maids or the neighbors or the very denizens of hell heard him. No answer came through the door, but still Francis sensed the presence of the creature waiting silently, staring with those eyes that had drowned in their own blood. No- there was something. A light scratching, like a sharp metal instrument scraping away at bone, came in long scores against the door. Francis saw in his mind's eye the ragged stump of bone that he'd left sticking out of Sabine's wrist and he gagged violently.

Suddenly he realized how stupid he had been to come back to his home without a plan, holding the very indication of his misdeed in his pockets. But there was still time for him to set the narrative in order. He simply needed to be rid of the evidence, and fast. Francis ran back to his room, sliding around the corner of the hall and bumping into the wall so hard that he yelped in pain. A portrait of his grandfather fell and the frame shattered against the floor, but Francis did not stop until the door to his room was closed and bolted behind him.

Alright, he thought. *Get rid of her hands, you get rid of her.* Francis laid his cloak on the ground and put another log on the fire, then another. While the wood smoldered, he turned the cloak upside down and Sabine's two hands fell to the ground with a heavy thump that unsettled his stomach. He halfway expected them to start crawling away but they simply laid there, palm down, silent and quite dead. Francis grabbed one by its thumb, then screamed and dropped it.

The inside of the palm was coated in wet paint that gleamed a glossy red.

He didn't stop to wonder what it meant or how it had come to be. Francis simply threw the things on the logs and grabbed the poker, pushing at the dying embers to try to bring back the firey teeth that had consumed the picture earlier. The ring would not melt in the fire, but it would be easy enough to drop it in the river once the skin and bones had withered away to nothing. That is, if he could just get the fire to start.

"Come on!" he instructed, but the fire did not respond to his order. Francis jabbed harder at the wood, his hands shaking so badly that he had to use both of them to direct the poker at all. He managed to produce a little smoke, but no flames. Why hadn't he remembered to throw another log on before he left? He had worked for nearly ten minutes with no results when a firm tapping at the door startled him so badly that he almost dropped the poker entirely.

"Your honor," came the voice of one of his maids. "Your honor, there is something I think you should-" her voice was cut off by one that was deeper and much less compassionate.

"You need to open up, right now."

Francis plunged into a fear so deep and cold that

he was unable to even formulate a response. He poked harder at the logs, but other than a stubborn wisp of grey smoke, the fire refused to go along with his ploy. The gold ring atop the logs glinted cheerfully, almost a wink, as the dawn sunlight tipped into the room and a murmur grew from outside his home.

Francis was still waiting for the wood to ignite a quarter of an hour later when the door to his room burst inwards with a tremendous crack. The constable, a giant of a man with whom Francis had collaborated on many arrests, ducked into the room amid a swarm of people who were either onlookers or thrill seekers or both.

"Your honor, there seems to be cause to believe that-" the constable started in his deep voice, but he stopped cold when he saw the fireplace and the hands lying atop the logs.

"It's true!" he roared, pointing. "The artist's hands, as sure as the picture! You murderer!"

"Wait!" Francis yelled. "You don't understand!" But the crowd that had packed into his house was at a frenzy now, and they didn't give him a moment to explain. The people that only the day before would have tipped their hats in respect if they saw him in the street now grabbed Francis roughly and pulled him from the room. They dragged him through the halls of his house, where his maids were watching with gaping mouths and wide eyes.

"What's going on?" Francis screamed. "What cause have you to break into my house?"

"What cause?" The constable repeated. "Look!"

He turned Francis toward his front door as they passed it.

In the wood of his door was scratched an image of Sabine from the waist up, smiling as she had in life and with her arms folded over her lap gracefully, but she was without her hands. Beside the portrait's head was Sabine's signature. The painted handprints were not even dry yet, and as Francis gaped at it he swore he could see tendrils of smoke rising from the cooling wax that clearly bore the imprint of the cat with the snake in its mouth.

"No! It can't be!" Francis screamed. "There's got to be some other explanation!" But the crowd did not stop, hooting and screaming behind him as the constable dragged Francis towards the jail where he himself had dealt with many impounded criminals.

As if he was the monster, not Sabine. As if he had disrupted order, not her.

The whole thing was insanity.

Trapped In Thought

Melanie Cossey

As my movements become cumbrous, in need of concentration and effort to execute, I know my destination is looming. I am descending that derelict staircase into a cellar flooded with fetid water. Each shot of whisky is a step and I am almost to the ripples. I will float at first, reveling in the buoyancy of numbness, where the illusion of an escape will cradle me, before I cross that barrier into the very depths of my torment.

Once the drink catapults me into the abyss, I will be embraced by the very demons I seek to escape.

But I ordered another whisky anyway.

It falls hard over my tongue, burns itself down my throat. And my soul yearns for her, for my Jenny. Oh, in the swirl of my bitterness I cling to the sodden, sinking wreckage of equanimity.

I see her face before me. My dearest, my only sister Jenny, her hand slapping mine away as I once reached to pull the curl from her blonde hair. Oh, how I fought against her journey from innocent girlhood into the inevitability of womanhood. Into that treacherous place that steals freedom from the female species and trusses it up with straight back, cold nods, and restrained laughter stifled behind fans of lace. I knew then that time would steal my childhood companion into that world of falseness and decorum, turn her pagan soul into the very model of Christian propriety, and I could not stand it.

"Another drink!" My request leaves my lips like a surly bellow as my line of empty glasses shifts and sways on the bar top's surface.

"I'd say you've 'ad enough, sir," the barmaid's closed-fist face scowls as she reaches for my drained glass.

"I'll tell you when I've had enough." My graceless mitt swipes for her deft wrist.

"'Ere now, let go me arm, ya drunken letch, and get the ef outta me establishment."

It is as if a great kraken rises from the bottom of those dark depths, for the flood waters of my soul part like a typhoon, and the leviathan breaks the surface. The barmaid screams and the glasses that held the measured increments of my demise pitch to the floor and burst. Fistfuls of taffeta and the starch of crinoline tears the webbing between my fingers and the tangle of words drown in my throat, netted by the whiskey and rage. And then the waters seal over my head, pulling me under.

When I emerge again, I am stood up against the stone siding of my family home in Kensington. The splatter of frigid October rain penetrates my stupor as it strikes my face. Enough of my senses have survived the drowning to discern the blue coattails and top hats of two of London's local constabulary. One holds me by my scruff while the other bangs the door knocker.

Some hazy moments pass, and the door opens, leaking lantern light onto the threshold. The flickering vision of my mother appears in the foyer, and I wrench myself from the bobby's grasp and ooze my way inside. Sliding onto the divan in the drawing room, I lay my pounding head on the cool silk cushion.

From the direction of the foyer, the hushed whispers caress the mahogany wainscoting and it amplifies them enough, so I hear.

"He's just lost his dear sister, Jenny. We all have. Please show a hapless brother some mercy."

"We'd like to, ma'am. We'd certainly like to, under the circumstances, but you must understand, it's up to the barmaid whose dress he all but tore to ribbons. As I'm sure you can appreciate, she may not be all that willing to pardon the incident."

"The incident," I repine as I sit up, clutching that pillow to my chest like a life preserver. "The incident is that those dresses ought not to be worn by *any* woman at *any* time and certainly not a fifteen-year-old girl."

And the great sea beast inside me once again ascends to the surface.

"Mother, tell them what happened to our little Jenny. Come on, let's be out with it."

Through the thinning fog of my inebriation I see mother's face sink two shades paler as she stammers, lowering her eyes and the volume of her voice.

"It ... it was a fire."

"What's that you say, Mother? But a mere fire? Untrue!" I rise then and start toward the figures in the foyer, although the unsteadiness from the momentum of standing overtakes me, and I half-crash into the arm of the divan before righting myself. I continue advancing undeterred. "I shall tell you gentlemen proper. My sweetest flower, my darling sister Jenny was imprisoned in that tomb of voluminous ruffles and flounces that London society regards as a dress.

"She stood stoking the fire in her bedroom when a draft, caused by her movements, stirred under her crinoline and fed that greedy flame. It ignited that abomination of female fashion and she became a roaring fireball. Do you hear? A screaming, roaring ball of flesh-consuming, bone-melting fire!"

"Lucien, stop." My mother's hands raise to cover her ears, her face wet and contorted like a bawling baby's.

"All right, that's enough now." One bobby stiffens, grips his truncheon, and takes a step toward me as the other takes Mother's arm and sweeps her aside. With a scowl, I retreat, turn and quit the room, grabbing a lantern left on a table by the door in my haste to be rid of this pretentious drawing room with its heavy drapes, its embroidered screens and stained glass, blockading the stain of tragedy from the west wing, lest it try to seep in here.

"Oh, leave him be," I hear my mother sob, and the hallway behind me is absent of sound until, after a moment, the gentle clunk of the door latch brushing the strike plate reaches me. I pause to light the lantern, then resume storming down the length of the hall, my limbs pendulating in a military cadence that steadies me. Turning left at the end of the corridor, I make my way towards the forbidden, towards the lingering trauma, the unfadeable sorrow, of Jenny's bedchamber.

The odor of rancid smoke affronts me as I near, but I drive myself on until I'm trembling before her door.

Preventing me from entering is an assemblage of boards nailed in violent disorder to the frame. I set the lantern down and with a roar I fling myself upon them, tearing off these guardians to my love, my Jenny.

As I yank open the door, the acrid wisp of a bitter smoke, sour with the taint of Jenny's burnt flesh, leaps for me, closing around my throat in a stranglehold that makes me sputter and cough. I cross the room for the window that was left open, the tattered sheer dancing a ghostly rain-sodden waltz with the cold and storm. I rip the damned thing down. The metal rod disturbs the silence as it clatters to the floor. A gasp escapes me as I throw the sash open to its widest, the toothless black maw looks ready to consume me. I gulp electric air, its cool blackness relieving my senses of the horrid odor of a life consumed by fire.

Holding the lantern aloft, I allow this innocuous flame to illuminate the room. My chest tightens as I dare my eyes to look to the hearth, where the murderous flame had accosted my precious sister.

Dear God! What a sight fills my vision. Singe marks mar the once-rich mahogany floor. It's the perfect charred outline of her petite form, sketched on the floor in an indelible black ink. The scorching spreads up the Doric columns of the hearth, blackens the once aqua tiles, to defile the mantle and scar the ceiling.

Oh, my Jenny, what hellish chariot came to bore you away to the afterlife? And why was I not there to halt it? To drive those demon horses away. To shoot them between the eyes if I had to. Anything, so that you would not be taken from me. Oh, why had I allowed myself to be detained in London upon that night? If I had only declined to meet my solicitor for an ale and instead hurried home to be with you, you would have never suffered such a fate. For I would have insisted upon yet another game of pinochle, and you, never able to deny me such folly, would not have retired early, not have stoked your own fire. Your chambermaid would have gone about the task and all would be well.

I pound my fist against a table and curse.

"Oh, Jenny. Jenny!"

At this, the calling of her name, a blaze of lightning illuminates the mantle, and there upon it, amongst the patina of char and soot, a miniature visage flares.

I gasp at the likeness. My darling Jenny there, immortalized in a tiny figurine of white porcelain. I cross to the fireplace as the parched floor beneath me rumbles with my steps and the booming clap of thunder. I snatch the ceramic likeness and hold it up to my face, trying to discern its shape in the flickering lantern light. My fingers trace its grooves, the cold cheek, the piled hair, the ringlets falling down its back, and then the fullness of the skirt.

That cursed, vile, devil-inspired cascade of billowing fabric. The very model of the gown that had imprisoned my Jenny in an inferno of inescapable flame. With another burst of electricity, the figurine blanches and I see my tender Jenny, amassed in white hot flame, and her cries shriek in my brain, searing it.

"I curse you!" I shout. "I curse the flame. I curse the char. I curse the soot and the smoke, and all that took my sister from me. May the devil take you!" With the violence and ferocity of all that consumes me, I hurl that china Jenny into the firebox, and it returns to me in a shower of shards, piercing my skin with tiny lacerations. I raise my hands to my head, feel the trickle of blood down my arms, my cheeks, as I grab fistfuls of my hair and release a caterwaul to rattle the bones of those long dead in their crypts.

"My sweet sister, where has your beautiful spirit gone? Did it fly away up the chimney? Then I wish to go after it. Oh, with my very soul I beg to depart this world and fly after you, for a curse be upon this life. I shall conscript myself to the soot and ash and bind myself to the fury and the outrage your death has wrought."

Another blaze seizes the room, the electrical energy igniting me as a great force within, a surging heat, from the seat of my belly rays upwards and then outwards. It singes my innards as it bursts from my chest whole. With it, I feel a splitting of my soul into two parts. Then, to my horrified and confused mind, I witness a form, a crimson fire bolt, shoot towards the open firebox and set off up the chimney and, in tandem, feel the sensation of shooting up that chimney. It takes some moments to realize that I have become both the occupier of the interior of the chimney flue and that of my body stretched out on the floor below. The part that took its leave also took with it the strength of my emotions, my rage that burns with a crimson heat in violent agitation.

That I could experience this splitting of consciousness cages my mortal spirit in a trap of fear so encompassing that it sends my body into paralyzing trembling. I cling to my body in bewilderment for a few draining minutes while the hands of my sobbing mother fall upon it, palpating my chest. Her shouts of direction for my father and my oldest brother to hoist my body and carry it to my bedroom down the hall cause me to recoil, as her fear for my life, for the possibility of losing me in death, combine with the fear trapped within me and magnify it to an insufferable degree.

Upon this, I commit myself to solely encompass

the alternate consciousness that occupies the chimney: that of the fury and indignation I feel for Jenny's death. I vow never to return. The power of rage is always preferable to the vulnerability of fear.

So, I flee to my wrath and in it, I reside. These interweaving curved threads of emotional disturbance build for me a kind of cocoon. A Kama-Manas of humming anger. A cradle in which I sway to the rhythm of violent aggression.

My acerbity is made stronger by the fact that my Jenny is not in the flue. I am not able to touch her, to reside with her in the spirit realm. Perhaps Heaven is many dimensions away. And so, the hum grows louder within my soul and my form, that of the bloodiest stain, is sustained and I revel in it. If I ever have a mislaid thought of returning to my weakened body, it is at once dismissed, as a sideways glance toward my bedchamber reveals a significant growth in the fear that surrounds my cast-off body. Fear, offered up as food from those friends, doctors, and relatives who would visit my comatose figure and weep and pray that my family shall not lose another. No, I could not bear to return to the form that expanded in such treacherous paralyzing dread. And so, I learn to find comfort in the rage.

Every one of these perpetual moments, one on top of the next, and the next, spin me end-over-end in the pitch of this eternal crimson blackness where I am cut off from all I know. Death would have been better, but death is not reachable from where I am. I am ethereal, possessing no way of ceasing my existence, no way of harnessing myself. I am a free, untethered form without destiny, cut loose from my body. One half of a whole.

I cannot cry out, I cannot feel anything except my own torment, my anger, made worse by the segregation from the love I once had with Jenny, the love that yet remains in the earthly form, by the visitors that gather around my bedside. I breathe the fury in like oxygen, I drink it like whiskey. It is my food, it is my rest, my tonic, and my sexual fulfilment. I cannot abandon my course. I am stranded.

In such a state, it is impossible to assess the passing of time. Such a thing is the stuff of the higher emotional forms, where one must temper and balance time with the labour of love, charity, and peace. But here, the emotion of anger serves only itself. And the master must continue to feed. Such is the way of these treacherous thoughts. But even if one knows not the rate, one knows that the logic of time insists that it must advance. That human forms continue as they have.

And in whatever moment this is, I am aware of an infiltrating noise. From below me comes the sound of Jenny's door opening and the footsteps of two, no, three people entering the room. At first it is the clomp of my father's riding boots, followed by the light, hesitant step of my mother, with the clack of her maid's wooden heels following close behind, as is her custom.

Then I hear the rush of a tiny gasp and my father's voice, "Don't look at it, my darling. We shall have that mantle hacked to pieces tomorrow and the floor ripped out. The whole lot shall be replaced by next week. You shall never be reminded of what took place here, if I have anything to do with it."

My father's statement is followed by a choking sob.

Expunge her? They are going to excise her like she'd never existed?

There follows the light spring of a latch—the armoire popping open—and the scrape of hangers on metal, screeching in protest, then the soft whomp of heavy clothing falling to the floor.

"Box these and bring them to the church, Molly. I can't bear to look at them. There are women who have fallen on hard times that could use them. And those hair adornments too. Gather them up. Gather them all up."

Worse! They are going to give away those horrid dresses with their flammable crinolines to poor unfortunate women, so they may also meet their demise in the flame, or tangled in the wheels of carts, or under the hooves of horses, or poisoned in arsenic green, or pierced by exploding hair combs.

No! my heart shouts. My soul ignites in the heat of protest, and the flame of rage sparks anew, and from the churning, grinding, stiletto-pointed dart I become a flame as white hot as the sun and set alight the creosote lining of the chimney.

Within moments, a downdraft sends the tendrils of that lifeless gray smoke into dear Jenny's former bedchamber.

"Dear God, Augustus, the chimney's on fire! Do something."

The memorable wooden scrape of the lifting of the sash, and the faraway cries of "Soot-Oh Sweep," and my father's yelling, "Boy! Boy! Come extinguish this fire. Hurry...," all infiltrate the flame of my rage up the crackling flue to my inferno. I writhe in the grip of this searing, burning fury. This complete consummation of my soul. It has fanned to such intensity that I am merciless, beyond any agency. A spinning tempest set on destruction.

Then, something scuttles beneath me. The tender scrape of skin on brick, the soft coughing choke of a climbing boy, inching toward the blaze of my rampancy. Eyes in the dark have found me here. Eyes that are accustomed to seeing the blackness of things. Eyes that are seeing what I wish no one to see.

No! Stop! My combustion is unstoppable.

His eyes grow wide in the brilliance of it. They say it is bigger than he thought, it is hotter, so forcibly hotter, like none he has ever extinguished before. And there I see the very glance of at first panic, and then at once I know I am seeing the same look that passed Jenny's eyes of cornflower blue in the last moment of her life. The look of acceptance and then of gladness, of reverence and finally peace, as she saw what I suddenly understand that all children see when they pass: the glory of the Lord coming to carry them home. And in this moment my rage dissolves, and I weep at last.

The journey back to my body is like fighting the tides, like swimming for where you think the surface is after a tumble from a boat. It's that watery film that filters the light and shapes, and as you near it, you pray you have enough breath to succeed in breaking its surface, and that you don't drown before you do.

What I take for ocean waves on my face are tears. And my gasps for air are but tender sobs.

Into my brother's bewildered, yet joyful face I sputter between sobs, "Hurry away to Jenny's bedchamber. Tell mother I'm back. And that the climbing boy has perished. Oh yes, and that the fire has been doused."

"Oh, Lucien. I thought... I thought..." And he breaks away with a last squeeze of my hand to run down the hall.

How easy it is to become trapped in our thoughts, I think, before the deep sobs for darling Jenny, that I could not before now cry, overtake me.

RETURN UNTO THE
LAND

R.E. McAULIFFE

19th September, 1799

A GHASTLY NIGHT TO BE BACK.
I am already beginning to regret my decision to accept this commission. Surely it was some foolhardiness that tempted me into it. Why else would I undertake the rebuilding of an Irish manor house, a project spurned by the rest of my profession for the obscurity of its setting?

And I thought I had left my flirtations with danger behind me when last I departed these shores, so many years ago now.

Despite the season, it was lashing with ran when

the stage-coach set me down. The driver was a sullen scoundrel.

'This is as far as I go,' he kept saying, when I protested at the weather and the dark. 'Phelan will be along for you.'

And with that, he cracked his whip and drove on.

Who the d---- Phelan was, he did not care to tell me.

A rough structure loomed in the dark, set back from the roadside – an abandoned shepherd's hut, I thought, or the ruins of a burnt-out church. In any case I headed straight for it, hoping to find some shelter. Only when I drew nearer did I realise that it was a circle of standing stones, clawing up through the earth like ancient finger-bones. Even after all these years, the arrangement struck fear into my heart: such is the power of folklore imbibed in childhood. But a deluge of rain holds more power still, and I put my foreboding aside to huddle in the lee of those sinister monoliths.

Little did I know the trials the night still held for my nerves.

Cold and hunger had kept me sharp throughout my journey, but now the hammering of the rain must have lulled me into a doze, for I woke to a roll of thunder. Recovering my wits, I realised that what I had taken for thunder was in fact the galloping of a horse's hooves. Phelan, I imagined, come to rescue me at last, and out I stepped to flag him down.

Hoping for a carriage but prepared, by now, to settle for a donkey-cart, it was with some surprise that I saw a lone horseman charging towards me. I waved to signal my presence, but he appeared not to see me.

Within minutes, horse and rider were upon me, near enough for me to see the foaming of the horse's mouth. Its breath blew hot and acrid against my face, but it was not that which transfixed me. I might have fled the rank odour of putrefaction. But the ragged stump of the horseman's severed neck, the foul skull clutched beneath his arm, skin flayed to reveal festering tissue that swarmed with maggots: these were sights too singular and appalling to comprehend. And so I stood, immobile, as the horse hurtled towards me.

At the last minute, the rider swerved, and vanished into the darkness. Shaken finally from my trance, I stumbled back towards the standing stones. But before I could reach them, the sound of returning hoof-beats nearly stopped my heart.

I knew I mustn't look back. I grew up with stories of the dúlachán, the headless horseman who rides abroad to cull men's souls. The age of reason had not been enough to unseat those tales entirely, and if there was one thing I knew, it was that I mustn't look back, and I mustn't be seen.

I had to find somewhere to hide.

My limbs were leaden and my breath laboured, but if I could keep moving forward, keep going long enough...

Unable to heed the warnings coursing through my fevered brain, I looked back.

The cloud-dimmed moonlight picked out the billow of a white shirt, the glint of tackle. Life tingled back into my veins as I realised that this was not the same horse, nor the same rider, relentless as their pace might be.

I scrambled out of their path just as the rider snarled, 'Away with you, now.'

Of course, my earlier vision can have been nothing but the trick of a mind starved of food and comfort. My return to my native land is not without trepidation, after all, although I come back to a part of the country where I am not known, and travel under an alias to boot.

The sooner I finish this assignment, the better. This land is no longer my home.

It was some time later when a brisk clopping and a rumble of wheels heralded the arrival of a horse and cart. It drew up on the road, leaving me to make up the distance between us.

'What in the name of all that is holy are you doing, lurking by those accursed stones?' spluttered the driver.

'I take it you are Phelan?' I said. The man nodded, patting the neck of his cart-horse, a skittish beast, I thought, for its type.

'I'm Edward Deane.' I held out my hand in common courtesy, but the churl merely stared at it, and growled, 'Who else would you be?'

He refused to help me fetch up my luggage.

'You'll not catch me going in there,' he said. 'Hard enough getting Peggy this close, the poor creature,' rubbing the horse's mane with a tenderness greatly at variance with his manner towards myself.

Chide him as I might for his superstitions, it was left to me to heave my trunk back to the road, cursing myself, not for the first time, for packing it quite so full. The continuous rain left the ground boggy underfoot, and several times I sank ankle-deep into an unseen hollow, or had to manoeuvre the trunk out of some mud-clogged rut.

When at last I hauled the trunk onto the cart, Phelan begrudged a few inches of his seat for me, at the same time smacking the horse's rump, so that I had only just time to scramble on as the cart jolted forwards. No doubt the villain hoped to see me topple.

'So you work for the Fitzalans?' I asked, making a mental note to report his behaviour to my new employer as soon as I got the chance

Phelan spat out of the side of his mouth. 'It's another devil I work for. His lordship is neighbour to my master, or would be, if my master was ever at home. But I believe they're friends of long standing.'

Not another word did we exchange for the rest of the ride. Once we had put some distance between us and the standing stones, the horse's pace slackened to a plodding gait more typical for an animal of its heft. Ignoring the chattering of my teeth, Phelan made no attempt to speed up.

Eventually we reached the brow of a long, steep hill, dominated by a sprawling skeleton of crumbling walls and unroofed gables.

'Welcome to Cashelifrinn,' said Phelan, his teeth flashing in a sneer which even the night couldn't hide.

'Yes, yes, this is the work I have come for.' My patience with the cur was near exhausted. 'Pray take me now to my lodgings.'

'Why, here we are.'

I stared about me, aghast.

'But – this is a ruin...,' I uttered, when at last I could speak again. 'Surely you cannot expect me ... on a night like this...'

'It's good enough for his lordship,' said Phelan, 'so I daresay it's good enough for you.'

He let the horse trot through the remains of the manor house, until we came to a small section which was relatively unravaged. The walls at least seemed sound, although it was only a matter of time before the weight of the adjoining ruins caused them to buckle. There was even a door, charred but functional. No roof, of course.

Phelan alighted from the cart and put his shoulder to the door. It opened with a creak, sloughing off a chunk of wood as it did so.

'Rotten,' observed Phelan. 'Like everything else here. Well, get your trunk and come in.'

Stumbling beneath its weight, I lugged the trunk from the cart and followed him.

He lit a candle, and set it on a small table which appeared to be the room's only furniture. The floor was strewn with rushes, and a straw pallet had been made up beside the table. I picked up the candle to cast its light further through the room. A gust of wind chilled through the scrap of tarpaulin hammered across the nearest window-frame. Beyond the candle's reach, something scuttled across the floor. There was then a whinny, and holding up the candlestick, I made out the outline of a horse, tethered in the far corner.

'Would Fitzalan lodge me, then, in his stables?' I demanded

'Mind you don't waste that candle,' said Phelan. 'You'll not find another here.'

I turned towards him, to look upon his face for the first time. It was bony and wrinkled, and livid skin puckered around a scar that ran from his left temple to his nose. Worse, though, was were the knots of mutilated flesh on either side of his head. The wind raised the candle to a sudden flare, in an instant illuminating the full horror of the wounds. Phelan's ears had been cut off.

The next second the candle was out. The return of darkness stamped the image of Phelan's disfigurement onto my retinas.

'Did you see all you wanted?'

The voice rasping close by made me start, as the candlestick was snatched from my hand. In another minute it flamed again. As my eyes grew accustomed to the dazzle, I saw Phelan holding the candle up to his disfigurement.

'Take a good look, now,' he said.

'I'm sorry,' I said. 'I hadn't realised... it being dark...'

Phelan set the candlestick back down on the table.

'Well, you know now, and let that be an end to it.

His lordship left you some bread, but the rats have been at it.' He pointed at a hollowed-out crust on the table.

'I'm not hungry,' I lied.

Phelan shrugged. 'That's just as well, then.'

He made for the door.

Some long-harboured guilt, it must have been, that compelled me to utter, 'Thank you for picking me up, Phelan.'

'It's what I was paid for. You wouldn't drag a living soul out on a night like this, otherwise.'

'A dead one, perhaps,' I murmured.

'What was that?'

'Just a fancy – a horseman crossed my path, and for a minute I took him for ... '

'A horseman?' Phelan paused, turned back to me.

'No doubt some local ne'er-do-well.'

Phelan nodded. 'Peadar Bán and his gang are abroad, then. A fine night for it, and good enough for them.'

'Rebels still at large?'

'They call themselves the Children of Sadhbh Amhaltach, say they're fighting for the rights of the people.'

'And aren't they?'

'They're fighting for themselves, just like we all are.'

With that, he was gone.

Try as I might to sleep on this pallet, between the cold, the rustling of the rats, and the chomping of the horse, sleep eluded me for hours. When it did arrive, it was fleeting and fragmented, plagued with images of Phelan's scarred head, which in turn summoned phantoms I had thought long buried. How long must I make expiation for misdeeds committed in the folly of youth?

Shivering now over my journal, the candle-light sickly and the ruined house groaning and whispering about me, I can't help thinking I'd have found more rest out there beneath the standing stones.

20ᵗʰ September, 1799

Despite the words with which I closed my last entry, sleep must have found me last night, for I was woken up this morning by nothing less friendly than a kick to the ribs.

Before I could curse my assailant, I heard the words, 'So you're Deane?', in that clipped accent so familiar to me from the voices of my own father and uncles. I looked up to see a tall man standing over me, holding the reins of the horse that had shared my sleeping quarters.

Past associations made me scramble to my feet despite myself.

'Lord Fitzalan?'

'You took your time getting here.'

'The crossing was delayed ... the weather ... '

'Yes, yes, the weather is what it is in this godforsaken land, and sailors are as superstitious a bunch of imbeciles as you'll find among the natives here. Speaking of which, I hope that scoundrel

Phelan treated you well? I fear any conversation you attempted must have been one-sided.' Fitzalan tugged at his own earlobe and guffawed.

'Who did that to him?' I asked, although I knew the answer.

'Rebel scum, worked into a frenzy by that upstart Wolfe Tone.' Fitzalan spat. 'Well, we sorted him out. As for Phelan, he's a turncoat, no better than the blackguards who marked him for it, but of more use to us. My own man, Hennessy, has gone to fetch the building materials, so Phelan will have to do. Now hurry up, man. There's work to be done, and not much daylight to do it in. I brought you some breakfast.' He thrust a hunk of bread towards me, suspiciously similar to the rat-nibbled offering of the previous night. I confess that by then I was too ravenous to care.

'You can eat while we walk,' commanded Fitzalan, and I followed him and his horse out, tearing into the bread as I did so.

'Our quarters, as you can see, are all that's left of the old house. I intend to keep it until the new structure is habitable, then knock it down for good. No sense hanging onto the past, eh?'

Fitzalan strode across the ruins, marking out the boundaries of the house he wished built, considerably larger than the original. Every few minutes, he punctuated his orders with the utterance, 'That will teach the blighters.'

'Right then, I'm off,' he said abruptly. 'Phelan will be along later to check up on you. You'll be relying on him until Hennessy returns. I keep no horse but my own these days, and she's carrying me to Castletown.' He patted the roan's left flank.

'Castletown?' The name shook me; I had not expected the past to cross my path so close.

'Two counties east of here. Some friends of mine have a spot of bother there. I said I'd help.'

The last thing I'd admit to Fitzalan was that I knew Castletown well, almost certainly knew Fitzalan's friends, and quite probably knew the parties that were bothering them. I tried to still my nerves. After all, no-one in Castletown would be looking for Edward Deane. By now, surely, no-one would be looking for me, either. Twenty years change more than a name can. Even a wanted man's features, I told myself, are erased by the next generation's feats and iniquities.

And yet, when I thought of the unfortunate Phelan, it shocked me to realise how little had changed.

'When will you be back?' I said aloud.

Fitzalan waved away the question, seeming irked by my concerns at being left so rudely in a strange land. How little he understands of me.

'I'll take as long as I need,' he said. 'You've plenty to get on with here. I expect to see good progress when I return.'

'And Hennessy?'

'Should have been here yesterday, but I expect he suffered the same hold-ups as you did. I can't hang around waiting for ever.'

With that, Fitzalan swung himself onto the saddle and galloped away.

And I am left here, to my own devices.

I will spend the day measuring up the ground and revising my drawings. Already I can see that the design I first submitted to Fitzalan, with its classical proportions and gently sloping roof, has no place here. In fact, it confounds me that the man can have hired me on their strength. The gables need a steeper pitch against the rain, and turrets placed here and there will break the force of this treacherous wind. Those earlier drafts belong to another country, one of sun-blessed order and reason: a country I have never visited, not even in my dreams (ah, would that my dreams had ever been so gentle). The style for which Edward Deane is acclaimed might pass in the bucolic masquerade of southern English estates, but not here. Looking down now from the hill-top at the vivisected countryside, its hedgerows and dry-stone fencing off ever more desperate grasps at subsistence, I know that this house demanded something fiercer.

Night-time, 20th September, 1799

Such strange happenings have occurred that I am driven to commit them to this journal, if only that I may peruse them more collectedly once daylight has returned.

I worked as I had intended, stopping only when a wash of blood-streaked gold over the west told me that the day was over. Only then did I realise that, apart from the morning's stale bread, I'd eaten nothing since the day before. I guessed to reach the village would take an hour and a half on foot, maybe longer in my weakened state, with no guarantee of sustenance when I got there. But Phelan had not come, and for all I knew he might not bother to come again, with Fitzalan out of the county. I needed food, and candles, too, for the fever of inspiration was upon me, and I intended to work through the night.

I was some way down the hill when I heard the hoofbeats. A group of horsemen cantered in my direction. The riders were preceded by a marching band, a piper and a fiddler and a troupe of ragged women and children, sounding sticks and pan-lids and the sheer force of hands and feet and lungs. I crouched down beside a clump of bushes and watched. As they drew closer, I saw how gnarled and emaciated the marchers were, little more than a danse macabre of jerking skeletons.

The horsemen lent their voices to the discordance, a few raising bottles to toast their progress. They all wore white shirts or chemises, and I knew the rider I encountered the night before was among them. Bringing up the rear, a man on foot struggled to keep up, cursing loudly, his arms bound tight to his sides. The other end of the rope was held by the last horseman, who tugged on it every now and then, so that his prisoner stumbled. At this the nearest horsemen would jeer, and lay bets on how long it would take the man, now being dragged along, to find his feet again.

I held still, waiting for the grim procession to pass him by. They, too, were heading for the village. Following them now seemed abhorrent; my hunger had abated, for a while.

Just below me, to the west, huddled the standing stones that had sheltered me the night before. Remembering Phelan's superstitious dread, I reasoned that they might provide me with refuge again, at least from the villagers' grotesque revelries.

No sooner did I rise from my hiding-place in the undergrowth, than a hand was clapped over my mouth, an arm gripped me in a stranglehold, and I was pulled back down. As I tried to break free, I felt the earth vibrate as a cudgel struck at the bracken a few yards from my head. There was a ululation, somewhere further back, and then, right beside my ear, it seemed, a voice called, 'Over here.' Feet pounded towards me. I froze.

I felt the beat of my captor's heart as we lay entwined, still and silent. Above and beside us, the hunt exploded into sounds of thrashing and whooping and snarling. A drop of something thick and hot splashed onto my temple. Looking up, my eyes traced the point of a tongue, a slack-jawed muzzle, a fox's head dangling from the gash across its throat, a hand wrapped around the stiffening paws. Voices rose in an excited patter I couldn't understand, and gradually faded, with the footsteps, into the distance.

Only then did the hands across my mouth and neck let go.

'What are you doing here?' said Phelan, behind me.

I struggled to sit up. 'I was walking down to the village,' I said.

'And what business have you there? Didn't his lordship say I'd look after you until Hennessy gets back?'

'You didn't come. I had no food, no candles even.'

'I've provisions for you in the cart. I was on my way just now. I've a day's work to do besides looking after you, mind.'

'That's why I was going to spare you the trouble.'

'And get yourself into more? Have you any idea what that lot would have done to you if they'd seen you?'

'I'm just here to do my work. They have no grudge with me.'

'Would you cop on to yourself. You're his lordship's lackey, and that's all they'll see you as. There's no love for the English here.'

'I'm not English,' I said, 'I come from - ' I stopped myself just in time.

'Nor for those who help them,' Phelan continued, 'wherever they come from. The Irish who help get the worst of it, believe you me. Or did you not get a good enough look at me last night?'

He led me to where he'd hidden the cart, tucked in behind a screen of gorse. Only as they were driving up the ruins did he speak again.

'Is it the old house you were running away from?'

The moonlight filtered through the clouds,

lending a purple tinge to the sky's inky black. The ruins of Cashelifrinn might have been the aftermath of some cosmic battle, lopped-off limbs of an army of malignant giants, semi-vanquished and waiting to strike back.

I dismissed the eerie fancy. Hunger, I reasoned, wreaking havoc on my imagination.

'If so, I don't blame you,' said Phelan. 'The place is cursed, all right.'

He'd measured my consumption by a meagre standard, but he'd brought me a full loaf of bread, at least, and candles. Some milk and butter too, four eggs, and blood sausage. By the standards of the last few days, a feast.

'His lordship paid for it, no doubt he'll be taking it out of your pay. But that's between yourself and him to settle. In any case, I won't be back tomorrow. They're bringing the harvest in, what there is of it with this accursed rain, and I'll need to collect my master's due.'

'Your master's a churchman then?'

Phelan snorted. 'His parish might not know his face, but they still have to pay what's owing to him. The people starve, but the tithe gets paid. And when all is said and done,' he dropped his voice, mumbling more to himself than me, 'must I and mine starve too?'

He jolted the reins, and the cart-horse set off.

But I could not let him go like that, and found myself trotting behind them. 'That man,' I called, 'the one they'd tied up, who was he?'

It was a few minutes before he replied. 'Another proctor,' he said. 'Name of Magee. Working over by Holywell, that one. They march them through all the villages, just to remind us that they're everywhere.'

'Violence will do their cause no good, and the man is as much of a victim as ... should we not try to stop them?'

Perhaps my words rang as false to Phelan as they did to my own conscience, for he merely sighed, and whipped the horse on.

Morning, 21st September, 1799

Little did I imagine, when last I set down my journal, that the events of the night were far from over.

From my newly acquired provisions, I prepared himself a dinner of bread and sausage. But when I went to eat, the smell brought back to me the fox's protruding tongue and blood-stained, stiffening limbs. Repulsed, I scraped away the meat, and tried again. The first bite of bread lay solid in my mouth, cold and dead, until, unable to swallow, I spat it out.

Nausea made me restive. I tried to work some more, but my pen wandered off into strange arabesques and meaningless curlicues, or spiralled out in some other-worldly rage.

Weariness got the upper hand, and then I struggled against the vortex of a fever-dream: a procession of crazed villagers, their forms growing and dwindling like flickering flames, dancing in a circle; and within that circle danced a troop of faceless, white-shirted horsemen, I myself at their head; and at our centre, a cavernous pit. Beneath the singing and whooping of the dancers, the earth rumbled, and from the pit rose a skeletal hand, grasping for something to hold onto. I ran to it, and stamped on the brittle fingers, bones crunching to dust beneath my feet, the horsemen and villagers cheering me on. At last the mud rose to swallow what was left of the hand, and then I was sinking down with it...

I woke to find my cheek resting on a page of my drawing-book, damp with a mixture of saliva and spilled ink. The new candle had burned down to half its size. A few inches away, a rat munched at the remains of my dinner. It eyed me as it ate, whiskers twitching with disdain, then ambled off the table and into the darkness.

Panic gripped me. The dream - half-memory - this frenzy I had just been part of - it demanded a response.

I should have acted sooner, of course. What matter that I am a stranger to these parts; or that I was one against many? What matter that I have my own reasons for wishing to stay hidden? When I saw that man dragged along by a mob, I should have done something to help him. Else how can I truly claim repentance for my own crimes?

Perhaps, I told myself, there was still time. The wind and rain had abated, and I had no more excuses. Not this time.

The moon was swathed in clouds. Unable to find the track, I slithered down the muddy hill-side, clutching at tufts of bracken to slow his progress. The throes of my nightmare still gripped me, making my heart race, yet driving me inexorably on.

I do not know why I made for the standing stones. They seemed somehow inevitable. I was nearly upon them when a gust of wind swept the clouds from the sky, and the moon poured its fierce clarity across the land. At that moment I spotted the horse charging towards me, its rider a dark silhouette against the pale stones. I cast about for somewhere to hide, before the full procession bore down on me, but the land about here was barren. Then I saw that the horse was alone, and for a second I felt the world slip away from me. For now, in the relentless moonlight, there was no doubt about it. The rider's neck was bloody and truncated, yet somehow he spurred the horse on, faster and faster towards me, and from the mangled head clutched by the rider's side, there issued a ferocious scream.

As the horse drew ever closer, I knew that in moments I would be trampled, and yet I could not move. Now the rotting face was a hand's breadth from my own, its staring sockets and gaping mouth a mockery of my own horror. The stench of rot made me gag as I tensed for the impact.

And then, the next second, the dúlachán had passed me by.

Instantly released from my paralysis, I spun round to watch the horse ride off, but in that moment the moon clouded over, and I could see nothing at all.

I crumpled to the ground, letting the sodden

grass chill me into a semblance of calm. I could not deny what I had seen, and yet, as the minutes passed, I convinced myself that it has all been part of the ghastly dream that had dragged me here; that somehow I had never fully woken, and that the care and fatigue of my recent travels had induced in me a fit of somnambulism, from which I was only now recovered.

It was then that I became aware of a noise, the repeated clink of metal on stone.

I'm awake now, I told myself, rising to follow the sound. I'm awake, and in this world. By the dim light of the shrouded moon, I made out a horse and cart, drawn up some yards away, and beside them a figure stood digging at the earth.

'Who's here?' I called, as he approached.

'Is it Edward Deane again?' came Phelan's voice, although the man didn't look up. 'You may as well help, now you're here.'

'It appears you were expecting company,' I said, taking a second shovel from the cart.

'There seems to be no getting away from you this night,' said Phelan. 'And you'd know he was here, if anyone would.'

'Why do you say that?' I started scraping at the loose top-soil.

Phelan watched me for a minute. 'You know not to dig too deep, too,' he said, returning to his own work. 'You know how it's done, all right.'

Hoping to distract his attention from myself, I began: 'Had we not come for him...'

'They'd have been back by morning to let him out. This was a warning, not an execution.'

I started at the word. But Phelan did not notice, for he was seized by a violent shudder of his own.

'In all conscience,' he said, 'I could not leave him in here a moment longer.' He dropped his shovel and held up a hand. 'I have him here.'

Together we scrabbled at the soil with our hands, unearthing here a shoulder, there a foot, until enough was exposed to heave the body out.

The proctor Magee's chest heaved as he gulped at the air. We set to work on cutting loose the rope that still bound his arms, and brushing the dirt off his face, so that he could breathe freely.

'The bastards,' he sputtered, when at last he could speak. 'The bastards.'

'I can take you as far as Waterfall,' said Phelan. 'You'll need to make your own way home from there.'

I helped Phelan lift Magee onto the cart. As we settled him down, Magee turned his glazed eyes onto me.

'You're next,' he said, his voice still hoarse. 'They said they'd be back next for you.'

'Get some rest now, while we drive,' said Phelan, and climbed on.

I gripped Phelan's sleeve. There was a question I had to ask.

'I don't suppose you noticed anything, while you were out here?' .

'What sort of a thing would I notice?' said Phelan.

'Pay him no heed. What man wouldn't rave, after what he's just been through?'

'Not the men who abducted him... no, I meant... did you see anyone else?'

Phelan met my eyes at last. 'You mean the dúlachán?'

To my shame, I shuddered at the word.

'You saw him the night you arrived, did you not?' Phelan continued. 'He's after you.' He searched his pocket, then pressed something into my hand. 'Here,' he said. 'Keep this safe. The gold will keep him away.'

I ran my fingertip across the small medal in my palm, remembering another medal I'd found, clasped in the hand of a dying man, as I dug his grave twenty years earlier, and two counties to the east of where I am now.

'Remember,' said Phelan, as he drove off. 'The third time will be your last.'

-- September, 1799

Time, it appears, has outrun me, and I can no longer be sure of the date.

The last few days it has rained continually, and I have spent the time most profitably, in drawing. My vision of the new building takes shape beneath my hands: sheared to the elements, thin and sharp, and high too, reaching above and beyond the storm-sculpted landscape.

Transcendent.

This is what is needed.

On and on I worked, pausing only when I could no longer ignore the need to eat, or later, to light and trim the candle.

The rap on the door came as a shock.

Phelan shouldered his way in, and nodded at the sheets of paper littered across the table.

'Hard at work, I see.'

'I wasn't expecting you so soon.'

Phelan lit a fresh candle from the stub burning down by my hand, and held it up to scrutinise my face.

After a few seconds, he sniffed, and said, 'You'll have your joke, no doubt. I've said to you before, I've my own work to be getting on with. The tithes have been hard to gather, this quarter, thanks to Peadar Bán's crowd. Ah, but it's been a poor harvest, too. In any case, I see you've made the food last.'

He nodded toward a hunk of bread and meat, which I at some point had started to eat.

'But you're back early,' I said. 'I thought you'd not be back before tomorrow.'

Phelan's eyes glinted in the candlelight. 'I've not seen you this past week,' he said. 'Have you not left the house since then?'

He leafed through a pile of my discarded drawings. 'So this is what's to become of the place.'

Eager for another opinion, I thrust my latest sketches toward him. 'I've finally got it,' I said. 'I've captured what this place needs. What do you think?'

Phelan looked long and hard at each page. 'I

think this place has captured you,' he said at last, 'and you'd do well to get away from it, if you still can. In these drawings, I see a crazed house, fit for a crazed and evil land, and such this is. Lordship or no, fate cheated the Fitzalans when they seized Cashelifrinn. Damned this place has always been, and damned it will always be, and more pity on you, if its insanity has you under its curse.'

Accustomed to his ignorance as I believed myself to be, the effrontery of the man surprised me, and I could do no more than order him to leave.

'It's a bright night,' he said, as he moved away from me, shocked perhaps by my sudden vehemence. 'You should get some air.'

'When does Hennessy get back, with the building materials?' I demanded, eager to get on with my work, now that I understood what the place needed.

'I dare say he'll be a while yet.'

'What in the world can be keeping the man? We have work to do, and his lordship will want to see progress.'

'I'd say his lordship will take his time before heading home, too.'

'There's the labour to sort out too – I expect Hennessy will take care of that – we need to be well under way, before winter sets in...'

'Time, indeed, for all of that,' said Phelan. 'But for now, why not take a turn about the place, clear your head?'

'My head,' I said , 'is perfectly clear. And I have work yet to do – the details still, of the turrets...'

'You say you understand the place, but you won't truly know what it needs, until you've seen it by moonlight. And the moon is near full tonight. Come away now, and walk with me.'

I followed Phelan to the door.

'That's right, said Phelan, 'come along.'

He stepped out.

I paused on the threshold, blinking in the sudden light.

'Go with you?' I said. 'And listen to your infernal stories and ignorant suspicions? Go with you, and let you poison my mind against this land, you traitor? Never.'

With that, I slammed the door shut, letting the rain-warped wood muffle Phelan's imprecations. After a while I heard the cart roll away.

I returned to my drawings, but the visit had broken my concentration. My line wavered. Rummaging in his pocket for a wad of caoutchouc to erase a mistake, my fingers closed on a piece of metal, and I pulled out the medal Phelan had lent me. The infernal cheek of the man, I thought, casting it from me. Trying to drag me back into the ignorance and filth I sacrificed my misguided youth to defend. Trying to turn me against this far worthier project, when clearly it was meant for me, and I for it.

Still, it struck me that Phelan was right about one thing. The house I was designing must look as magnificent by moonlight as by day. More so, in fact, for with its long hard winters, this is a country of night.

I took paper and pen with me, for the moon was as bright as Phelan had said. The ruins of the old house jutted from the hillside like a smashed mouth. It will be a kindness to erase it. And in its place, my new creation – no, the creation of Cashelifrinn itself; for this house will be in and of the land – the new house will take root.

I walked away, turning every now and then to sketch a fresh perspective, looking still for the best view, the vantage point from which I would see the whole picture. Before I knew it, I'd reached the standing stones. I stopped, suddenly tired. It seems I am grown unaccustomed to exercise these last few days, barely pausing to eat, at that. Besides, this was as good a spot as any to make a drawing.

I was caught up in the smooth vigour of pen across paper when a horse's whinny startled me. I looked up to see a cart-horse floundering in its traces, as its driver whipped it forwards. Soon they were close enough for me to recognise Phelan again, beckoning wildly.

'Get in,' called Phelan, as they drew level with me. 'For the love of God, get in.'

Alarmed, I let Phelan help me up onto the cart. 'What is it, man?'

Phelan's torrent of speech was all but incomprehensible through his wheezing. 'I saw it,' was all that I could make out, as they sped away from the stones.

'Saw what?' I prompted, when the other man began to breathe normally.

'I was wrong,' said Phelan. 'I should have left you alone in the house. And then, when I saw ... I was coming back up to warn you ... '

'Yes, but saw what?'

Phelan's mouth gaped. 'That,' he said, pointing with his crop, and I turned to look.

There was no mistaking the horse, nor its demonic rider, as they thundered towards the cart. Phelan's horse reared up in terror, and Phelan nearly snapped the reins as he wrestled against the beast, his entire body seized by the effort to stop the creature from bolting. Yet somehow he still found breath to mutter the repeated syllables of some prayer or incantation that I recognised from my long-buried childhood.

For, perhaps in reaction to my companion's fear, I found myself strangely calm, detached, almost, from the grotesque scenario unfolding before us. The horseman seemed more cadaverous now, its sternum sunken and its limbs disjointed. The head it clutched oozed its final sulphurous putrefaction. The jawbone slackened with a hissing stench, then roared out two words as horse and rider dashed past the cart and disappeared.

Phelan crossed himself, slackening the reins about his quivering cart-horse. He fingered a gold crucifix hanging around his neck.

'Well, thanks be to God, it was not my name the dúlachán called,' he said at last. 'Nor one I recognised, not from about these parts. Well, you're safe now too. Whatever it uttered, it was not Edward Deane.'

'No,' I agreed, 'it wasn't.'

'It's as well I lent you the St. Christopher,' Phelan was saying. 'I must get it back off you, before you go.'

I left him to prattle on. My thoughts were in another place, in a town two counties to the east, with a life I'd tried to leave behind, and a name that has followed me to a grave.

Michaelmas Eve, 1799

I have spend this last day working on my drawing. If nothing else, I hoped to finish this.

And now, as the light's final traces evaporate into the fog of night, I see that at last it is finished, and I see it for what it is.

Arches rising to a point that challenges heaven itself. Flying buttresses bearing the weight of centuries back down into the entrails of the earth. Traceries as fine and strong and lethal as a spider's web. Vaults fanning out like the wings of dragons. And through it all a lurking asymmetry, a subtle skewing of angles and tilting of planes, that just contrives to shift the scheme from majesty to unease.

With each stroke of the pen, I have called up, without seeing it, a malignancy so ancient that it pre-dates evil.

Now I hear a hammering at the door, and voices raised above the steady patter of the rain. Perhaps it is Peadar Bán and his gang, making good on their promise to the proctor Magee. Perhaps it is Lord Fitzalan, accompanied by my own kin and neighbours, here to seek justice for the crime I committed when I tried to redress the wrongs inflicted by my class.

Or perhaps it is a phantom, a headless demon shepherding me and the other lost souls to our eternal damnation.

It is all one.

I have returned, at last, to my end.

Enjoyed what you read? Don't forget to leave a review!

Visit us at:

deadsteam.wordpress.com

grimmerandgrimmer.wordpress.com

ACKNOWLEDGEMENTS

Bryce Raffle would like to thank William J Jackson and the members of the Scribblers' Den for their support in this endeavour. Further thanks goes to Derek Tatum and Leanna Renee Hieber for helping to get the word *dreadpunk* out into the world.

About the Authors

BRYCE RAFFLE
EDITOR/NEWGATE

Bryce Raffle writes steampunk, horror, and fantasy. He was the lead writer for Ironclad Games' *Sins of a Dark Age*. His short stories have appeared in anthologies such as *Hideous Progeny: Classic Horror Goes Punk*, *Southern Steam*, and *Den of Antiquity*.

He is a member of CWILLBC and the author of *The Littlest Dinosaur* & *The Littlest Dinosaur Finds a Home*. He lives in beautiful Vancouver, Canada, where he works in the local film industry.

Twitter @bryceraffle
Facebook.com/bryceraffle
Website: www.bryceraffle.com

ROSS SMELTZER
THE INVOCATION

Ross Smeltzer is a high school teacher, freelance writer, and occasional short story author living in Dallas, Texas. His published work has appeared in numerous dark fiction and horror anthologies, including *C.M. Muller's Nightscript, Volume 4; DeadSteam; A Midwinter Entertainment*; and *Into the Woods.*

E. SENECA
CECILIA

E. Seneca is a freelance speculative fiction author with a strong affinity for horror and dark fantasy. Some of her works include "Harvesters," published in Grimmer & Grimmer Books' first anthology DeadSteam, "It Lives in the Mineshaft," "A Specific Sort of Shared Madness," and "Haunt Me Like A Memory," published by Soteira Press in their Monsters anthology series, and "Glut" published by Sliced Up Press in their Slashertorte anthology. She has written original fiction since 2008, and can be found on Twitter @esenecaauthor.

ARTORIA SAHNOW
MOTHER OF ROTTEN REEDS & DUCKWEED

Artoria Sahnow is a Gnostic poet, music-maker and dreamer of nightmares. Her stories and poems can be found at jormunghast.co, and via Misery Tourism and APOCALYPSE CONFIDENTIAL. She can be found on Twitter @jormunghast.

CC ADAMS
AT THE END OF A PISTOL

London native C. C. Adams is the horror/dark fiction author whose work appears in publications such as Turn To Ash and Weirdbook Magazine. A member of the Horror Writers Association, he also holds a 2015 Honourable Mention from the Australian Horror Writers Association for short fiction.

Still living in London, he lifts weights, cooks - and looks for the perfect quote to set off the next dark delicacy.

Visit him at www.ccadams.com

ROB FRANCIS
A Living Cell

Rob Francis is an academic and writer based in London. He mainly writes short fantasy and horror, and his stories have appeared in magazines such as The Arcanist, Apparition Lit, Metaphorosis, Tales to Terrify and Weird Horror. Rob has also contributed stories to several anthologies, including DeadSteam by Grimmer & Grimmer books, and Under the Full Moon's Light by Owl Hollow Press. He is an affiliate member of the HWA. Rob lurks on Twitter @RAFurbaneco.

MACY HARRISON
The Color of Paris in the Spring

Macy Harrison is a horror and dark fantasy author based in Dallas, Texas. Her work has been previously published in *Novel Noctule*, and is forthcoming in several anthologies and magazines. She is currently finishing up her first novel, which is set in Victorian England.

JAMES DORR
THE GOOD WORK

James Dorr's The Tears of Isis was a 2013 Bram Stoker Award® finalist for Fiction Collection, with his latest book, *Tombs: A Chronicle of Latter-Day Times of Earth*, a novel-in-stories from Elder Signs Press. While primarily a short fiction writer, he writes some poetry too, working mostly in horror/ dark fantasy with forays into mystery and SF, and currently harbors a Goth cat named Triana. For more information he invites readers to visit his blog, at http://jamesdorrwriter.wordpress.com Facebook: https://www.facebook.com/james.dorr.9

DAVID LEE SUMMERS
THE SUN WORSHIPER'S GHOST

David Lee Summers is the author of a dozen novels, two novellas, an indie comic book, and over ninety published short stories and poems. His writing spans a wide range of the imaginative from science fiction to fantasy to horror. His most recent novella is a World War II-era fantasy called *Breaking the Code*. His short stories and poems have appeared in such magazines and anthologies as *Realms of Fantasy, Cemetery Dance*, and *Straight Outta Tombstone*. When not working with the written word, David operates telescopes at Kitt Peak National Observatory. Learn more about David at http://www.davidleesummers.com

KAREN J CARLISLE
BLOOD TIES

Karen J Carlisle is a writer of steampunk, Victorian mysteries and fantasy. She was short-listed in Australian Literature Review's 2013 Murder/Mystery Short Story Competition. The second book in her cosy fantasy mystery series set in Adelaide, The Aunt Enid Mysteries, is due for release in December, 2021. Her short stories have featured in the 2016 Adelaide Fringe exhibition, 'A Trail of Tales', 'Where's Holmes?' and 'Deadsteam' anthologies.

Karen lives in Adelaide with her family and the ghost of her ancient Devon Rex cat. She's always loved dark chocolate and rarely refuses a cup of tea.

Webpage: www.karenjcarlisle.com

RENEE M.P.T. KRAY
THE ARTIST'S HANDS

Renee M.P.T. Kray grew up in Michigan with eight siblings and several really dumb dogs. Having been homeschooled from a young age, she was able to experiment with writing and quickly fell in love with the art. She earned her BA in Literature from Ave Maria University, her MFA in English and Creative Writing from Southern New Hampshire University, and has self-published two collections of short stories: Think Again: A Captivating Compendium and Restless: A Year of Ghost Stories. However, none of these pursuits have been as challenging as trying to get her pug, Potato, to stop eating dirt.

MELANIE COSSEY
TRAPPED IN THOUGHT

Melanie is a writer, poet, and freelance editor, holding a certificate in editing from Simon Fraser University. She has twenty-five years experience as a content writer for magazines and the internet. These days, Melanie writes in the fiction genres of gothic horror, historical, magical realism, paranormal, and women's fiction.

Her debut gothic horror novel *A Peculiar Curiosity* was published in 2018 by Regal House Publishing. Melanie's short stories can be found in several anthologies, including *Quoth the Raven* and *Love Among the Thorns*, both edited by Lyn Worthen. Melanie's gothic horror short fiction, *Midnight Rider*, was nominated for the 2021 Poe Saturday "Visiter" Award. Melanie belongs to the Horror Writer's Association and teaches writing on Vancouver Island.

R.E. McAULIFFE
RETURN UNTO THE LAND

R.E. McAuliffe is an emerging writer of short-form speculative fiction. Her stories have been published in The Mechanics' Institute Review Anthology and in Red Cape Publishing's A-Z of Horror Anthology series. An Irish writer, she now lives and works in London.